WATCH OUT FOR ME

SYLVIA JOHNSON

WATCH OUT FOR ME

First published in 2011
Copyright © Sylvia Johnson 2011

All rights reserved. No part of this book may be reproduced or transmitted in any form or by any means, electronic or mechanical, including photocopying, recording or by any information storage and retrieval system, without prior permission in writing from the publisher. The Australian *Copyright Act 1968* (the Act) allows a maximum of one chapter or 10 per cent of this book, whichever is the greater, to be photocopied by any educational institution for its educational purposes provided that the educational institution (or body that administers it) has given a remuneration notice to Copyright Agency Limited (CAL) under the Act.

Allen & Unwin
Sydney, Melbourne, Auckland, London

83 Alexander Street
Crows Nest NSW 2065
Australia

Phone: (61 2) 8425 0100
Fax: (61 2) 9906 2218
Email: info@allenandunwin.com
Web: www.allenandunwin.com

Cataloguing-in-Publication details are available
from the National Library of Australia
www.trove.nla.gov.au

ISBN 978 1 74237 670 7

Internal design by Sandy Cull, gogoGingko
Set in 12/17 pt Bembo by Midland Typesetters, Australia
Printed and bound in Australia by Griffin Press

10 9 8 7 6 5 4 3 2 1

The paper in this book is FSC certified. FSC promotes environmentally responsible, socially beneficial and economically viable management of the world's forests.

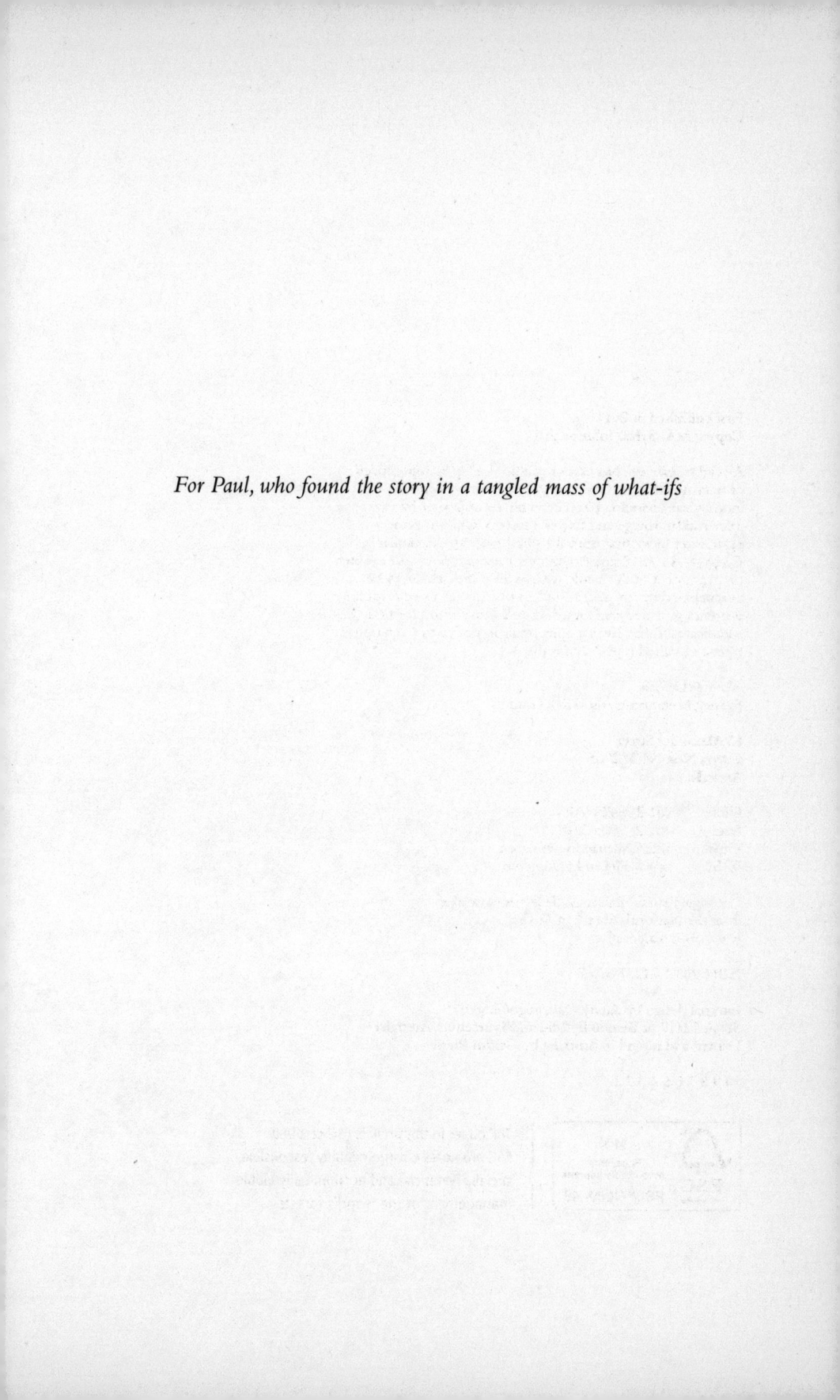

For Paul, who found the story in a tangled mass of what-ifs

On the jetty, near the lighthouse, is a boy.

He leans against the guardrail, shielding his eyes from the sun.
But the guardrail is old and terribly dangerous and
when you look again

the boy is gone.

GUARDIAN, FRIDAY, 26 AUGUST 2005

Armed police officers fired at Jean Charles de Menezes for over 30 seconds when they killed him at Stockwell Tube Station, according to a witness statement made to independent investigators and obtained by the *Guardian*.

The witness says the shots were fired at intervals of three seconds and that she ran for her life fearing terrorists had opened fire on commuters.

And from then on, blood.
PABLO NERUDA

BOOK ONE

The Lighthouse

There is darkness. There is light. Between darkness and light there are shadows and imprints; impressions, interpretations. A man boards a train. He sits. He looks out the window. Remember him.

You will hear a sound, running feet, a shout—you will turn towards the noise. You will obey the orders, you will stand and run and when you look back you will see him surrounded by gunmen and pushed to the floor and you will not help him.

Remember. Remember his face. You will see it explode like a flower, a soft red flower. Remember him.

It's a long story, this, a glimpse of a longer story. There will be blood and fear and anger and there will be darkness.

And there will be light.

I

Toby Woods
SYDNEY, AUSTRALIA, 1967

When he went with the others to tell the story they had agreed on, people were already gathering at the police station. It wasn't a crowd yet, because everyone knew each other—but to him, being new, they were almost-strangers, and what they were going to hear rose up in his stomach and made him sick. It was the first sign he had of the power this lie would contain: in the rising and churn of his gut, he could feel it beginning. But it was not the kind of warning a child could interpret—and after all, he was only eight years old.

Once, long ago, he'd been shown a goat moth caterpillar. The cordyceps fungus had grown inside it, eating the grub alive bit by bit, turning the soft fat body into wood. He had touched the caterpillar husk, the wooden wrinkles and folds, the wooden mouth.

The parasite shoot had pushed through the creature's head, and it was still growing.

INTERVIEW SGT MARRON 7/1/67

Peter Woods My name is Peter Woods. This is my nephew Toby. He is eight years old. He has been staying with us for the holidays. His mother's been ill.
Toby Woods My name is Toby Woods. I am eight years old. I am staying with my cousins. They are nice. My aunt is nice. My uncle is nice. [My cousin] Hannah is nice. [My cousin] Richard is nice. [My cousin] Lizzie is nice.
Toby Woods I did go to the park yesterday morning. I went with the others. I do not know what time.
Toby Woods We played in the shed. I do not know where else we played. We played at the spaceship first and then we played up at the shed.
Toby Woods We did not play at the sandpit. I did not see a baby at the sandpit.
Toby Woods I want to go home.

Interview halted.

Lizzie Woods
FÈS, MOROCCO, 2005

The gates are closed. For the first time, I'm really afraid. It's 4.30 am, still dark, and the streets are empty. I've been all the way down to the Bab R'cif gate and back again on my own. I'm up on the roof but I can't see across the medina. The town is blacked out and it's cold, so cold my hands are shaking.

When I was eight, I thought fear could make me invisible.

I followed along the walls till I got to the square. The gates to the square were blocked by military trucks: outside the walls there was screaming and I could hear gunshots. In forty-six years, I've never heard terror like that.

The tourists were packing and leaving Fès all through yesterday. The Spanish group left as soon as the rumours began. The New Zealand family never came back from Sefrou. Most of the tables were empty at dinner last night.

The Germans—the bus group—left an hour ago, in the predawn blackness. They crept down the unlit stairs, not speaking, not even whispering to each other. Ali was waiting for them—he was frightened for once into silence. I watched them count heads and slip through the doorway and into the alley outside. They were very quiet, they were wholly terrified. They only took what they could carry themselves.

Ali was there to lead them down through the black maze of lanes to the gates.

He is eight years old—he can't be dangerous.

There are things I need to explain or you won't understand; there are things you have to know about this place. You have to know before you come in that Fès is an ancient town, small, medieval, walled; that there are four entry points through the walls, four gates which are huge stone arches. The gates don't shut but they can be blocked. The walls stretch around us, encircling the Old Town entirely; and the cobbled alleys and lanes inside the walls are so narrow and twisting that cars can't come in at all, only donkeys and carts. Sometimes the lanes become tunnels, lost in the darkness of ancient houses that clasp at each other and form a roof four or five metres over the cobbles—so if there is fighting, tanks and trucks won't help. It will be all on foot, lane to lane and alley to alley, and there are children.

There are children. They run through the Old Town, steering the tourists through tracks and tunnels that can't be learned, can't be remembered. They are watchful, resourceful, they know the town, and Ali can't be more than eight years old.

'*Allahu Akbar!*' God is great!

The mosque is calling. The muezzin sings the call at the first sign of daybreak; but he catches the morning star from the top of the hill. Down here in the Old Town we're still in the grip of the night.

'*Allahu Akbar!*'

When I was eight, the cottage burned down, and I slapped Ray Kane who grew up to be *that* Raymond Kane, the radio shock jock—tough on border control and anti-asylum seekers, unmoved by the plight of refugee children and babies. When I was eight, the war began between me and the nuns who wouldn't believe in my grandfather's little moss piglets.

The Germans never mentioned they were leaving. We were together at dinner last night and they said nothing, not to me, not even to Kate, or she would have been down there this morning to see them off whatever the hour, because they were guests and she would have been loading them up with tea and bread and fruit for the journey. I was awake in the darkness, I heard them, I opened my door and saw them gather and leave. And then, because I am a foreigner too, because I don't belong in this town, because there is no-one here to watch out for me, I slipped out and followed them down.

INTERVIEW SGT MARRON 7/1/67

Elizabeth Woods My name is Lizzie Woods. I am eight years old. Yesterday I was down at the park. I went with Hannah and all of the others. Hannah is my sister.

Elizabeth Woods We played on the spaceship and then on the merry-go-round. We played on the centipede swing.

Elizabeth Woods There was a pram near the sandpit. A big girl was minding it.

Elizabeth Woods I don't know who the big girl was. I don't know her name.

Elizabeth Woods She might have been the baby's mother. I don't know.

Elizabeth Woods I did not see the baby. I saw the big girl crying, but that was later, that was after the baby had gone.

Elizabeth Woods I didn't see where the baby went.

Hannah Woods
SYDNEY, AUSTRALIA, 2005

Wasn't this all supposed to *change*? I'm sorry, but *wasn't this all supposed to change*? Did we not have a War on Terror—and excuse me for pounding the point here, but did we not *win*? Because things are not going well, my friend, the teamwork is sadly afuck, the whole point has been lost if some cretinous Yank with a badge can stand in the Opera House car park—in my fucking *car space*—and tell me I can't park my car. This is not a happy start to my working day; this does not augur well.

Death and terrorists woke me this morning, death and terrorists and a brutal but well-deserved hangover. The hangover I can deal with, but honest to god I have had it up to *here* with the bloody terrorists. Bad enough we've got the global forum meeting in Sydney this week; bad enough that the place is wall-to-wall Asia-Pacific heads of state; bad enough that we had to invite the American *president*, so we're suddenly flooded with flags and anthems and motorcades, but last night the terrorists whacked a US government building in Africa. And that, of course, has just driven everyone *crazy*. All over the airwaves they're spreading the news that security here has been *doubled*—not for *us*, you understand; let's be clear about this—for the US contingent. Which would be a pain in the arse at the best of times, but it's tragic tonight because tonight they're all coming here for dinner and a show at the Opera House. Which is where *I* work, which is why I decided not to come in till the peak-hour carnage was over—and even so the whole trip was awash with cops and press and security agents. When I did get in, the boom gate down at the car park tried to behead me and then some American badge-wearing *twat* appears out of nowhere waving a *gun*. Waving a *gun*!

This, you see, *this* is the thing I hate most about terrorism. One little bombing and everything falls to pieces.

This is not going to be a good day. I've got Satan's own *fuck*worthy hangover, the heads-of-state lot are a haemorrhoid on the tight-buttocked arse of my life—and that's not all. That's not all. I can taste guilt in the mix. I can taste guilt in the mix and I know where *that* comes from. That comes from yesterday—that's Post-Lunch-With-Toby Remorse. That's knowing that somehow I've done it *again*, I've been suckered, I've marched myself into a minefield, because *yes*, I'm stupid, but also because I was drunk and that's not my fault, that's Toby's fault for not drinking his share and for being so helpless and *teasable*. God alone knows what I said, but I made him cry, I know that—he's got to be forty-six years old by now, same as Lizzie, but I made him cry, there were definite *tears*. So today of course I feel like I've kicked the head off a fluffy wee *kitten* and the thing is that's not who I *am*! I'm *not* mean and nasty and brutal—oh alright, I *am*, but not all the time. I have a *human* side for chrissake—I was trying to be nice! I was trying to be *nice*, I was trying to *atone* because his dad has just died and Richard had suckered me in with one of his terrible brotherly emails, he'd already suckered me, softened me up. '*We shouldn't abandon him, Hannah. We should make an effort at least, he's our cousin—we should welcome him back to Sydney. He's* *only got us now.*' Which is fine for Richard, of course, who's safely in Rome, and fine for Lizzie, who's all post-divorce again, doing a midlife PhD in *Morocco*—it's fine for *them* because I'm the one who's going to get stuck with the Family thing.

Oh, sweetjesus*Christ*—the lift's gone on strike. It won't take my passkey ... Swipe and Enter it says and I'm standing here swiping away like a swiping *fool*—Swipe. And. Fucking. *Enter*! Damn it— I will not take the stairs, I am not in a stair-taking mood! They've changed the *codes* or something, they've screwed the mechanics— they've broken the *building*. It worked last night, I was here last night with Toby and everything *worked*—the doors, the car-park entry, the lift; everything worked, everything *functioned*, everything *opened*. Then the bright day dawns, the place is overrun with America's Finest and—total *stuffage*. It's fucking Iraq, all over again.

We shouldn't abandon him, Hannah. Jesus. We shouldn't *abandon* him? And then with one of those Richardy twists of the knife that he does so well, he says: '*Try to be nice. We ought to atone.*'

Try to be nice. That's how they get me, you see. That's how they sucker me in every time. Try to be nice. When everyone knows I have no gift for niceness; it scares the *crap* out of people whenever I try to be nice, they think they've got three months to *live* or something, they wait for the snark to jump them. But hey, I tried. I did the right thing. Not straightaway, of course: I didn't *stalk* him, I didn't *descend* on him, I didn't turn up at the funeral or anything—but last week, when I got his text message, his why-don't-we-meet-up-and-here's-my-phone-number message, I did the right thing. Not all that thrilled that he had my number, of course—but I guess that's the sort of thing you can find if you work high enough in the government. So, I called him back, I said all the nice things: sorry to hear about your dad, we should have lunch or something, all that sort of thing. Made plans, set a time and a place, cleared a spot in my schedule for yesterday—and I almost got away with it because he was late and I almost walked out, but suddenly there he was by the door and, god, there was *nothing* left of the boy, not a flicker and who would have guessed, I was thinking—hand-made suit, Rolex watch, he's got the total *Diplomatic Immunity* look; but then—just that odd little frown and the tentative eyebrows, the quick anxious glance around the room, and suddenly underneath it all, there he was, dear little Toby; dear little sweet little Toby, all shy and forlorn—like a poor little kitten fished out of the waves with a bloody great *rope* round its neck, attached to a bloody great *brick*. The decades just slipped away and he was eight years old again and it was Christmas and '*Poor little bugger,*' Dad said. '*He's been through the mill alright, he's really been through it. Poor little coot.*' So I stood up, I waved him across, swapped coffee for champagne and champagne for vodka and the last thing I know the wagon is galloping off again into the sunset and that's eleven long days of sobriety shot down in flames. So thanks for that, Richard.

I will get through today. I will walk up the stairs to my office and lock myself in and relax—and no-one will miss me, no-one will need me for hours because everyone's focus is stuck on the heads-of-state dinner tonight; the whole *building* is preening and polishing flatware and watching for terrorists.

I will hydrate. I will breathe. And later, when the sun has gone down, when the hangover's been thrashed by the twin gods of time and Tylenol, there will be opera and dancing and fireworks and life will be good again—or if not good, at least not *insane*, at least not beturded with guilt and remorse and buggered-up passkeys, and SWAT cops with guns and aggro and unfulfilled neo-con yearnings.

Above all, I will not trawl the past, I will not *strand* myself in the mire of long-ago memories. I Will Not Be Lizzie. Because life is a valley of tears and injustice, but let's take it on like the bastard it is and to hell with fucking *atonement*.

He should never have come to us in the first place.

He should have stayed home.

INTERVIEW SGT MARRON 7/1/1967

Hannah Woods My name is Hannah Woods. I am thirteen years old. Richard is my brother and Lizzie is my sister and Toby is my cousin. I am the oldest.

Hannah Woods We went to the park after breakfast. I do not know what time. We went on our own. Me and Richard and Lizzie and Toby.

Hannah Woods I was in charge.

Hannah Woods We played all together at first and then the Hampdens came up and the Kanes and we played with them.

Hannah Woods The little girls went on the merry-go-round with Lizzie and then on the centipede swing. The boys played up at the spaceship and then at the shed.

Hannah Woods I didn't stay with the girls—I played with the big kids up at the shed.

Hannah Woods I did keep an eye on the little ones. I kept an eye on them but I wasn't playing with them, I was up at the shed.

Hannah Woods I did not see the baby. I did not see where it went.

Hannah Woods We did not leave the park. We stayed there all day.

Toby

Home had closed behind him a lifetime ago—in his mind he could see it collapsing in on itself and disappearing. 'It won't be for long, mate,' his dad had told him. 'Just till the end of the Christmas holidays. Things'll be settled by then.' And, 'They're staying down at the beach, you know—that'll be great fun, won't it? You'll learn how to swim—all sorts of things . . .' And then, a little more quietly, 'You liked the cousins, didn't you—Richard and Hannah and little Lizzie? You all got along like a house on fire at Easter . . .'

In the train, eyes closed, pretending to sleep, he had taken the picture of Easter out of the book of his heart like a photograph. It was full of bright colours; candles and singing at church and jokes and laughter at lunch and then shiny-wrapped eggs hidden all through the garden like treasure. There'd been a present as well, one for each of them, and his was a torch that was red and heavy with batteries inside. Later, much later, right at the end of the day when the grown-ups wanted to talk, they'd shooed all the kids out to play: and then the streets became full of buffeting boys and squealing girls from the houses around. The evening light had left the sky and they still weren't called in, and suddenly it was quite dark and there was a moment when Toby stood frightened and wanting to pee—and he'd turned his torch on instead and like moths the other children had swirled and clustered around him. Suddenly he'd become the focus of the group, which split into girls who hid and boys who ran in a pack, and the beam of his torchlight jumped through the dark and ducked and swerved around fences and bushes and houses. When a big boy tried to grab it from him Richard had pushed him away, and the other kids joined in too till the big boy knew he'd been beaten at last and gave up the battle. The memory of that night was full of magic and if something rotten lay deep in the core, he'd managed to hold it at bay all this time and out of the reach of the light.

In the train he examined their faces as he'd done every night since Easter; but when they charged to the gate to meet him, the three of them, roaring and surging and grabbing his suitcase and pulling him into their current—when they charged to the gate he was suddenly thrown by how far they'd moved from his memory, how perfect they were. His father looked down at him, thinking the boy might be lost in this bright race of cousins, but Hannah grabbed him in a hard-angled hug and Lizzie picked up his haversack and swung it around her, pivoting with it in her delight at this unexpected addition to their holiday, and then Richard pulled him away from the girls and said, 'I'll show you where we're sleeping. We sleep out the back.'

Bad things just happen. That's what they said at the funeral a few weeks later: bad things just happen and no-one is really to blame.

But after the funeral his dad had taken him home again.

INTERVIEW SGT MARRON 7/1/67

Richard Woods My name is Richard Woods. I am twelve years old. We are staying here for the holidays. We come up here every year, just after Christmas.
Richard Woods I like it here. I like the beach. I like the park.
Richard Woods I did go to the park yesterday. With my cousin and my sisters. My cousin is Toby Woods.
Richard Woods Some other kids came as well and we played with them. We played at the spaceship and up at the shed. We played there all day.
Richard Woods We did not play at the sandpit. We played at the shed and under the shed and in the bush that's around the shed. We played Phantom Agents.
Richard Woods We stayed at the park. We did not leave the park. We stayed there all day.

Toby

It was Richard he loved the most—Richard, who was impossibly strong and clever, impossibly brave. Richard was twelve years old to Toby's eight—tall and already muscled, fast and fearless, a ruthless tackler, a scaler of trees, a clandestine smoker. Richard never thought before he acted, never foresaw the consequence, was not afraid; to Toby, whose life had been roped in by fear and prophecy, Richard was godlike. And Hannah, the eldest, who idolised Richard, who followed him into every crisis and every act of nobility, every battle—Hannah was second in Toby's heart. They pounded through the house ahead of him, hurtling down the length of the hallway, straight through the kitchen and out the back to show him the screened-in verandah that the boys would share. He stopped on the threshold behind Lizzie and strained to look in through the door—and everything was perfect, as perfect as Easter, was just as he'd dreamed it would be.

It was a rickety little room, tacked on, never really intended for a bedroom. There was a chair of frayed cane, a wardrobe that stood on three legs with a small pile of books for the fourth, a bureau and two ex-army stretcher beds, one neatly made up with sheets and a pillow, the other already strewn with boy-detritus—a sleeping-bag, a pocket-knife, socks and swimmers, still wet, and a towel with its own trail of sand. Lizzie dropped the haversack onto the visitor's bed, and Richard flung himself down with abandon onto the tumult of the other.

'No-one else is allowed in here,' he said, and Lizzie's 'Yes we are' was half-hearted at best and vanished into the silence. Because this was a boy's kingdom, Richard's kingdom, shut off from the world of sisters and parents and rules, and everyone knew it. Electricity hadn't made it this far. There was a hurricane lantern, matches on the bureau, and instead of glass in the windows there was nothing but mesh and a canvas blind to pull down if it started to rain. 'Make yourself at home,' Richard said with some magnanimity and, as if to underline the sanctuary, Aunt Susan's voice called suddenly down the hallway, 'Hannah! Lizzie!'

And that was that. Toby said a rushed goodbye to his father, who had to shoot back to the station to catch the last train, and then he ran back through the house to unpack before Richard could change his mind.

INTERVIEW SGT MARRON 7/1/1967

Osman My name is Faruk Osman. I came from Turkey. I am 34 years old.

Osman I can speak English. I can speak some English. I can understand you.

Osman I know a child is missing. I understand what missing means.

Osman I work for the council. I was at the park yesterday morning. I was working.

Osman I was clipping the hedge. I was doing the gardens—the roses. I was fixing the tools. I clean up the tools in the shed.

Osman I can read. I can write.

Toby

At some stage, on his own first day perhaps, Richard had also unpacked, claiming the space with his own array of possessions. So the shelves—not really shelves, just a wooden box painted and nailed to the wall with a little round mirror beside it—held a torch like Toby's own torch, a Coca-Cola Master Series yoyo, a bottle top scraped to silver, a stick of green chalk. Toby looked without touching, keeping his hands in his pockets. He was torn between the thrill of acceptance and an acute awareness of the potential for being a nuisance. The bureau had a book as well as the hurricane lantern and there were two other books and some comics on the floor beside it. A hook on the back door held a rope fashioned into a lasso or maybe a noose imperfectly tied. A haversack almost identical to his leaned against the metal leg of Richard's army cot, and sandshoes and socks and clothes lay just where they'd fallen.

Toby undid the straps of his pack and emptied it onto the bed. The clothes went into a drawer of the bureau, but there was a box of Fantales too, and his pair of binoculars. He put these on the end of his bed, in a gesture that invited sharing but not too eagerly.

Richard ignored them.

Toby sat.

The back door closed the verandah off from the main part of the house. There was a low wooden door, three feet high, in the furtherest wall, which could have been a closet or could have led anywhere and he imagined exploring it in secret, just him with his torch, but Richard read his mind and said, 'It's locked—I've got the key.' And then he sat up suddenly, hooked Toby's haversack up with one foot and pulled it over onto his bed. He checked it closely, pulling the straps about, testing for strength, and when he was satisfied he threw it back to Toby's bed and said, as one connoisseur of packs to another, 'It's genuine army. Like mine.'

He made the thumbs-up at Toby and life was perfect.

On that first night the mesh window melted away and the stars began to move across the sky. Richard lit the lamp as soon as the sun had set, holding it up by its wire handle, swinging it with studied fearlessness. 'You can't see yet, but later this whole window disappears. At night, it's not like a room at all, it's like being outside in a tent.'

But it wasn't like being in a tent—it was like being in a cave whose unguarded entrance let in all the wild and enormous night. The hurricane lamp couldn't burn forever and when the yellow flame sucked itself back to the wick and sputtered a moment and died, they were left in the darkness. Small noises crept in from the blackness outside. They could smell the woody, grassy dew and the ash of old fires. They whispered across to each other, plans for midnight hunting trips, bonfires on the beach, dawn raids down at McCauley's to swipe the bottles of soft drink left at the back of the shop, but the darker it got the more Toby wished they were inside the proper walls of the house, or the beds were closer together, or there was light. When the spaces grew bigger and it sounded like Richard might be asleep, Toby would rouse him with more questions until it was very late and no-one whispered back across the silent room and Toby knew that he was the only one left on the planet. Soon he was adrift himself, in a grey and abandoned world with his eyes closed, trying to remember himself and the anchor of home. There was a knot in his stomach that might have been fear or might have been sadness but it vanished almost at once because Richard was shaking his shoulder and outside the darkness was just giving way to the dawn ...

And that morning stayed in Toby's mind forever. He'd only known the overprotected life of a solitary child—and now he'd survived a night without walls and was outside at sunrise, unwatched and unguarded, with this soldier, this boy-king who knew all the bush tracks, who ran without tiring, who climbed the unclimbable, who aimed and fired at sounds in the bushland that could have been anything.

Because that was the other thing, the most dangerous thing. He'd brought the air rifle with him.

INTERVIEW SGT MARRON 7/1/1967

Osman There were people at the park. Many people.

Osman I do not know how many.

Osman There were children in the sandpit. I do not know how many. There were babies, little babies. There were big children, boys and girls.

Osman There were one or two adults. One or maybe two. Maybe three.

Osman I did not talk to them.

Osman I did not talk to the children.

Toby

The rifle had come at Christmas, after months and months of pleading, but already Richard held it as though it was part of him. They had whispered about it last night, and now Toby thrilled at the sight of it—shiny and powerful, full of the threat of danger. The barrel was cold and so grey it was almost a taste, as bitter as iron; the tiny V of the sight was meticulous, pitiless. The strap was still stiff and the butt was perfectly curved to fit Richard's shoulder. It had grown into him already; against all the rules, he carried it loaded in one easy hand, ready to shoot on a split-second impulse. He could jump and spin and aim and fire off a shot in a single movement and he knew everything that there was to know about hunting. 'You can't be afraid,' he told Toby, that very first morning. 'You have to be quick, you have to be *certain.*' Because that was what having a gun was all about, this *certainty*; that was what transformed a boy into a hunter. 'If you just wound a pig, it'll rip you apart with its tusks,' Richard said, and he said it casually, sighting along the rifle's barrel. 'You have to be sure you can kill it with just one shot.'

'Have you killed things?' Toby asked, and Richard looked beyond him into the middle distance, considering how much knowledge could safely be shared. He turned away without giving an answer. But later that morning he handed the rifle to Toby and taught him to aim and fire, and Toby shot at tree trunks and ran up to find the little grey pellets embedded right into the bark of the wood, all crumpled and dead. So you probably couldn't kill a pig with this rifle, but that didn't matter. What made Richard heroic was the thing that he knew in his heart—that he *could* kill a pig, and that if he did he would do it the right way, all at once and without any fear. And maybe Richard had killed with a different gun, a bigger gun. Toby pulled the pellets out of the bark, and later, when the sun was properly up and they were hungry enough to head back to the house, he carried the little grey talismans home in his pocket.

And after that it didn't matter about the screen wire that vanished as night fell and left the verandah exposed and unprotected or about the long, long train ride that stood between Toby and home. The days developed a pattern, a plan of action. In the mornings, Richard would shake him awake in the piccaninny dawn and they'd race across the grey garden and over the fence and lose themselves in the scrub. They'd build a fire before the sun was properly up, using kindling and grass and the matches they pinched from the house. Most of the time it was just the two of them—Hannah didn't like mornings—and most of the time they brought bread down to toast, and sometimes potatoes and eggs. The bread fell off the sticks and the potato skins burned and were too hot to touch, and the eggs exploded or stayed depressingly raw—but with nobody there to laugh they could still be warriors. The fire would turn to ashes as the sun rose, and they could imagine they'd been there all night, that they'd been camping out in the wild, surviving beasts and battles and capture. They made spears and practised throwing them; they practised flicking the pocket-knife, first at trees, but then at each other and you had to be quick to dodge it in the sand. They practised ambushing and tracking and hunting, they made weapons and stockpiled them under a cover of fallen branches and leaves at the foot of a tree. They talked about what they were doing, but never about themselves. Richard thought up the plans and ideas and Toby helped carry them out. They were a team—and if one of them was less strong and less quick he wasn't a girl at least, and they could rely on each other not to go bleating to grown-ups if someone got hurt . . .

Every morning they'd see the sun fire the world into life; wallabies crossed the tracks in front of them, possums tightrope-walked along the telephone wires. Once the track was swathed in spider webs covered with dew; they thrashed the webs down with sticks. 'We should bring some petrol next time,' said Richard, 'and burn them out like Dad burns the bull ants at home.' But they didn't have petrol so they fired the little grey pellets into the bushes just as a warning.

Within himself, deep in the private places, Toby knew he was growing stronger and less afraid—but then his father would phone and take a bite out of his heart. 'You'll be back before you know it, old son,' his father would say. And, 'Everything will be right as rain again soon.' Well there was nothing right about rain, and the longest he could stay was till school went back, so why did he have to be reminded all the time?

Morning after morning they raced through the dawn and started their outlaw fires and when the fires had died they'd destroy the evidence, pulling the brightest sticks from the embers and stomping them into dust. Hannah would join them once the morning had properly begun; and one day—when they knew they could trust him—she and Richard took him down to their secret place, the abandoned lighthouse.

Hannah

Oh, someone will *die* today I swear, with my lanyard wrapped round their neck they will *die* if this lockdown fiasco continues. The car park, the lift, and now I'm locked out of my office. Who the fuck is in charge here? I mean it—who is in charge? They've closed the rehearsal rooms, the hallways are packed with sopranos hurling high Cs around and it doesn't help that my head is full of *Vikings*, and it doesn't help that security's discovered the PA system or that there are people all over the place doing room checks and blocking things off with ropes and steam-cleaning *carpets* for fuck's sake and none of them knows how to whisper, none of them knows the value of SILENCE! Above all it doesn't help that they've not only locked up my office they've closed the *bar* as well, can you believe it? Locked up my office and closed off the *bar*, and Jesus they'd better not keep it roped off much longer, because I'm not feeling great after last night, I'm not feeling top of the world, and some juice with a dash of vodka would do very nicely at this stage, would even things out for a while, put bits of me back together. A drink of some kind might settle my head—and some Panadeine and a Valium too, if you're buying.

Guards all over the place. All through the corridor, wall-to-wall guards and guns and security. I can't stand it—steps must be taken. It's time to head down to admin, to throw myself upon Lydia once again, prostrate myself before the jealous god of replacement passkeys. We've been here before, me and Lydia—we have a ragged and bitter history with passkey replacement. It's not very long since the last time I turned up, not very long since the last time she dragged out the sodding Serenity Prayer. Oh, I have supped at the table of Lydia's Discontent, I have drunk at the well of Aggrieved Displeasure—but this time at least I can tell her to fuck herself, this time I'm totally blameless; I'm sober, I have the key in my hand, and if my access code is screwed, well, that's clearly security's fuck-up—not mine.

GUARDIAN, SATURDAY, 23 JULY 2005

At Stockwell, bewildered eyewitnesses told how they had witnessed the moment, shortly after 10 am, when the suspect was repeatedly shot. All described the man as wearing a bulky winter coat, despite the warm weather, and at least one said he thought he spotted a belt with wires running from it.

The Messenger
SYDNEY, AUSTRALIA, DECEMBER 2005

These are the facts.

At 11.15 am, give or take, a middle-aged man of average height, clean-shaven, dark-haired, pushed a pink square of thin cardboard over the counter at Lawrence Dry Cleaners inside Wynyard Station. This had been planned.

The woman behind the counter matched the card to a garment. She was not a garrulous woman, not the type to push herself forward; later, when the media descended on Lawrence Dry Cleaners, she closed the doors. But she did remember, privately, that he looked like a nice bloke and that he was sweating. It was a terrible day to be carrying a thick woollen overcoat wrapped in cling plastic; although now that she thought about it, he'd removed the plastic and asked her if she had a bin or a place to put it. He had handed the plastic over, and thanked her.

This too was planned.

He left the dry cleaners then. He walked through the heat of lunchtime. He passed two bus stops and the maximum number of people. He carried the coat in front of him, draped over his arm like a curtain. Sweat dripped from his tight red face and was lost in the thick stiffened folds of wool. In the bin, his name waited, scrawled on pink paper, tangled and strangled in plastic. All this was planned.

He had already triggered alarms; he'd been caught on camera the night before in a well-guarded, sensitive venue. He was known to possess a stolen security pass.

An alert had gone out, a background report was being created; his past examined minutely; his movements were being discussed.

This, too—all part of his plan.

II

Lizzie

There should be men on the streets. The mosque is calling. There should be men on the streets, wearing robes and making their way up the hill to devotions. My first morning here, and each morning since for the last five weeks, every morning I've watched as the song from the mosque has called men to walk through the alleys, to climb up the hill to pray.

'Hayya 'ala-salahh . . . As-salatu khayru min an-nawm.' Come to prayer . . . Prayer is better than sleep.

The streets are still empty.

Listen—you need to know this. The walls of the Old Town are fifteen metres high and there are four gates, four *bab*s for entry. But listen—the gates, the *bab*s, are blocked by military cars. I know. I was down there. Outside the Bab R'cif, the square was crammed with soldiers and trucks. There was light from the trucks, light blazing all through the square, and I could see things. I could see this—I could see the tour bus in flames. Inside the bus there were people and outside the bus there were soldiers with guns and the door at the front of the bus was burst open—exploded or shot through perhaps, I can't be sure. There were trucks at the gates and trucks coming in to cut off the streets to the New Town.

I saw a man burning inside the bus, one of the men from the German tour group; I saw him screaming and trying to push his way out through the door. I saw him shot. I saw him fall. I watched him burn and smelled him burning and inside the bus the other people were screaming louder and louder and then the bus itself started screeching and twisting and more and more soldiers were running up, training their guns and shooting in, shooting in through the windows.

I watched as the bus exploded. It exploded slowly, pieces flew slowly, scattering flames and hitting against the walls, the trucks, and skittering over the ground.

We're trapped in the Old Town now. The walls are surrounded. The exits are sealed.

I saw one other thing. I saw Ali, watching, down at the edge of the wall, and the light and the flames were reflected again in his eyes. I think he saw me. I held out my hand, I tried to speak. He slipped past me, back in through the barricade, up through the gateway, tiny and quick as a fish; he slipped through the alleys and disappeared into the blackness and chill of the Old Town.

He led them there and then he watched them burn.

I know what the silence is. The generator that throbs like a heartbeat just under the chaos of sound is dead.

He is eight years old. He can't be dangerous

Toby

The lighthouse had long been forgotten because of the park. The park sat on a spit of land above the harbour, with swings and a merry-go-round and a wooden fortress. Behind it, to the north, a pathway gave access to two real cannons, left over from a time when war had seemed threateningly close. Further on was an anchor, huge and heroic, embedded in concrete; further still the mast of a ship, and a telescope pointing across the water; and then even further than that, Richard told him, was the start of the tunnels that led to the underground rooms where bombs and grenades had been stored in the time of the war and where graffiti carved into the walls held the long-ago dates of the sentry watch and soldiers' initials. Beyond the tunnels the trail widened out and led down to a little cove with a sandy beach and a chain of rock pools. That was the western side of the spit.

The eastern side of the spit was a different matter. It was a dangerous, unloved place—off-limits, forbidden. The track from the edge of the road was hard to find and covered with blackberry bushes. There was no real path, just a wombat trail overhung with huge knotted fig trees and tangling lianas. At man height—even at boy height—it was uninviting terrain, and doubly so when compared with the west-side treasures. There were no cannons and anchors here, no soft sandy coves for swimming in—only thorns, and rusted fence-wire covered with more thorns, and instead of a path a tripwire of vines and a spillway of rock that fell into the water, covered by stinking green weed at the foot of the jetty. What clearing had once been done had been eaten back up by the bush years ago, and the descent was treacherous and steep and threatening.

Toby did his best to swallow the thorns and stings of the track, but the clawing of blackberry bushes left him near tears. 'They don't hurt that much,' Richard said to him, not with disdain, exactly, but with some impatience. 'I've had heaps.' He showed him his big boy's hands, all scratted and puckered with scars. 'We can go back if you like,' said Hannah, but Toby shook his head and pushed on.

And it was worth it after all, worth the blackberry thorns, worth the welts on his shins from the tangle of wires, the sting of sweat in his eyes, it was worth it to stand with these two, alone, at the edge of the spit where people hadn't been, so Richard said, since the end of the war; to be there when Richard passed him the water bottle from the camping kit and said with a mixture of pride and threat, 'If a boat crashed on these rocks, no-one would know it was here.' Except us, he meant, and it was worth the perilous clamber, worth it just to be included.

From above, the rocks at the water's edge had looked jumbled and stuck together—but now he could see there were spaces between them to find a careful footing. There was a little rock ledge that was hidden, just off the end of the track, and the water below it was cold and clear with tiny fish darting through it. He watched them slip through the seaweed, playing follow-the-leader and hide-and-seek—and then they scattered all in an instant as Richard led the way over the shallows and up to the jetty.

The jetty was rotting; the gaps where planks had long been missing were easily wide enough for a boy to slip through. Even Richard was cautious at first, fitting the haversack onto his back and strapping it firmly. He handed the water flask to Hannah and she crossed its long strap diagonally over her chest. The flask itself fell heavy against her hip.

'Be careful,' said Richard, and Toby would have frozen but Hannah took hold of his wrist and led him safely along the splintering remnants of wood. At the base of the lighthouse enough of the platform remained to give them a place to sit and they unpacked their lunch, legs dangling over the water, and they talked and laughed and ate and made balloons of their paper bags, dropping them onto the water to float in the current.

They climbed up the ladder and rattled the old iron lock at the battered door; they scratched their initials into the paint of the lighthouse. They lay on their stomachs and watched the jellyfish drift under the gap-toothed pier.

'This is government land,' said Richard. 'It's illegal just to be here. We could be shot.' He pointed to a rusted white metal square by the rocks at the shore, hanging unevenly, scarred, almost covered with blackberry. It was an official government sign, and though most of the words had been lost with the peeling of paint, it still held authority. But Hannah, suddenly impatient, got to her feet. 'They only shoot children in Russia,' she said. 'And nobody uses this place any more. The light hasn't worked for years.'

'They'll use it one day,' said Richard. 'They'll fix the light and they'll find our names on the door and they'll know we were here.'

Hannah left them then, and Toby, still on his stomach, watched her step carefully over the gaps and jump down from the end of the pier. She was growing more quickly than they were, he suddenly realised; she was taller and thinner since Easter and brothers and cousins and lighthouses wouldn't contain her for long. His heart lurched at the thought that she could leave them behind like this, and he was suddenly frightened of the drop to the water and gripped the wooden planks to steady himself. She turned, and stood with a finger raised in the air in a gesture that always meant *listen to me*: 'You should show him the cross,' she called to Richard. And then she was gone.

The cross wasn't really a cross any more—it was just a piece of wood that had once been painted white, cemented into a little mound of concrete. When Hannah had found it, years ago now, it had at least been complete—a white wooden crucifix marking a death or a burial; but the writing, if there was writing, had long since peeled off, and there was nothing to show who was being memorialised. That first year, Hannah had cleared the space around it of rocks and thorns to make it respectable; but when they came running to see it the next year, the weeds had grown back and the crosspiece had splintered and split and was lost in the undergrowth. Each year the weeds and thorns grew back and each year the marker was harder to find, but the children would clear the space around it, right down to the mound of cement with the hole that Hannah had found with her probing, insistent girl-fingers.

The mounded cement domed up to a few inches clear of the ground; a cavity angled in at forty-five degrees. 'We think a flag went in there, but we never found it,' said Richard. He took Toby's hand and bunched three of his fingers together to slip them into the opening and show him the grooves at the bottom. 'We think a soldier's body is buried under here. If it's a soldier's grave, you'd need somewhere to put the flag.' He sat on the ground suddenly and pulled off his shoes and socks and then he threw off the rest of his clothes and high-footed down to the slippery rocks. He hauled himself up on the jetty again, and sprinted along it as though the planks hadn't rotted, as though nails didn't stand up rusty and lethal and hungry for naked feet; and then, at the very deepest edge, he hurled himself into the water, his knees clutched up to his chest. The splash was enormous. When he surfaced, he cut through the water neatly, swimming the length of the jetty, moving from pylon to barnacled pylon—a shark or a dolphin, strong and completely fearless, entirely at home in the ocean.

'Come in!' he yelled and put his face right down again into the water without even closing his eyes. He pushed away from the pylons and looked up and yelled, 'We should have brought the snorkel and flippers,' and then he disappeared down in a duck-dive that took him right under the jetty, right into the shadowy places. Toby was panicked, holding his own breath, counting the seconds in case there was danger, in case there was something down there waiting, in case there was terror and screaming and blood, but suddenly there he was, bursting up through the surface, grinning and shaking his head, the droplets of water flying away from his hair in a crown of tiny lights, an exploding halo. 'There's a really big fish down there! Really big! We should've brought a spear gun.' And he was gone again, diving back down to the blackness under the shade of the jetty.

And that was the wonder of them. Everything that they did was reckless, heroic. Not just Richard, all the cousins, Hannah and Lizzie too. When they did the washing-up, they didn't take care and mind the glasses—they twisted the tea towels up to use them as whips on each other, with the ends all knotted and wetted to make them sting. They played with matches all the time—stealing them from the stove or the box near the hurricane lantern, striking them and flicking them at each other, lit, and jumping out of the way just in the nick of time. They were never where they said they'd be, they ran across roads and they played wherever they wanted and no-one was watching. To Toby, raised in the web of his mother's illness, this was astounding. Her sickness had stretched like tentacles, pulling him away from the world, back into the safety of home. He had learned to be quiet and terribly vigilant because even on good days the world outside was hedged about with danger, and on bad days he would wake with a start to find her sitting across from his bed, watching him, sleepless and terrified. Her terror infected him. It was impossible to know whether he was being watched or watched over, if he was the threat or the target of threat— and if he woke to find her watching he knew that days would pass before she would sleep again, days of watchfulness followed by nights of talking and praying and sometimes shouting.

But the cousins were fearless. Things would get broken, and nobody cared that someone could lose an eye. Living with them was like living inside a volcano, like walking right up to the edge of a hundred-foot cliff and not falling, it was like playing with fire and not getting burned and he knew that little by little he was forgetting to be afraid . . .

Lizzie

We noticed it yesterday, the new unfriendliness down at the market. The cries of 'Hello, come in' were missing; the insistent offers of *thé menthe* and biscuits were gone. Two of the men from the bus group had come back early, with talk of trouble down near the tanneries. But perhaps it began before then; perhaps it had already started. Perhaps it began on the night that we watched a tangle of boys flitting neat-footed, nimble as goats, across the flat roofs high over the Old Town.

It was Kate who spotted them first—Kate who owns the *ryad*, who's lived here for years now, part of the old medina. My New York professor had suggested I email her for some contacts for my dissertation; but then there was all the sad to-ing and fro-ing of my divorce and it wasn't till later, until that was finally all behind me, I found her website again—with all the alleys and markets and fountains, the colour, the cobbled squares and the mosque at twilight. And I thought perhaps this was the angle I could take: not the wandering tribe, but the tribal settlement, the town that evolves, the walls that enfold them; and besides, I thought, it looked like a place to rest, just to *be* for a while. My professor approved the changes, I booked a ticket, a room at the *ryad*, and from the first morning and for weeks afterwards I found myself asking: how will I ever leave this?

And then just a few nights ago, in the rooftop courtyard, as Kate poured the coffee—in the chatter and mix of languages I saw her waver, become distracted. I followed her gaze to an artist's dream silhouetted above the thrum of the market—a tribe of boys running hard along the flat rooftops; a palette of smoke and shadow and movement. Young voices lifted clear of the chaos, wafted across the tumultuous dusk in a burst of shouting and laughter and I thought it was a game perhaps; hide-and-seek, or chasings. But then I saw the gang was half-grown, was too old for children's games: and the boy in front was dark-skinned and clearly afraid.

He vanished into the tangle of roofs. They followed hot on his shadow and didn't return. I turned to ask what had happened, what we'd seen, but Kate shook her head.

'Somali,' she said to me, but she said it quietly.

Perhaps it began then—or even before then. Perhaps it was already building.

Of course it was.

The darkness is lifting now. The houses begin to stand clear of the shadows. They are mud brick, ancient, built up against one another; they lean out over the alleys and laneways, jostling their neighbours, creating the walkways and tunnels that only the donkeys can master. There should be growers pushing their carts to the market on top of the hill. There should be charcoal fires burning down in the street at the places where merchants gather. There should be the ribbon of light that marks the roadway outside the Old Town walls, the warm pools of orange spilling into the misty blue overlay.

I don't know where Ali is. I don't know what's happening outside the walls. I came back through the empty, dark streets to the guesthouse door, which is more than three metres high, made of wood and iron, and shut it behind me. I walked back up the narrow dark staircase that twists like the Old Town itself, back and back and back again, till it reaches the door that leads to the rooftop courtyard. And I am there, now, waiting for day, and my hands are shaking.

I've never known the *ryad* to be so silent.

The Messenger

From Wynyard Station, he walked down to Circular Quay, still pushing the coat in front of him. It was a hot day. Witnesses said that he seemed intense; that he walked briskly; that he bumped into other pedestrians from time to time, '*but not like a drunk—just like a man in a bit of a hurry*'.

At the Quay he approached each of the ticket booths in turn, asking which was the ferry for Bradleys Head. He ordered a cup of coffee at the milk bar and drank it in one gulp with his coat across his knees. He walked through the crowds again—asking over and over for directions to Bradleys Head.

At about three o'clock, it was later reported, he put his overcoat on, bought a ticket and boarded the ferry.

Deep in the heart of the city, he was already under discussion. Threats were being assessed. Emergency plans were considered.

'*You don't think, do you?*' a woman said on the television news the next day. '*I mean, we've seen all the ads on TV, but you don't really know what you're looking for. He might have been sick, you know—just a little bit crazy.*'

Hannah

Oh *god*, I'd forgotten she'd have the radio on. I'm always astounded by Lydia's tragic fixation with Mr Ray Kane. We may work in one of the most beautiful buildings in the world, we may be home to Australia's most uplifting music, but the constant ambience from Lydia's office is the vile faux-political *vomit* that Kane whips up from the sat-upon suburbs. I don't know where he gets his audience from. He's not an attractive guy, but they flock right to him.

I knew him years ago. He was a small and borderline loathsome kid and he's grown even viler with age. Today, of course, it's the global forum he's targeting—more specifically the antiforum brigade.

'*Is the police commissioner going to cave in to these thugs and troublemakers? Or will he have the guts to finally stand up to them? He should refuse them a licence. He shouldn't let the idiots march!*'

He should let them march and then have the Americans shoot them. Ray Kane would love that.

I've got to start taking an interest again. I've got to start reading the paper again for fuck's sake. Somewhere there'll be an answer, somewhere deep in the bowels of Hansard or something, somewhere they will explain, our fearless leaders, just when it was that we signed the whole bloody country over to the good old US of A. Somewhere, I'm sure, they'll explain why we can't throw a *party*, for chrissake, invite the neighbours for dinner, discuss some business, hear a few songs without filling the hallways with gun-toting Homeland Security types. I'm not against guns, you understand, or taut-bodied jocks in jackets—but this is *Australia*, people, and sanctioned thuggery brings out the worst in us. The Asian heads of state always dropped by before without all this drama. The British PM has been over; we didn't drag out the water cannons for him and fence off the fucking footpaths. So I don't see why the American president gets all this palaver. I don't need the global explanation, I don't need a DefCon briefing. I'd settle for local answers—I'd settle for where the fuck's Lydia?

I used to be informed. No, really. I used to read all the papers, I used to be up to the minute. I had concerns and opinions and everything. And then I just lost interest and I'll tell you why. There's this thing called a Gordian worm. It lives in the stomach of grasshoppers, but in order to breed it needs to be swimming in water, so what it does, it makes the grasshopper search for a pool of water and dive into it and drown. So think about that for a moment. Somewhere inside the Gordian worm there's a gene that knows what a worm should do in order to make a grasshopper drown itself in a fucking pond. A *gene*. In a *worm*; inside a *grasshopper*. And here's the thing: you think about the Gordian worm for long enough, about how it controls the grasshopper, how it makes the insect drown itself so the worm can breed and multiply, and all of a sudden it starts to sound very familiar. You find yourself mulling over the whole al-Qaeda issue. Suddenly there's us and America and Britain and large bits of Europe all flailing and thrashing around and looking for new ways to drown our democracy. Warrantless searches; renditions—extrajudicial imprisonments ... Look out the window now, with this heads-of-state gathering set for tonight, look down there at Circular Quay, at the barriers, loudspeakers, sniffer dogs. There are *water cannons*, for god's sake. *Water cannons!* In little Australia! Take a look out there and tell me the bad guys aren't winning.

And then, of course, it's a very small step from genes and grasshoppers to tequila slammers and after one or two or five of those, the fact that you live in a country that's run by a Gordian worm from a cave in Afghanistan seems, I dunno, somehow less special ...

She's not here. Lydia's not here. Lydia *lives* in this office, she *has* no life, she's *never* away and just when I *need* her, when I could *use* her, she disappears. And all her people have given up entirely; come over all helpless and pointless and thrilled to be ordered around by Americans. And by Ray bloody Kane.

Toby

No-one noticed when they all got back from the lighthouse—no-one had known they were gone. The doors were flung open as soon as the day began, and stayed open and unlocked all day. The kids were shooed from the house like so many spiders, swept up and shooed outside. They didn't come back to the house till the light began to fade, and in the clamour of teatime the first of the lies was born. 'What did you do today?' the father asked Toby, and Toby was frightened, seeing again the barbed wire, the NO TRESPASSING sign; he retracted himself in the way of the sea anemone. But the others had no qualms at all. 'We went to the tunnels,' said Richard, 'and guess what we found?' He held out his hand and a marble lay there, cool and mysterious, green as the sea, smooth and dull on his palm. His father took it and rolled it across the table, polished it, held it to catch the light. 'Well, that's really something,' he said. And that was the wonderful thing about Richard. He carried the burden for all of them.

Later, in the little verandah room, Richard flicked the marble over to Toby's bed. 'It's really rare. It could be made of emerald,' he said; and then, as Toby turned it over in his hands, 'I wasn't lying. I did find it in the tunnels.' But not today. Today had been all lighthouse, all glint and mirror of sun and water, and dazzle of

Richard and Hannah. Toby flicked the marble up with his thumb and Richard caught at it, quick and careless, and dropped it onto the mantelpiece. 'If you like, I can show you the tunnels tomorrow,' he said, climbing into his bed.

Lizzie

I can see more clearly now; the light is blue and the shadows are purple and yellow like bruises. The streets are still full of last night's rubbish. The sweepers should have been through by now; the donkeys should be hauling the refuse away.

I need to describe the guesthouse I'm in—the *ryad*; the *ryad* is something you need to understand. You mustn't think of it as a guesthouse in the Western sense—it's not. It's fifteenth-century Islamic architecture; built on a large square floorplan, four storeys around an open interior courtyard. There are two main staircases, set into two of the corners. They are terribly narrow, these staircases, and terribly steep, eighty-one steps cut into sections of nine—so nine steps, and then a turning of ninety degrees and then nine more steps and so on. Do you understand? The stairwell is dark, tiled in dark blue and white, and the risers so steep that your legs will ache on the way from the ground to the rooftop. As you climb through the storeys, the rooms become bigger, more beautiful, more ornate, and there are little hidden chambers, secret annexes tucked under the turn of the stairs where the women could sit behind pretty carved fretwork and watch the play of life below without being seen themselves. But these are traditional, common in every house; you mustn't think of them as safe hiding places.

The wooden interior doors are three metres high and carved and painted, the floor and walls are tiled and the pillars too, all beautifully tiled in *zellij*. I can't begin to tell you how captivating, how peaceful and gentle the whole effect is. But there is only one way in and one way out—just the door to the street. To be safe in here, you need to secure the entrance. When the door is locked and the windows are shuttered, the house shows a solid, unbreachable wall to the street.

From the top floor another staircase leads out to the roof. The roofs are flat. People sit up here in the evenings, drink coffee or sweet mint tea, and talk and watch the sun set low behind the hills.

Why is this important? So you'll know this is not like home, this is not what you think. So you'll know what to look for, you'll have some idea how to find us . . .

The light from the mosque is fading. The shadows have gone.

Listen. There could be guns on the roofs. There could be snipers. There could be children with stones. A stone hurled down from the roofs could kill you.

I think the Italians got out—Carlo and his girlfriend. I think they did—I don't know. I haven't seen them since last night. They were young, they were not wealthy enough for the *ryad*; they stayed at one of the houses up by the old Jewish quarter, the *mellah*. There are two Americans staying here, Jenna and Tom. Jenna is a TV presenter from one of the National Geographic shows; Tom is her cameraman. There's a young French couple, Luc and Brigitte, barely into their twenties. There are four older people from Spain and some others, some Europeans I think, who came in yesterday while I was still down at Bhalil. Someone should be keeping a tally of all the guests; Kate will know. There are servants—two or three local boys, and the teenaged girls in the kitchen. The girls are Somalis, refugees, from the camp on the edge of the town.

I keep thinking: are we the only ones who saw the bus burning, Ali and me? Does no-one else know? Then why is the Old Town locked down? Why is every door shut?

They know. The locals know. They are staying off the streets, staying in their houses, keeping the shutters closed and their huge doors bolted and locked because they know.

My face is bleeding. I hadn't realised. The blood has congealed in the cold. There's a bump on the side of my temple. I can feel it throbbing.

I must have fallen, down at the gates.

I saw Richard in Rome. Not that it's relevant now. Or maybe it is.

The night has faded. All the blue shadows have burned away in the dawn. There's no sound coming up from the streets. Perhaps they're gone. Perhaps it's over.

Will anyone come? Does anyone know that we're here?

Toby

'If you like, I can show you the tunnels tomorrow,' Richard had said, but there were too many other things to do, too much to see, and it was Uncle Peter who took them up days and days later, when he wanted to try out the flash on his newest camera. 'How about you pack something to eat and we'll have a picnic,' he said to Aunt Susan; and Lizzie overheard, as she always did, and broadcast the news. 'We're going on a picnic! We're going on a picnic!' she chanted, beating her hands on the kitchen table—and because there were adults the rules had changed, and they could be skittish and silly again, even Richard.

'We'll take the bikes and meet you up there,' Richard said, but to Toby's secret relief the adults said no.

'It's going to be a scorcher, mate,' Uncle Peter said. 'And we'll want to take a trip down to the beach on the way back.'

It was a very short car trip—ridiculously short, only five minutes or so—but Lizzie's silliness infected them all, and they sang and jostled and tickled each other all the way. When they got to the headland Richard and Hannah tore off, disappearing into the mouth of the tunnel, shouting and screaming and whooping up echoes that tumbled into the silence. Aunt Susan took the car rug and spread it out on the grass and unpacked the basket, and

Uncle Peter got his two cameras together and tested his little light meter and fiddled around with the flash.

'Ready,' he said, and Lizzie and Toby set off beside him.

Toby didn't like the tunnels. They were dark and they smelled of the wet earth floors and the air was trapped and musty. Richard and Hannah knew their way through the dark but to Toby the burrow of rooms was sad and bewildering, and the press of earth above him was disconcerting. Outside, in the shade of the trees, the cannons stood high on their battlements and the day was sunny and full of blue sky and birds; there were sparrows and willie wagtails up there and tiny grey lizards skipping across the stones—but in here the paths that began in the sunlight soon turned into high-walled canyons that sank ever more deeply into the earth till roofs formed above them; and then they were gloomy and chill and dank and though the light sliced through in bands from the grids in the roof the bands grew further and further apart and it seemed that the earth was closing in all around him.

He hung back with Lizzie while Uncle Peter used the flash to photograph eerie grey chambers and the light that speared through the grids. There was nothing here any more—the shells and bullets had gone long ago, and the paths through the tunnels had been tamped down for years by thousands of sandshoes and sandals; but Toby imagined the soldiers, standing alone with their guns at the ready all through the night, imagined them watchful, perhaps afraid—and maybe they didn't like being soldiers anyway, and maybe they didn't like being so far from home. He knew the sadness that had seeped into the walls along with the rain and the trapped air and darkness. Children's hands had rubbed along during games of chasings and blind man's bluff, so that three feet above the ground the rock was smooth and almost warm, but the tunnels themselves were lonely and full of hurt.

They stayed close to the father, the little ones, one on each hand; and when the light disappeared completely, when the track grew into a tunnel, they moved closer still. Lizzie grabbed his left hand as often as she could, and when he needed it to work the flash for his camera, she twined her fingers around his belt. Toby, less assured, kept his hand on the edge of the camera case that was slung from his uncle's shoulder. Without recourse to complaining or whining they slowed his progress so much that he retraced their steps to the place where the last slanting grid of light had been and he told them, 'Stay here in the light. I'll be back before you can count to twenty, okay? And we'll go back to Mum.' He jogged away into the darkness—but just when he was about to vanish from sight he turned and lifted the camera to get a shot of them, taut and alone in the tunnels, and then he changed his mind, and didn't take the photo, didn't even press the shutter. He came back and crouched down in front of Toby and said, 'You're okay, mate. You're okay. Tell you what—we'll go back, hey? I think Aunty Susan will want some help sorting the lunch out.' He took Toby's hand this time as well as Lizzie's and when they got back up to the picnic rug he said softly to Lizzie's mum, 'God alone knows what she's done to that poor little kid, but he knows about terror.'

Later, back at home, they heard him give Richard and Hannah a bollocking. 'You're meant to watch out for him, you two,' he said. 'You're meant to look out for him.' Hannah said, '*I* didn't know he was scared of the dark,' and Uncle Peter snapped, 'You should have known. You should have noticed the first time you took him down there. And I'll tell you something—you're not going down there again. The tunnels are out of bounds for the rest of the holidays.'

Richard and Hannah were outraged and Richard said, 'But that's not *fair*—' and Uncle Peter, loud-voiced and angry, said, 'Don't you argue with me. You'll do as you're bloody told, or I'll have that rifle back. You can think of somebody else for a change. You're meant to look after the little ones.' Then he softened a bit and said, more like his usual self, 'There's plenty of other places for you to explore.'

Mrs Monckton

You'll be able to see the heads-of-state fireworks thing from here a bit later, if that's what you want. That's where the view is, straight across to the Opera House, over the harbour. Better to watch it from here—they said on the radio there would be all sorts of trouble with all of the protestors. Thugs and troublemakers, that's all they are. Shouldn't be allowed to march, if you ask me. The police should get more powers. They should get tough.

There won't be too many people up here tonight, though. Not like New Year's Eve. The crowds on New Year's Eve are dreadful ... same every year. They come in from everywhere, from all over the place, come in in the morning and grab all the best spots with their picnic rugs and things—tables and chairs, some of them! All over the place. It's a pity I think, because all the locals miss out and of course it's the locals who pay the taxes.

I've lived here all my life, ever since I was married. It was, oh, a lovely little place back then—very pretty. So quiet. So friendly. It's still lovely, of course, but the values have gone through the roof now. It's the views, you see, and the beach, and it's so close to the city. But it's changed. It's different. I don't know anyone now—it's all different people. Stockmarket people. Eastern Suburbs. Once one of them buys in, of course, they all want a piece—it's not like it used to be. And there's crime now. Alcohol problems. Road rage. Graffiti all over the place. Didn't used to be crime, before. Just the one crime, that once. Just that once, the time when the poor little baby went missing.

The Messenger

On the ferry he went first to the cabin and stood for a time blocking the aisle as he folded his overcoat, placing it down on an empty seat. He moved to the windows then, crossing the ferry from side to side to change his view. At some point he took up the coat and moved outside. He wandered the periphery of the boat, pushing his way past the seated passengers. '*He was sweating and angry-looking,*' one person said; '*trying to find somewhere to sit perhaps, but all of the seats were taken.*'

He was noticed by most of his fellow passengers; as the journey continued he became increasingly agitated. A tourist on the ferry was concerned enough to ask if he was alright, and later one of the passengers said she had made a verbal report to the ferry's captain. The captain had passed the information on to authorities, stating he had seen the man who seemed 'very stressed out'.

'*I was alert,*' the ferry master said later. '*I kept an eye on him. I was alert, but I wasn't really unduly alarmed.*'

III

Toby

Hannah's call had come out of the blue, a gust of bright air on a day that was almost suffocating with lawyers and real estate agents. At first he'd thought it was Jen or one of the kids, calling in from Cambodia, but the number on the screen was a local one and unfamiliar. And then—'*Toby!* I don't believe it! We thought we'd lost you forever! It's *Hannah!*' she said; and his heart jumped suddenly, suddenly edged about with uncertainty.

'Hannah,' he said. 'I'm sorry—*Hannah?* I wasn't expecting—'

'Of *course* you were!' she said 'I wouldn't *ignore* you! And, listen, you're practically famous, aren't you? God of Cambodia or something? I suppose you forgot all about *us*,' she said, before he could get a word in. He hadn't heard from the cousins since childhood, but he could almost remember a summer, bright with laughter and sunlight and magic. 'We're hideously impressed,' she said. 'We tell *all* our friends—we bore them to *tears*. And, oh hell, I forgot to say—' and her voice was different, all of the tease was gone, she was real for a moment '—Toby, I'm sorry about your dad. I sort of remember him. He was one of the good ones.'

Which was nice of her. And nice of her, too, to make the call. She was teasing, of course, about being impressed, about the Cambodian thing, but they'd always teased—hadn't they always teased? And besides, he'd done very well, as a matter of fact, climbed a long way up through Senior Administrative Support. He had some good stories to tell. Assistant Trade Commissioner was nothing to sneeze at. And he'd been within striking distance of the ambassadorship.

'Blood's thicker than water,' she said. 'We have to have lunch, I'm afraid. You can't say no. We can't keep on *stalking* each other . . .'

Well, it would make a change from the endless clearing and packing and stowing away of his father's estate. They could make it late afternoon coffee instead of lunch and if it was awful he could always duck out, say he had somewhere to be, a meeting or something, sorry to run off, sorry to bolt—

But as things turned out he'd had no desire to bolt. She'd jumped up as soon as he walked in and thrown her arms around him and she was still utterly gorgeous, still stunning to look at (he'd forgotten how pretty she was) and wilder than ever, and funny and warm and she would have known him *any*where, known him at *once*, he was *just* the same, just exactly the bloody *same*, but what was he doing all those years, and how had life *treated* him—and how could he leave them like that?

By the time she'd stopped for breath and ordered coffee and cancelled it and ordered a bottle of champagne instead and a mezze plate, he'd been sucked in completely—he'd been buffeted, overwhelmed, drowned in her big-sister safety. 'It's great to see you again,' he'd managed, and she'd nodded, 'Isn't it? Isn't it?'

He'd wanted to ask about the others, about Richard, but the afternoon light was shimmering behind her, like a halo, a green glass halo catching her hair in the light off the water and he was suddenly silent again and awkward just like he used to be. He was tempted to pull out the photos of Jen and the kids, except that she'd think the children were his and he'd have to explain then, and explain why they weren't coming over, explain that it hadn't worked out, the family he'd tried to build in Cambodia that just never took, that wasn't well tended enough; and she might smell the failure on him and he might lose a bit of his shine. The walls had tightened around him, damp and constricting; he picked up his glass and set it down, brushed at the sleeve of his jacket, hoped she might notice the quality band on his watch—but when he'd looked up she was smiling, the light had settled, the room had righted itself, was balanced and stable again. And then she was laughing at him as she always had done—but kindly now, with the distance of years between them. 'We loved you, you know,' she'd said. 'From the very first moment we saw you, we loved you . . .'

She hadn't asked about his job; she'd just talked and in talking became again the brown-legged girl he remembered. She talked cinematically, visually, remembering details, so the decades vanished and the screen door opened and children swarmed out like blowflies—out to the side of the house to grab the wheezy old bikes and ride down to the park; and if Toby spent as much time walking as pedalling they were patient and didn't desert him, riding back again and again in long lazy loops to keep him in sight and encourage him on. 'You and that bloody red bike! Do you remember?' she'd asked with a sudden laugh at his stubbornness, his breathtaking lack of ability. And he did remember, the triumph of learning to ride it, the fierce way he loved it . . .

And once the floodgates were opened, they were open. The screen door banged once, twice, three times and he was one of the gang of children again, hurtling along the side of the house, the morning already ripe with the promise of heat, each breath carrying the faint salt sting of the sea. His sandals slapped against the bitumen and the red bike was big, too big for him, but it was a girl's bike and he could climb onto it unaided. He couldn't reach the pedals from the seat, and he couldn't keep up even with Lizzie even though she was only a girl, but from the first he made up his mind to rise to the challenge, to be like the others. He remembered the sweat that pinpricked his forehead and out of the past he heard Richard's voice as clear as the day. 'You have to practise. You have to learn or you won't keep up with us.'

And *keeping up* had become a sacred goal from then on. He had never been part of a group before; he was drunk with the thought of belonging, intoxicated. He wanted to meet any challenge they set him, to prove his love, to be worthy—because Richard was clearly the best, the most admirable thing. Richard taught him to shoot, set a fire, to keep secrets. Hannah taught him cards, and how to captain the centipede swing, how to cross his fingers for safety when he lied—but these were girl things. Running like a boy, letting his bike fall to the ground, wiping his face with his hand instead of his handkerchief—these were lessons that only Richard could teach.

So he practised everything every day—the bike, of course, but also whistling and shouting and climbing the spaceship, because the spaceship in the park was where plans were made. There were areas in the park, delineations, that were invisible to grown-ups and outsiders. The spaceship was the centre. The centipede swing was okay, but a boy had to ride it alone and standing upright, never seated. The shed at the back was for older kids to hang around behind, smoking and swearing. The oval was boring. The seesaw and slippery dip were for little kids and girls. The sandpit was only for babies. He learned to read the distinctions, he practised the codes.

'You run like a *girl*!' Richard had told him once, in the early days, and they'd added running to the things he had to master. Richard made him race against Lizzie and he was left so far behind that he stopped, bent over and gulping for air. Then Richard had walked back to him slowly, without any comment, walked back and stood close in front of him, punched him hard and quick in the shoulder, sent him backwards into the dirt. The punch had left a red mark and had hurt all day but he didn't tell anyone; and the next day they'd practised running again and he'd stopped waving his arms around and run straight like an arrow and not up and down like a girl. Lizzie still left him for dead because he was slow, but Richard said later, 'You know what's good about you? You don't give up too easily.'

'They were good days,' Hannah had said and yes, she was right. They were good days.

Lizzie

Up on the hill, the mosque is steady and achingly white. The call to prayer was almost two hours ago now. The streets are still empty.

I met Kate on the stairs. I was on my way down; she was running up to the roof, panicked, unsure of herself and of me. 'The bus group has left,' I told her. 'I heard them out in the hallway, hours ago, I saw them leave.'

She has gone down now to wake the others, to see who has gone and who is still here. 'Come with me,' she said. 'I need you, you'll have to help me, you'll have to explain.'

And you are going to ask why I'm here then, still here on the roof. You are going to ask why I didn't go down and help her. Alright and you can ask. You'll say, *I thought you liked her, I thought you were friends—or if not friends, then allies at least; I thought you trusted her.* And it's true that last part. I thought I trusted her, too. But listen—there is this between us now: she doesn't know what I saw. She doesn't know that I watched them burn in the square. *Why didn't you tell her?* you ask—and I can't explain; except that although she's a Westerner, she lives here now, she's married to Hama, a local, and I don't know her, not really. Her loyalties can't be assumed.

And there's more, there's something more and you need to know this. She was already frightened, there on the stairs, when I met her—she was white, she was shaking with fear. She was running up to the roof and she crashed straight into me, grabbed my arm, pulled me up here beside her, back through the door to the rooftop.

She was already scared. Do you see what that means? She knew something was underway, she knew there was danger.

On the roof she went straight to the eastern corner, the furthest away from the mosque. She leaned over the wall and looked down through the cold silent morning—not out, as I'd looked; not out past the centre of town to the gate, to the walls—but down, straight down, past the jumble of lattice and through the gaps to the alley below. She moved slowly along the wall, along the whole length of the wall, looking over the parapet, and I looked too, though I couldn't see what she might be looking for down on the cold cobbled street twenty metres below.

And then, quite suddenly, I could.

I've watched morning after morning break up here. I've seen the skyline when only the mosque is visible, blazing out like a lighthouse against the blackness. I've seen the way the blue shadows gather and move in the predawn, rising, shot through with the golden glow of occasional streetlights. I've heard the ruckus of the donkeys waking on the hill, and birds, and the roosters . . .

You know what I keep thinking about? My grandfather's little moss piglets. They're real after all, if naming things makes them real.

It's cold. It's early. It's morning. The shadows are gone and the mosque has faded. It's time to go back downstairs.

There is blood in the air.

Red

That Ray Kane bloke's all over the radio today, with this heads-of-state meeting—all over the airwaves, shouting and whipping up aggro, hating the Muslims, making his point. I heard one person take him on, just one person, called him a bloody racist, phoned him up on air and said, 'You're inciting hatred, you're ramping up fear. You should be ashamed of yourself.' Well, he didn't know Ray Kane, of course. Got him a terrific bollocking, then Kane cut the line and went on a tirade about appeasement and political correctness—dragged Hitler in, and poor bloody Chamberlain and all the rest of it; said it wasn't racist to be aware of the very real threat, that fear was more than appropriate, all things considered. And they lapped it up, the rest of his callers—all on his side, all full of praise for his comments.

Talkback radio—I'm not a fan. It's not something I listen to, normally. Today, though, when they told us where we'd be working—that's why I listened. As soon as they mentioned Bradleys Head, his face came to mind—Raymond Kane. I knew him there, just for a little while, when we were kids there back in the sixties. It was just for a couple of weeks, I think, but I never forgot him. And that was strange because we were army, my dad was posted all over the place and we never set roots down, never stayed long enough to make friends with anyone. So I've forgotten more people than most men have ever met, but I never forgot him. There was a power to that kid. He was a mean little shit, but the adults loved him—thought he was straight up and down, well-mannered, decent. Decent! He had them fooled, alright. He was a bully is what he was—he was more than a bully. He was—Christ, he was not a nice kid. Not at all.

I've come up against his type a couple of times since then. You get them in my line of work. Not that often—although, to be honest, soldiering can bring out the worst in people as well as the best. I've seen nice guys eaten alive by their demons, guys who were decent men get a taste of power and lose themselves utterly. But this Kane bloke—no, that's a different thing. He was a bully from the word go, sadistic, a baby thug, and he hasn't changed, not a bit. And I don't like the stuff he's spouting all over the airwaves today. I don't like it at all.

The Messenger

Once he'd left the ferry, he became indecisive. He hovered between the bus stands, reading the destination boards and the framed timetables. He looked lost, people would say; he looked unsure, uncertain—and he held his heavy coat as though it were a talisman, or a compass perhaps, a buffer against the world, as though it were armour.

'*I thought he needed help,*' one woman said. '*But I didn't like to ask. I wasn't sure.*'

A man reported that he was '*checking out the buses. He was lost, but he looked, you know, angry. I didn't know if he spoke English. He looked sort of foreign.*'

And a woman: '*He didn't speak. We didn't know what, but something was wrong. And he was hot, you know, his face was red and sweating. He didn't look right.*'

In the event he didn't take either bus, but set off up the road to Bradleys Head on foot in the baking heat with no hat, no water, the heavy coat softening now with the weight of sunlight caught in its fibres.

Hannah

I've solved my access problem, thanks to a terrified minion. She handed the master key over with barely a whimper. There'll be trouble about that later, but in the meantime I've achieved ingress to my office, I have unearthed my emergency Panadeine, I can start *work*, and yes, it's a later kind of start, but there's hours to go till the shit hits the fan. Plenty of time. Put a call in to Rob, find out how the staging's going, hop down to the workshop, hurl some abuse around, beg a couple of Valium. Because Valium is my friend on days like today. Valium will help me not mind about things like security jocks in my car park. More importantly, it can help me not mind about Toby.

I don't want him back.

I don't want him back. There—I've said it. I don't want him back in our lives. He brought all the bad things with him—Lizzie said that. And she was right, even then, as a child, because his mother was mad as a hatter and somehow he carried her craziness *with* him, he couldn't *escape* it; she'd scored her fragility deep into every soft little inch of his skin, every tiny white cell. And it was still there yesterday, oh Christ it was, still on show in that terrible *eagerness*, that awful way he has of *glancing*, of checking the shadows. There's no *need* for it, that's the thing—even all those years ago there was no *need*. We were perfectly nice little kids, we were *good*, we were perfectly normal and friendly. Then he appeared out of nowhere, glancing and checking, anticipating—and he just *broke* things, he broke our *childhood*, he smashed it to pieces for god's sake, just by being so *breakable*.

Nothing escaped that summer. Nothing was left untouched.

I shouldn't have called him back. I should have just ignored his text. *I'm back in Sydney—here's my number*, as though I had nothing else going on, as though we'd been waiting to hear from him all these years. Richard had no right to push it—he knows what I'm like. And the thing is, I don't *hate* Toby, I really don't hate him—except that I talked too much last night, asked too many questions and stuck the knife in a bit; and I know he felt it—and then I felt *bad*, of course. So I brought him back here, sneaked him down to the workroom to show him my canvas, the beating heart of my tortured soul. And you know what? He loved it. He *loved* it. He thought it was wonderful, thought it was *Art* and I gave him the leftovers, too, all the stimuli, all of the duplicate photos and stuff. I wouldn't have done that for someone I hated, would I? So no, I don't hate him.

But I don't want him back in our lives. It's all just too *fraught*.

I was thirteen years old, the year that we met. Richard had just turned twelve and Lizzie was eight. He came to us suddenly, out of the blue, at Easter—and then again, later, just after Christmas at Bradleys Head. Our parents used to rent an old house there every year, down near the beach—a rickety place off the main drag, down on the road to the cove. It's gone now, the house, transformed into glitzy apartments with full glass walls and harbour views; but Bradleys Head was a backwater then, almost empty except in the summers with the influx of holiday people. We were holiday people.

I remember those days, still. I do remember those days. We were always the first family there and a week or so later the Hampdens and Kanes would appear, and then, of course, the holiday really began. By nightfall the suburb was ours—the beach, the park with its blistering slippery dip; the bright jacaranda mornings, the sand and saltwater afternoons, the splinters and bee stings, sunburn and bindii—and the tumbling southerly buster that raced through the houses at five and slammed all the windows and doors. It was glorious stuff! The days were long and blue and hot, and full of the shriek of cicadas; and in the evenings the families would meet on the beach with fish and chips or meat pies and cordial. After dinner we'd play hide-and-seek in the dusk, or cockylorum or Phantom Agents. Sometimes one of the fathers would light a bonfire of driftwood and seaweed, and at least once there were sparklers and crackers and tiny jumping-jack fireworks. And finally, to farewell the huge dark deeds of the day, we'd join forces and dig a trench in the sand as a break-leg trap for intruders—because we were territorial, too; we guarded our sacred places. Every summer was just the same stretching all the way back to *before you were born* years; there was just room enough in the world for us and the Hampdens and Kanes—and oh, they were glorious, glorious days.

And then Toby came; shy and watchful and twitchy and scared. I think—I still believe—we were good for him. We brought him out of himself and that was something he really needed. His family was odder than odd. His mother was crazy, quite literally a lunatic—I think at the end she was sectioned.

I didn't mention her at lunch yesterday. I probably should have. But I had this sudden guilt that we might have teased him about her as kids do, just in passing you know, without meaning very much by it. But he was such a *teasable* kid; so terribly heart-on-his-sleeve.

Crazy about Richard, totally worshipped him, not that anyone minded—*everybody* loved Richard. We were a tribal mob, and very tight-knit, but when he appeared we just moved aside to make room and coalesced round him again and it was good for him, I do believe that. No parents watching, no schedules, no rules that couldn't be scrambled around. It was summer, 1967, it was Australia—it was the perfect way for a little boy to learn how boys should be.

That's how I remember it, anyway. That's what I tried to build up on the canvas. That's what Richard took such great exception to just before he went off to Europe, the last time I saw him, a year ago now. Nobody wants to believe it these days—that childhood was innocent once, was somehow more fun. It's not *acceptable*, it's anti-*feminist*, white-picket-fenceish, politically dubious. But that's how I remember it. It was a happy time. There were tragedies and accidents, just like there've always been—but we were good little kids, all in all, and we were happy. And I put that down on the canvas, and last night I showed it to Toby. And he liked it and he should know. So screw you, Richard . . .

There's such a *mood* in here today, the whole bloody *building* is cranky. And Lydia's going to feel like a fool when she finds out her lackey's handed the master key over. No bloodshed—total surrender. Score one to me, I think! I ought to tiptoe down to the concourse now, slip into Bar*Ista* and order a coffee or two. I need to suck back one of Marcus's Yirgacheffe specials, admire the harbour and channel some Eckhart Tolle—and maybe a baby martini or two—and wait for the headache to go. Just be quietly at peace, like a smiley little emoticon.

Lizzie

Kate locked the door to the roof a few minutes ago. She came close to me, touched the red mark on my face and then locked the door to the roof. In all of the bedrooms she's closed the shutters and pulled the latches across. All the rooms are as dark as night, but here in the *ryad*'s centre, the unroofed courtyard, we can see that it's morning outside.

Last night we all agreed we'd wait it out. The boys had come back with the talk of trouble brewing, and we all agreed we'd stay inside until things calmed down. There had been small outbursts already by then; one of the guests had been spat at down in the marketplace. One of the Germans had had his camera pulled out of his hands and smashed on the cobbles. At dinner, people were talking of groups of young men harassing people, shouting, hissing at tourists and women in Western dress; and the merchants closed early.

Teenagers, Kate had said last night. *It's just kids coming in from the New Town. It flares up now and again, but it settles down quickly with no harm done.* She'd promised she'd keep us informed. *You'll be perfectly safe*, she'd said. She was smiling as though it was nothing, as though there was nothing to worry about. *You are our guests*, she'd told us. *You are like family.* So we were family, last night. We cleared the tables together, all of us, guests and Kate and her husband, Hama, as well; but when the pair from National Geographic TV decided to go out suddenly, to pick up some night-time shots, she wasn't happy. *Don't go stirring up trouble*, she said, and she'd said it lightly, as though she was joking; but the rest of us stayed and helped with the washing-up.

And yes, I thought we could trust her, yes, I thought we were friends.

Breakfast is over now. Kate has offered the last of the cheese and figs. The mood has changed; there is no talk of teenagers any more, no talk of kids from the New Town. So many chairs are empty and the guests that have stayed are on edge.

'There's a problem,' Kate says, and her voice is strained. She doesn't tell us we're perfectly safe any more, and she doesn't say we are family. 'It's just a political thing,' she says. 'It's not personal. You should stay inside for the morning. Just for the morning.'

We didn't see Hama at breakfast. We don't ask where the others have gone—the German bus group, the New Zealand family, the people from Spain. Nobody wants to count up the missing faces. We need to pretend; we need to believe we can trust her.

She hasn't told them what we saw from the roof. And you can ask why I said nothing when she locked the front door and the door to the roof as well, when I found that the windows were shuttered—and this is why: because earlier, on the roof, when I could see what she saw, the body limp and dead on the cobbles below where the blind woman sits every morning, her life tattooed on her face, with bunches of herbs all around her, chanting to people to touch, to smell, to buy—when I saw him, Carlo, the young Italian man, and the pool of blood that was thickening next to his head, and the rock that had been used to batter his skull still lying where it had rolled, leaning into his shoulder; when the world dipped and lurched and spun away from me, I saw Kate leaning across the wall with her hands biting into the stone and she was sobbing, 'Thank God! Thank God.'

I keep thinking about the Italian girl. I keep wondering where she is. They were on their gap year, working for an NGO, she and Carlo, terribly young, and assigned to help the little group of Somali refugees who camp out at night in the ruins. Kate had introduced me to them one afternoon by the flute-maker's stall. They had offered to take me up to the camp if I'd shoot a few photographs for them. And then Kate ordered *thé menthe* and we'd sat in the square and told stories and laughed at the worst of the tourists.

GUARDIAN, FRIDAY, 22 JULY 2005

The Metropolitan police commissioner, Sir Ian Blair, said the man shot dead at Stockwell Tube Station in South London was 'directly linked' to yesterday's failed attacks by four suspected would-be suicide bombers.

Toby

'They were good days, weren't they?' Hannah had said. 'Good times.' And she was so beautiful yesterday, backlit, with the afternoon shimmer of light on the water behind her and light in her hair and her face so bright with remembering, that if he'd just pressed the shutter then, just pressed it once and disappeared, he could have framed that long hot summer and it would be perfect. It would be just like it was on that best of all days, the day when they'd gone to the lighthouse, the day he'd braved the terrible trek through the scrub in the heat, with the flies that stuck to his face and the tangling thorns. The world had been empty that day, except for him and Richard and Hannah—and in an instant he was back there again, remembering ...

'I know something,' he'd whispered long ago into that hot and tidal silence.

The children had already finished their sandwiches, blown up their brown paper bags, dropped them down through the gaps in the jetty to watch them float like jellyfish, drift and drown through the water. Now they were counting the grey little fingerlings that darted for crumbs in the shadows beneath them. 'I know something,' he'd whispered. 'There's a germ that lives under the earth. If you breathe it, you turn into wood. It's true. My granddad showed me it once—'

Beside him Hannah stretched with studied indifference. 'We already know about that,' she said. 'He's our granddad too, don't forget.'

'Anyway, it's a fungus, it isn't a germ,' Richard told him. 'Granddad showed us it *years* ago. And all the other stuff, too, the little moss piglets and stuff, all the stuff in his study.'

Toby's confusion was so clear on his face that Hannah laughed and sat up to slap him. 'We're *cousins*, stupid,' she said. 'We have the same granddad. Don't you know even *that*? Granddad practically *lives* at our place,' she boasted. 'He's told us the same old stories since we were *babies*. There's *nothing* you know that we don't know already!' She was crowing, triumphant, wonderful, and behind her the light was shivering green on the water. She lay down again, stretched her bare legs out on the splintered wood of the jetty.

'We know something, too,' she said, and the sly way she said it had made the jetty tilt under him. 'Your mother tried to burn your house down last year. She tried to kill you.' He felt the lighthouse slip, coming loose from its moorings. The water was all around him, silver and green; the hot sky beat down and the air was thick and heavy, too heavy to breathe. Richard's 'Shut up, Hannah,' was so soft he didn't know if he'd imagined it, but Hannah turned her face to her brother, shrugged and looked away carelessly and said, 'Well it's true. She's crazy. Everyone knows that she's crazy. It isn't *important* or anything.'

The water splashed against the supports of the jetty, against the base of the lighthouse, whispering secrets, threatening to sweep the whole world away.

'It doesn't matter to us,' Hannah said. 'Our aunt's crazy as well.'

There was silence for a moment and then Richard suddenly erupted in a great guffaw of laughter and Hannah kicked her feet together, pleased at how clever she'd been; and when Toby had worked though the logic, realised his mother and Hannah's aunt were one and the same, he felt the earth settle again. The water slipped back to its proper place, behind him the lighthouse stretched and relaxed and he laughed out loud too, and kicked his feet, watched the tiny fish dart away from all this funniness, and inside he thought he might cry; but Richard had sat up then and said, 'Hey—do you want to see something amazing?'

It was secret, really secret, Richard told him. It was so secret it couldn't be taken away from the lighthouse, so secret it had to be left down here, in the sacred place where they'd found it. He wriggled up closer to Toby, still on his belly, and said to Hannah, 'Hold on to my feet,' and then, being careful of splinters, he worked his way further and further right off the edge of the jetty, leaning down to examine the underside, where the old wooden pylons were. He gave a victorious, upside-down yell, and Hannah kept holding his feet while he wriggled his way back to safety. He sat up all flushed and out of breath; in his hand lay the blade of a dagger of some kind, rusted and thick with power.

Toby reached out to touch it, but Richard held it away. 'It has to stay here. If we ever take it away something evil will happen. The lighthouse might fall on the person who took it. A tidal wave might sweep them out to sea. Something like that.'

'Or there could be haunting,' Hannah said, and she was serious now so he drew his hand back, away from the thing.

'See how its point is broken?' Richard asked—and yes, the very tip was snapped.

'That's how we know it was used,' Hannah told him. 'That's how we know it's got power.' And it was clear that they knew the whole story true and entire—and clear that this was a treasure only they could read.

'Now that you've seen it, you have to make a vow,' Hannah said. 'You have to swear to keep this secret as long as you live.'

Richard nodded. 'It has to be secret,' he said. 'This is government land. We're not even supposed to be here.'

They were always so full of secrets. Not just the predawn forays into the bush, but the times when Richard would disappear without a word, and return again still without a word. And the low wooden door that Toby had opened once with Richard's key, during one of those absences. It was full of the very things secrets are made of, candles and matches and ropes and a pocket-knife, boy things, powerful things.

'You have to swear,' Richard said. 'Close your eyes.'

Toby closed his eyes. Behind his eyelids the green of the world went to black and red and yellow and Richard's voice seemed to come from the air, from the lighthouse—

'Swear that you'll keep all the secrets we show you. Say that you swear by the knife.'

'Yes. I do swear.'

'You're supposed to say you swear *by the knife*,' corrected Hannah, and Toby opened his eyes but Richard said, 'Close your eyes, we're not finished.'

So he closed his eyes again and Hannah grabbed his wrist and held it steady and Richard said, 'Don't flinch. We have to draw blood.'

His eyes flew open and he tried to pull away, but Hannah was ready, and she held him still and Richard grabbed his hand and forced the fingers open and suddenly there was a rough metal bite on the palm of his hand and then Richard had gripped Toby's hand tightly in his own, palm to palm, and said, 'Wait. Our blood has to mix. I cut my hand too,' he explained, 'and our blood has to mix for ten seconds and then it will heal like magic. If you can be trusted.' He counted slowly to ten and then released Toby's hand and when Toby looked, sure enough, his palm had already healed; there was no sign of blood, just a thin brown line like a scar where the knife had been. So that too was magic.

'It's healed. You can be trusted,' Richard said, and then he grinned. 'And now you're not just my cousin, you're my blood brother, too. And Hannah's blood brother.'

And that was the day, the best of all days, because after that they'd climbed up the ladder, they'd scratched their names on the lighthouse door, and Toby knew he would never betray them because they were blood brothers, cousins, and he was protected and drunk with their power. He knew their secrets and they knew his and if there were lies and larger secrets ahead they would always be safe with each other and they had the same granddad . . .

So where had that gone, that memory? Where had it hidden, for all these years? Because it had startled him, yesterday, the sudden clarity of the past—the way it returned after forty-odd years, fragmented, disjointed, but sharp at the edges; that one childhood day rising up to the surface, called up by the sound of her voice.

'You haven't changed a single iota,' she'd drawled as their drinks arrived—and the drawl itself had seemed chosen to offset the dance of the light that was all around her. The drawl, like the swearing, was new—but he remembered that light, remembered the way that she'd painted herself into his mind, so that she skipped over rocks, along the jetty, as though she was made of music, as though she was wings and air and nothing else, a sunbeam, a butterfly . . .

She drank fiercely, much more than she ought to, he thought, certainly much more than he did—but it made her chatty, enlarged her, made her shine even more; and he loved her all over again for her toughness, the long strong brown-legged barefooted honesty of her. And hours had gone by and drinks had turned into dinner and dinner was over and still they'd sat on and the waiter had brought them liqueurs 'on the house', which Toby was sure meant *please leave, it's late and we want to go home*, but she was oblivious. The light outside the window had faded to black, and candles were burning low on the tables and she played with the softened wax, pressing it, tucking it into the flame and watching it melt and she talked and talked and talked.

'You should have stayed in touch,' she said finally, sadly. 'Dad worried about you after they sent you off to school. But you never wrote. After all the trouble we went to, trying to turn you into a boy, and you never wrote!'

She was teasing, surely? The flame from the candle jumped and flashed green in her eyes; he blinked at the strength of it. She continued, heedless and unregarding. 'You were meant to be ours, you know, once your mother went loopy. You were meant to come live with *us*. But you just vanished and we never heard another thing from you. Dad was shattered—imagine ditching *us* for some fuck-awful boarding school. He felt terrible for you. But you were very young, I suppose.' She looked up then, sly, catching him when he wasn't prepared, and suddenly: 'Oh my God, you didn't *know*? Oh, you're kidding! Oh fucketty-*fuck*—I've spilled the beans!' She was mortified—or delighted—by her clumsiness. 'Oh, *toujours ma grande* fucking *bouche*!' she said and, 'It was just a *plan*, an idea—it obviously didn't go through.' She was scrabbling to shore up the walls of his childhood around him. 'Honestly, it wasn't *agreed* on or anything. It was just at the don't-let-the-kids-overhear stage. I don't even know how *I* heard—I expect it was Lizzie. Remember Lizzie? Like peas in a pod you two, you could have been twins.' She pushed his drink at him and tried to skip the stones across his memory, to make ripples that would flurry the implication of carelessness. 'She's in Africa or somewhere—some hideous place—doing a PhD. Gets politely divorced quite a lot—she's not much of a fighter. We never see her, of course—she hates us to bits. But you should call her—you were like peas in a pod. Don't you remember?'

No, he didn't remember.

'Oh *yes*! You were the *good* ones and we were the *bad* ones. You *must* remember.'

She could look cruel, he realised suddenly, and he remembered the shock of the first time he'd noticed. But not cruelty, surely, just a sharp edge at the corner of her eyes and she certainly couldn't help that. She looked up and caught him watching her, and she smiled and the sharp edge was gone, but he felt the held breath and had to release it in order to speak again. And before he could, she was picking up the bill, was reaching for her wallet, and she held out her hand to him, not terribly drunk perhaps, but not sober either, and said, 'I'm sorry. I am. I'm sorry. Listen—come back to work with me. No, come, come back to work. There's something I want to show you, I want you to see. Come back with me.'

It had gone, the glint in the green of her eyes. And if something was broken, she hadn't commented on it.

The Lighthouse

I t didn't begin, of course, with the man in the overcoat.
It doesn't end on the underground train.

The man is a paragraph only, a shape on the page that makes up the story—a phrase, something less than a phrase; a word, a morpheme.

He takes his tiny place in the *Guardian*, in the *New York Times*, in the *Sydney Morning Herald*, and you can find him there still, a bricklayer's son, born in Brazil, 1978, died of gunshot wounds at Stockwell Tube Station, in London, 2005.

He looks out of the page, darkly handsome; but the myth absorbs the man, creates him a winter overcoat, a hat, a bomb belt.

What is a bomb belt? you might ask.

He had Mongolian eyes.

BOOK TWO

I

Lizzie

This is not straightforward, this waiting, this not knowing. There are fourteen guests and Kate and the schisms are growing.

Jenna and Tom have left the *ryad* again this morning, and gone to the market. Kate isn't happy with them—they were energised, too excited, they're up to something. 'I think you should stay inside,' Kate said to them, more insistent than she was last night. But Jenna turned to face her directly, raised an eyebrow, daring her to go on, and Kate subsided, pinned between anger and fear.

So they do know—the Americans do know, I think; they know there is more to this. They know that it's worse—far worse—than Kate pretends.

They left, and we cleared the breakfast plates in silence.

The mood is awkward now. Luc, who used to tease me about my French, comes to stand beside me, stacking the pots on the highest shelves. He speaks softly, under his breath. 'I have not seen Hama,' he says, and the words sit heavy between us; and then Brigitte flares up beside him, her eyes hot in the chill of the kitchen. 'You are the friend of Kate and Hama,' she says in her awkward English. 'You are the friend of them, so then you must say to us.' Her voice cracks in fear, but she catches it back, takes a breath and says, more quietly, 'You must tell to us—can we trust them?'

I almost laugh. Trust them? The bus group trusted Ali, I want to say; or, go and look from the roof to the street outside the silversmith's shop. But I don't because it's too dangerous and because her voice has a rising note, a child's note, panicked and trying to keep in control. I've heard it before, the howl of fear in the tunnels, the wail of grief that curls through the church like incense . . .

Kate says Hama has gone to the New Town to contact our consulates. She says we are her guests and the guests of the town and we will be protected as family. She doesn't mention the young Italian. She might never have seen his body. She might never have clutched at the wall on the roof and sobbed *thank God, thank God.*

Nothing is moving outside. There is noise from the top of the hill; the donkeys are hungry and making a fuss about breakfast, the dogs are barking.

There is no noise from inside the walls. And it's six hours now since I saw the bus on fire.

Toby

'Work' was the Sydney Opera House, where Hannah drew the sketches that became sets and designs for stage shows. Toby wasn't the theatre type, and he'd become hopelessly shy all over again, despite the chardonnay, following her down the darkened concourse, nervous and ill at ease. She'd taken them into the Opera House through a service door, led the way through the underground corridors, ducked past NO ADMISSION signs and security cameras and into the warren of work spaces used by designers and carpenters.

'We're not supposed to be in here of course,' she'd told him. 'They're going insane with security because of the APCO thing.' But she'd stopped at a door that looked bleak and anonymous, just like all the others, and swiped with her passkey. 'Here we go,' she'd said, and she sounded suddenly nervous, almost uncertain; but she put her hand on the small of his back and propelled him through . . .

The lights flickered on, artificial and white, and he saw a workroom full of benches and shelves and beyond it a space that was stacked with squares and rectangles, covered with dust cloths. Hannah went straight to the largest, which leaned against the wall, facing it, and he joined her and together they wrangled it round so that they could see it.

'It's a foyer piece, for the front of house,' she said—as though that would make sense to him, as though he'd have any idea what she was talking about—and then she pulled the cloth away.

'Well?' she said. 'Be honest. Be brutally honest.'

Hannah

(And wouldn't you think I'd have *learned* by now? she'd thought to herself, though Toby didn't know that, not being a mind reader, not being privy to the last time she'd shown this piece off to someone she cared about, not knowing about the *bucketing* it had received. *Be brutally honest*, she'd said to Richard last year—and she'd been so *confident* then, so puffed up with her little success. Because everyone else had loved it, the *Herald* had actually mentioned it glowingly in its review of the show. So she'd sneaked Richard in, just like Toby, breaking all the rules, and uncovered the canvas. And he'd looked without commenting, looked without breathing a word, and she'd watched while he read every scrap of their childhood, studied each memory, touched every brushstroke. *Well?* she'd said then, unable to stand the silence. *Be honest—be brutally honest*, she'd said and, yes, he'd been honest, alright, and brutal enough for both of them. Just one word was all he bothered with, and the sting of the hurt was still there and the fear as well—because that was the last time she'd seen him and there'd been tears and shouting of course. And later, after a drink, or a few drinks anyway, she'd looked into the mirror that formed part of the artwork, the mirror that was meant to reflect the past back to you and show you what it had created, and she'd seen a face that was older than she'd thought and not as well camouflaged after all, one which always hoped that things had been different, had been better and sweeter and happier. That face again, and *toujours ma grande bouche!* she'd said, and she would have liked to make the grand gesture, hurl the glass into the mirror and shatter the artwork, rip it down from its frame and tear it into pieces, but it wasn't hers, it belonged to the show and the *Herald* had loved it. So she'd poured another drink instead and raised her glass to the face in the mirror and said ever so archly, 'Made. Bed. Lie.' And a few hours and the rest of the bottle later she'd passed out on the floor of the workroom. And oh! the next day, staggering out for a coffee as soon as Bar*Ista* opened, still drunk and dripping mascara, and there behind her of course was Lydia, cold with abstention and disapproval—and doubly so ten minutes later when Hannah discovered she'd lost her passkey down in the workroom the night before, had locked herself out of her office again . . .)

Well, maybe she should have forgotten the canvas entirely—left it alone in the workroom, covered it up with the dust cloth, its face to the wall. There were plenty of other pieces she had forgotten; and nobody needed it. Nobody else ever bothered to look at it. But it had stayed hard and hot like the spike of a thorn in her throat; she'd sneak down here sometimes just to feel the bubble of hurt rise up, to bite down hard for the sharp, bitter taste of triumph.

'Well?' she'd asked Toby last night, and he'd said, 'Oh, I like it,' so she was immediately angry, fired up and touchy because he was being *ingratiating*, because he clearly knew nothing about anything and didn't even have the grace to say so. He knew he was on rocky ground, and she could see him teetering, clawing at anything that would keep him from plummeting down to the rocks, from making a fool of himself—and God love him he kicked the ground further away with every step that he took. 'I like the mirror,' he said and he was a walking apology now, every fibre of his being screaming out that he didn't *know* this sort of stuff, wasn't comfortable here, had never seen a painting before with yoyos and mirrors and photographs stuck all over it and, *oh save him for fuck's sake*, she screamed at herself and she told him, 'It's about change, about time and childhood. It's one of those pictures we make for the theatre foyer, to set the mood for the show.' So he was released from the terror of Art and said, 'Oh I *see*.' And then, because he had some idea what the hell he was looking at, he could relax a bit, reach out and touch the bus ticket stubs, the bottle top scoured of its logo, shining and bright like a button. 'It reminds me of you,' he said suddenly, 'with your skirt tucked into your knickers, down at the jetty.'

Well there you are, then. And Richard had said it was whitewash . . .

Toby

It was huge, three metres by two, layered with painting and photos and textures—and other things too, trinkets and treasures—and now that he knew what he was looking at he could see what she had created. 'Childhood from the child's own view,' she said. 'A glimpse of the world that the child saw, inhabiting it.' And that's what the mirror was for, she explained, and all the other bits too. She pointed them out to him—the polio immunisation card, the school report. He didn't know much about art, usually didn't even know what he liked unless it was pointed out to him, but this piece came alive breath by breath as she explained it.

'Where did you get it all from?' he asked, wandering the length of the panel. He stopped to look at the tiny things, the old Legacy badge, the plastic walking elephant on a string from a cereal box.

'Garage sales, eBay—different places. I wanted to recreate the feeling of childhood, of what it felt like, childhood, back in the 1960s.'

Well, if this was what childhood was like, it was utterly magical. He flicked from image to talisman, captivated—but finding it disconcerting because he must have been part of this too, or of something like this, but he had no recollection now, there was nothing of this in the bites and grabs that were all he remembered of life before boarding school.

'And the photos?' he asked, and she slapped him, teasing, and then realised he was serious.

'They're Dad's, of course,' she said. 'You *can't* have forgotten the camera?'

But he'd forgotten much more than he'd realised; it must have all melted along with the lighthouse, because all these things remained stubbornly distant and totally unfamiliar. He stared at the canvas, willing himself to find some link, some way *in*, some way to claim the cicada's wings, perhaps, or the Argonauts' Pledge, or the secret notes in browned invisible ink—or the photos themselves, which were big and beautiful, part of the painting and yet not quite part of it; that were more like bystanders, more like echoes, reflections. Photos of unknown children at places he'd never seen, on outings he couldn't begin to imagine—groups and portraits, streetscapes, interiors, some of them black and white, some of them early coloured, and each of them capturing a time that was so mundane, so unnewsworthy, that it lay completely unnoticed under the weight of day-to-day living. A fun pier under a lowering sky, deserted and almost aware that it was reaching the end of its heyday; a ramshackle wooden bridge that buckled under the stampede of boys that was hurtling down it; a funeral gathering outside a church, the men in black, the women all hatted and gloved; a small girl's face turned back from the doorway to look again at the world outside.

Hannah smiled and said, 'Brings back memories, doesn't it?' and something fluttered along the back of his neck, soft wings like a moth or a warning—but her voice danced over it. She singled a photograph out, tapped lightly on the paper. 'Recognise him?'

Toby looked at the child and the earth swung away beneath him. It was a magnificent photo, a seamless merging of moment and technique; the light of a campfire on the beach at dusk reaching out across the water to the sunset billowing from the horizon. The sharp gradations of dying light burned across the restless water in a palette of silver and black and every possible shade of grey. And in the foreground, against the fire itself, magically delineated, the children, frozen in the act of turning away from the flames to watch the sunset. Everything about them seemed atavistic, elemental— wild hair matted like savages, jutting shoulders and collarbones, sharply angular limbs. The movement and wonder were captured and held in suspense, eternally. And in the foreground, slightly off-centre, one of the smallest children, a boy, looking bright-eyed and haunting up through the chaos, straight through to the camera's heart.

'Heathens at the dying of the light . . .' She smiled at the memory and was suddenly all business again. 'I've seen much worse in galleries and books—' And she mentioned a show that she'd been to last month which was *awful*, fuckmotheringly *dreadful*, full of pretentious effects and overblown sermonising. But he wasn't listening, because suddenly he knew it wasn't the dying of the light at all; he could feel again the crisp, clear air of daybreak, the coiled-spring excitement of being awake in the early light, with the wildness of water behind him. It was dawn, not dusk—the whole new glorious day was just beginning. He had been woken along with Richard and Hannah and Lizzie, woken with whispers and tucked half-sleeping into the car for the trip to the Point. It was dawn, the time for mulloway, bream and taylor, and though he couldn't remember a fish being caught, couldn't remember the reels and rods or the mucky and unfastidious baiting of hooks, he could remember the fire and the warm silvered water and shot through it all the fierce wild joy of freedom. All the childhood he'd lost was here, distilled and breathed into this picture.

'. . . and yet they're *reviewed*,' Hannah said, 'as though they were fucking *Michelangelo*. So, you know, you have to wonder how many of them are insiders, people who work for the ABC or something . . .'

He was back there again, in the magical first days, running along the cicada-shrill cove with his cousins. Aunt Susan looked after the food; Uncle Peter snapped photos. He was one of the children, climbing over the rock pools, crouched down to pick up the sea snails and starfish, or joined in battle, whipping long strands of beaded seaweed at the others while Lizzie yelled, 'Toby! Watch me! Watch me!' and turned a cartwheel over the sand, a proper cartwheel, perfect and poised, landing up on her little feet with a kind of a bounce. He was speechless with admiration, so then they were all doing cartwheels and trying to teach him how, and when they found out how ticklish he was they stopped trying to teach him and tickled him instead till he nearly died laughing. He remembered all the faces around him, laughing as if they were being tickled themselves, and Uncle Peter snapping photo after photo until the film ran out. Toby laughed again at the memory, delighted to find something so lovely, so precious, something he'd let slip away so easily, and Hannah laughed too and pulled out a folder full of photos from somewhere behind the canvas and handed them over and said, 'Here, then, take these—they're all copies and spares. Knock yourself right out.' And then she kissed him quite suddenly, lightly, just on the cheek and said, 'We all loved you, you know. We all absolutely *loved* you.'

Hannah

Quietly at peace—like a little emoticon. Did I say that? I said that, didn't I? I said quietly at peace and that's what I am. A little hungover, of course, so my old friends Disgust and Self-loathing are beating a path to my inner door, but you know what? I'm not going to let them in; I'm going to be mellow and happy. I'm going to count my blessings because I'm out of the office, and that's good; and Marcus is on at Bar*Ista* today and that's also good. And there are empty tables outside, and so what if it's only because of the fear and the firearms and hurricane fencing. The sun is shining; the harbour is sparkling and look!—there are snipers up on the roof and I've never seen that before. So isn't that *festive*?

Life, I've decided, is all about how you respond to things. It's all about whether your glass is half full or whether it's covered in crap. I mean, yes, we could bitch and moan about sniffer dogs and bag searches and civil liberties—but you know what? Let's not! Let's look on the bright side. Because they're going to do it anyway, so why not applaud? Life is a cabaret, my friend—especially tonight it's a cabaret—life is *show*time, tonight, its Head-of-State Night, it's going to be *huge* for frocks and fireworks and preferential Asia-Pacific–American trade blocs—and, quite frankly, if frocks and fireworks and preferential trade blocs mean taking a quick little dump on democracy's head, then I for one am happy to pull the chain.

Except I invited Toby back here again tonight, like the cretin I am. I told him I'd get him a ticket, I told him to meet me at nine for a place on the forecourt. I promised him music and drinks and crackers with caviar. I promised him sportsmen and TV hosts and lots of famous faces. I'll see you tomorrow, I said, and I waved and then I fell over. And there's no way they're going to let him into the forecourt tonight, there's security *ev*erywhere, there's no *way* I'll get him through. Why did I *do* that? Why couldn't I be a *belligerent* drunk like I usually am? Because I tried to be *nice*, you see, because he'd sent me a message, he'd gone to all the trouble of tracking me down so I tried to be *nice* like Richard told me. And now I'll have to be *un*nice and *uninvite* him and that means the whole of yesterday was a total waste of time and I should have stayed home.

Well, screw it, that's *quietly at peace* arse-whacked for today.

I wonder who else he's contacted? I'd love to know if he's planning to catch up with Lizzie at all, to track her down. They could rehash the old times. She'd love to rehash the old times, would Lizzie, she loves to compare the old stories. I hope he's not *judging* us, you know? I hope he's not sitting back somewhere and *reinventing* it all—because we were good to him, the little lost baa-lamb, we really were. Even though he was *flung* on us without any discussion, with *no* explanation—even so we were good to him. And he wasn't the easiest kid to be around. There was always that terrible sense of sadness about him, of tragedy waiting to happen. Kids find that unnerving. Sadness can rub off, you know—spill over; and it's not just kids—humanity at large has a natural limit to empathy, puts up some fairly unbreachable walls in the face of too much unfairness. It's worth remembering, that. It's worth bearing in mind. People are pretty much people and if we weren't noble, well, neither was anyone else. And they were good times, on the whole. And we were just kids.

I can't cancel tonight. My conscience would flay me. I'll tell him there's been a change of plans. We can go down to The Rocks or somewhere, have a drink, watch the fireworks from there. But that's it, then. That's as nice as I want to be.

INTERVIEW SGT MARRON 7/1/1967

Monckton My name is Maureen Monckton. I live at Bradleys Head. I have lived at Bradleys Head for thirty years.

Monckton I wanted to make a statement about the park where the baby was taken.

Monckton I was not at the park yesterday afternoon, no. Not actually there. But I know it well, I walk past it every day and I know it well.

Monckton I have come here to say that I think the park is dangerous. I think it's a dangerous place for children.
I think it attracts the wrong sort of people in general. That's all I want to say. It doesn't surprise me what happened. That's all I want to say.

INTERVIEW (RESUMED) SGT MARRON

Monckton Well there was another thing I wanted to be clear about. There are men at that park at night time. I've seen them. Men at a children's park. That's all I'm going to say.

Toby

As soon as he got home, he opened the folder she'd given him, hungry for anything he could claim as his, as familiar. She might want it back, after all; she'd probably need the photos for something, she'd kept them this long, she might change her mind. She'd been nice at the end, last night, and nice at the start as well, and only that bit in the middle had thrown him off-balance. She'd been pretty drunk by then—all that stuff about him being a *stalker* when, after all, she was the one who'd set up the meeting. But perhaps, he thought, she might have been nervous too; she might not have meant it to sound quite so accusing.

'You just *vanished*,' she'd said. 'Dad was *shattered*!' The mess of emotions had flooded inside him, but then she'd softened at once and touched his hand and said, 'Come on. I want to show you something. Come with me.'

Now, alone with the photographs, he was afraid that the magic was gone. Maybe it needed Hannah to be beside him, maybe without her voice the memories would keep themselves hidden. But he emptied the folder anyway, images spilling across the table in front of him, and he sifted through them one after another, and the memories came drifting back—slowly, because it was forty years ago, after all, but small and perfect and just as magical.

They were a riot of childhood, the pictures—they captured it all, all the things he'd forgotten. Everything Hannah had talked about; how wicked they were and unruly, how they ignored all the rules and went swimming at dawn, stayed up all night on the beach and lit fires in the bush and stole empty soft drink bottles from the crates in the yard behind Mr McCauley's, took them back up to the counter again as bold as brass to claim the refund. 'Oh, don't look like that!' she'd laughed. 'You were just as evil as us by the time we'd got through with you.'

And then suddenly there was one—an intruder shot; amateur, clumsy. It was hard and flat and the children were posed and static, frozen in place.

What's your name, little mate?

Was it up at the park? Was that where the photo was taken? He didn't like the shot; it failed on all counts. It was badly printed and bleached out. The composition was shoddy; instead of the kids being a focal point, they were all bunched up and the small boy alone at the edge of the frame was unsupported and incidental. Compared with his uncle's photos it was rubbish, and not only because it lacked the joyful ideal of childhood; on a purely technical level it was a disaster—it was a messy conglomeration of kids, undifferentiated, unremarkable.

What's your name, little mate?

Toby Woods.

Wasn't there something . . .? 'You just *vanished*!' Hannah had said—but, no, there was more to it than that. The worm of cowardice stirred inside him, and he put the photo aside, but picked it up again almost immediately.

They were all there, all of the older kids—and the names untangled, assigned themselves to the faces calmly, in order.

Hannah and Richard first, of course, but the other boys too, the kids they ran with: Sean and Kit and Lloyd and Matthew and the other one, the loud one whose name he'd forgotten, the thug, the bully. Lloyd was the biggest, but there was no doubt that Richard was leader. Or maybe there was. He caught at a fleeting memory—the slap of fists on flesh, the fingernails-on-the-blackboard squeal of cloth being ripped, blue and white edges coming apart at the seam and angry shouting—but it was gone, and there was only the photograph. Summer clothes, summer holiday haircuts, seven boys and a girl in an unforgiving sun, all knees and ears; and he was the little one, younger, head and shoulders below the others and off to one side.

Looking ill, perhaps, or scared, with the light in his eyes.

Lizzie

I heard them before I saw them. Kate's voice was quiet but very clear, determined and angry. 'You are not helping,' she said, and I thought she was speaking perhaps to the boys who sort the luggage. 'Don't tell me you want to help,' she said. 'I know what you want.' And I stopped then, out in the courtyard, because she was speaking English, speaking to one of the guests, and it was Jenna who answered, Jenna who must have just returned from the marketplace.

'We can do this without you. We don't need permission. We have all the contacts we need.'

'You're going to make things worse,' Kate said. 'You don't know what's going on.' There was a change in her voice, a fear—but the other cut right across it, tight, aggressive, inflexible.

'I know more than you think,' Jenna said. She was louder, piling the pressure on. 'I know there's been shooting down in the square. I know they've killed tourists. I know they've killed Westerners.' She paused for a moment; I waited, listening—spying. 'This is news,' she said. 'We can do news. You can help or not help, but you can't stop us filming—you can't stop us getting it out.'

She walked out to the courtyard then and saw me and stopped as though she would speak to me, but I stepped around her and into the kitchen and waited to hear her feet on the stairs.

Let me tell you about Jenna. She is articulate, she is clever, and more than anything else she is ambitious. She knows the opportunities fear can create.

She is dangerous.

Kate was alone in the kitchen, her face so deeply etched with fear that she looked liked a different woman. 'She wants me to unlock the door to the stairs,' she told me. 'She wants to herd everyone up to the rooftop. She used a helicopter crew a few days ago—they were shooting out in the desert.' I nodded. We had laughed about this the day they first arrived. 'She's calling it back,' said Kate. 'She thinks there's a story breaking, she thinks there'll be an attack in the town and she wants the pictures, she wants the guests herded up to the roof and she wants the chopper to fly over, filming. And there is no need for this, this will make things worse, this will only inflame—'

'The German bus was blown up in the square,' I told her. 'I saw it this morning, around four o'clock.'

She nodded, not registering shock or surprise or fear. So she'd already known.

'They were all there,' I said, and my heart was beating so loudly I thought it might burst, I thought it might rise up and choke me. 'All of the bus group,' I said, and my teeth were rigid, the words were breaking against them. 'All of them, shot and burning. Down in the square.'

She turned away.

'Ali too,' I said. 'Ali led them there.' I wasn't sure whether she'd heard me at all but she took a breath and it caught and tore in her throat.

'I don't know where Hama is,' she whispered. 'Carlo is dead in the lane, and I don't know where Hama is.'

Toby

'Good times,' Hannah had said, and they were good times. They were everything she remembered and more. With her by his side he'd been caught in the shimmer of water, the shrill of cicadas; only now, alone, he was stuck on the dissonant chord. He'd propped the photo in front of him on the cold, anonymous table. They were all there, all the kids, the whole tribe—so it must have been late in the holiday. In the early days there were just the cousins and him.

A baby was missing. The police had gone to the park with the baby's mother and cleared it out, and organised searches. Everyone said she'd be found before dinner, but the next morning Uncle Peter had said, 'Hop in the car, kids. The police want a bit of a chat with you.'

'We talked to them yesterday,' Richard said, and his jaw was tight and defiant. But Uncle Peter said, 'Well, they want to see you again. They were busy yesterday—they need to write everything down.' So they piled in the car.

It was a hot day beginning; a white sky, another scorcher in a week of hundred-degree temperatures. People were already gathering for the search. It wasn't a crowd exactly, because they all seemed to know each other, but, *You, the little bloke—come in closer,* the photographer had said.

In the photo now he could see the child that he had been, standing off to one side, his hands gripped tightly in front of him . . .

What's your name, little mate?

Toby Woods.

They'd been questioned up at the station, in the morning—that was it. That was where the photo was taken, on the morning after the baby was lost from the park.

You were playing with all the rest of them yesterday? Up at the shed?

There were so many people—the Kanes, the Hampdens and other people too, all the people who'd been at the park, or down at the beach or round at the shops. Uncle Peter had taken the children in one by one and when it was Toby's turn he had held the boy's hand and said, 'Speak up, Tiger,' very softly. 'Nobody's going to bite you.'

His shoes were still damp. His shorts had dried overnight but they still smelled of pee; they were stiff and they scratched on his legs.

Mate, I'm talking to you, the policeman said. *You were playing together?* And he was impatient and might have been angry so Toby said yes.

Yes, he was up at the shed.

Yes, he was.

There was something wrong.

Afterwards the policeman said he'd done a good job, good lad. And on the way home, Uncle Peter had stopped at McCauley's and bought them all iceblocks.

So where did it come from, this surge of shame and fury? Sitting alone in his flat he could feel it again, the chilly damp cling of wet shorts, wet sandals and socks. *You should never have vanished like that,* Hannah said, and her eyes shone green at the memory.

Bad things just happen. But after the funeral his dad had taken him home.

II

Toby

After just a few weeks with his cousins the green glass burst, and in the violence of shattered fragments his old world reclaimed him.

The days leading up to that point had seemed like heaven. No, not like heaven—like braving your fears to stand at the edge of a precipice.

'I wish I could stay here forever,' he'd said to them one unguarded morning. 'I wish the holidays wouldn't end. If it wasn't for school we could stay here and no-one would find us. If it wasn't for school I could stay here forever and ever and we'd be best friends.' That was the day that Richard got sick of him; that was the day that Hannah had given him a quick, unduckable kiss.

It was the kiss that made everything go wrong. Later, he would look back and see that that was the last time they'd all been together, the last day everything had been the way it was meant to be; and it had ended because of Richard getting mad and yelling at him and Hannah laughing to see him raw and hurt like an unguarded chick and leaning across and putting that kiss on his mouth. The light splintered green in his hands and that's when it ended.

They had been at the park in the morning, all four of them, up on the iron spaceship that was perfect for climbing on.

From the top of the spaceship the park was laid out all the way from the shed in the muddle of bush near the oval to the trees that shaded the sandpit along the fence. You could see patches of the road through the trees, and the scrub where the track led down to the secret lighthouse; and you could see the other way, too, you could see the road to the tunnels.

'The other kids come up tomorrow,' Richard told him, out of the blue. 'We're going to play wars. We always have wars. We'll have a battle to see who gets to be boss of the shed.'

The planet tilted beneath Toby's feet and he asked, 'What other kids?'

But Richard ignored him and looked up at Hannah and suddenly, out of the blue, he yelled, '*Shipwreck!*' Then he took off, running down the slide and away without looking back, and Hannah ran down the slide too, gaining ground all the time, catching up, her cotton dress dancing and skipping and showing her suntanned legs. Toby climbed down from his perch at the top of the spaceship and ran after them, but they'd already been swallowed up by the scrub before he'd even got to the road.

It was different this time. It was a long, long walk down the steep, thorny track to the lighthouse, all on his own with no hat and no water. The blood was pounding in his temples before he was halfway down, and his face was hot and burning. Sweat stung his eyes and the flies landed on his face to suck at the moisture there, and when he reached the end of the track, Richard and Hannah were already over the jetty, had already reached the lighthouse, had climbed all the way to the platform up near the top.

'You can come up if you like,' Richard yelled down to him. But he couldn't. Not on his own.

The water was barely moving. The skin on his face felt hot and tight from the effort of getting this far. He bent down to cup a handful of water to wash the sweat away, but the rocks were treacherous and he slipped and landed hard, jolting his body and scraping his thigh red and raw with a thin line of blood where an oyster shell caught it. Hannah and Richard could see him, and for a moment he thought that Hannah might come down and help, but she didn't move.

He wouldn't cry. Whatever happened he wouldn't cry. He stood on the edge of the scrub and looked over the water; pressed his hand on the bit of his leg above the scrape that was smudged with seaweed. He held it tight to keep the pain at bay and he didn't cry—and the other two stayed at the top of the lighthouse, whispering, giggling together, ignoring him. So when it was clear that he was unwanted after all, he turned back to begin the long walk home . . .

. . . And suddenly they were there behind him, running towards him, and he thought with relief that the game was over and they'd made him one of the team again but Richard banged him hard on the back as he ran past, yelling, 'That's for trespassing!' Hannah stopped and turned back and saw his desolation, and perhaps she was going to take his hand, perhaps she was going to make things the way that they used to be—but instead she ran up and grabbed his face like they do in the movies and kissed him hard on the mouth and shouted, 'We love you, baby—we love you to absolute *bits*!' and then she was gone.

Hannah

Well, there now. I've done my good deed for the day. I brought an espresso back for Rob, which is just how he likes it which makes me a nice guy because Rob said I was and Rob and I have a sort of a *thing*, an understanding about what constitutes *nice*. So that feels better. Besides, I always like Rob. He's the god of staging; he always installs my sets the way *I* want them done and he sides with me if there's ever any unpleasantness from The Director. He's my kind of man.

'Lydia's hunting you down,' he said, taking the coffee. 'She's up in your office. I'd cover my pockmarked arse if I were you. She's not a bit happy.'

'I borrowed her master key,' I said. 'And my arse, as you might remember, is blemish-free.'

'I'd return it,' he said. 'She's wearing her vampire face. She's out for your blood.'

I adore Rob. He always looks out for me. He's a *teensy* bit of a girl about things like OH&S but he mixes a wonderful Singapore Sling, he always expects the worst of me and he never *minds*.

Plus, he's probably right. I should head up and give the key back to Lydia's minion.

INTERVIEW SGT MARRON 7/1/1967

Hannah Woods We stayed at the park. We played on the swings and the spaceship. Some of the time we were up near the shed, but we stayed in the park.

Hannah Woods I was in charge. Of Lizzie and Toby and Richard—I was in charge.

Hannah Woods I could see Lizzie. I could see her from near the shed. I could see the little girls too.

Hannah Woods I wasn't just playing. I watched out for Lizzie as well, and the little girls too. You can ask her—she saw me. She saw me watch out for her.

Hannah Woods I didn't see the baby. I didn't go down to the sandpit. I wasn't meant to watch out for the baby. Just for my sister. And Toby as well.

Mrs Monckton

I was the one who called the papers, you know—just after the kiddie went missing. I was the first one they interviewed. My husband used to run the bowls nights up at the club; he met a lot of people through that and quite a few newspaper people of course, because they liked to report on all the social goings-on, so we were used to the newspaper people one way or another. So I thought, well, I'd ring them, just to make sure that everything was being done, everything possible, to find that poor little lamb. Because it's always important they have all the facts in a case like that, you see—not just facts, but impressions as well, you know: the things people know even without realising. It's the same today with this terrorist thing, isn't it? People hold back information out of fear and just not wanting to get involved, but you can't do that, you can't just keep quiet. You have to look after your own.

And I never liked that park. I wouldn't have let my own kiddies up there. But people would just shoo their children outside in those days, shoo them out of the house from morning till night. *Someone's going to get hurt on those climbing things*, I used to say; and someone always did, of course, or the little ones fell off the merry-go-round, and skinned their poor little knees, but nobody cared. It was the sixties, you see. Nobody cared about families any more—that was nobody's job. I didn't like the sixties. People think it was such a special time, the sixties, all civil rights, moratoriums, peace marches—well it wasn't. It was about selfishness, about losing control. That's when it started. Ignoring the rules, breaking the law—and no-one stood up to them, no-one got punished, no-one ever got more than a slap on the wrist. But once you lose respect for the law, you can't get it back. And that was the start of it, there, in the park with all the kids running amok and nobody caring. And the country was still crowded out with reffos from after the war—all men, all single men, all on the loose with their families millions of miles away. Couldn't speak English, and they'd work for nothing, and I'm not against immigration, but it has to be managed sensibly or it puts everybody at risk.

And then, of course, the kidnappings ... The little Beaumont kiddies, Graeme Thorne, those poor Wanda Beach girls. Terrible things started happening—terrible things ...

Hannah

They've taken my phone. Can they *do* that? They've taken my mobile phone!

I did what Rob said, I went down to admin, and they took my mobile phone. Not admin—not Lydia—the rednecks. They've got my phone. And she let them take it.

I don't like the way this is going, frankly. I don't like what's happening here. I want my phone back. I can't believe I *gave* it to them, I can't believe I *did* that—but it was really all kinds of ugly, it got sort of *threatening*. They really insisted on taking it off me, they practically *wrestled* me for it, and then they escorted me back up here and told me to wait in my office till somebody comes. So that's what I'm doing, I'm just ... waiting.

Also, my desk drawers are missing. I just noticed. And my computer, too, and my answerphone. Everything, actually—everything's just been pulled apart, the whole room's a disaster. They must have got in while I was down with Rob; they've been in and gone through the place. I mean what the fuck, am I being moved? Am I getting the sack? Are they spraying for *bugs*? They'd better not *sack* me, that's all—they'd better not try to get rid of me. Just let them try, because I have a couple of things I could say, there are things I could kick up a ruckus about. Let them try that on, because you know what? I'll be ready for that—oh yeah. I'll be ready.

Those drawers had stuff in them, by the way—personal stuff. What gives them the right to break in and walk off with my *drawers*?

I hope they don't go through my emails. I'm *screwed* if they go through my emails. Of *course* they'll go through my emails, that's what they took my computer for.

This is an arse of a day, all things considered. An arse of a day.

I want my mobile phone back. There are texts and things I don't want people to see. There's stuff I sent to Rob, for starters. I don't want to get him in trouble.

I'm guessing that this is all about sneaking Toby in last night, which is starting to look like it might have been an exceptionally lousy idea. We were probably pinged on their cameras. We didn't sign in, for starters; we didn't follow security's protocols and they're *huge* about protocols just now. I wouldn't have done it sober. Well, yeah, I probably would; I probably would have done it. But I'm not sure these blokes are going to view *rat-arsed* as much of a bloody defence.

Such a fuss over some bloody prank, some little *infraction*!

I should go home. I should just go fucking home. I should walk out the door, tell the guy to have Lydia phone me—I shouldn't kowtow to this crap. This isn't America, Soldier! This is bloody *Australia*! We don't go snooping through people's computers, we don't go *invading* their mobile phones. We have privacy rules, you know? We have civil liberties! I should just leave. Let the bastards sack me if that's what they want to do . . .

I should *breathe* is what I should do. I should relax. I should look out the window.

The Harbour Bridge is still there. The Oyster Bar is still there—probably loaded with tourists. The Oyster Bar is my personal Maginot line, I said that to Lydia yesterday. When the tanks roll into the Oyster Bar, I'll be out of here like a shot, but until they do, you can screw your sodding evacuation drills.

I keep thinking about that thing she said last week—the security speech. I thought it was Lydia being important, but now it seems kind of prophetic and pointed at me. *We don't have a sense of humour any more. We can't afford it.* And I laughed, of course, because, well, it was Lydia and she's never displayed any kind of humour in her life about anything. But now I'm thinking—what if the whole place has gone humourless? What if sneaking Toby in after hours has jumped the border from prank to *criminal*? But they'd *tell* us, wouldn't they? They'd have to *tell* us, they'd have to give us a *warning* . . . And then I think well actually, Lydia up at a rostrum delivering speeches, that could be considered a kind of warning.

I can see Bradleys Head, just across the harbour. I can see the lighthouse, too, just where it used to be. It occurs to me suddenly that I've never looked at it, never just stood at the window and looked through the view at that summer; and now that I do I'm bereft, I'm thirteen again, and I miss Richard . . .

The lighthouse is there, but the tunnels are what I remember—pitch black and enclosed, shot through with the thrill of silence. I'm thirteen and it's dark all around me, dark like the grave, and if I don't laugh I know I'll win like I always win. There's a trick to this game and I learned it the first time we played. The trick is *stay still*.

That's the one thing boys never think of. They scatter as soon as the counting begins. They can't *run* through the tunnels, because it's so black, it's so dark, and you have to keep count of the rooms, so you need your hands out or else you'll get lost or bash into walls—and the walls are hard, believe *me*. But they *scatter*, the boys, they try to get away from the soldiers as fast as they possibly can. Or they try to *hide*, as if *hiding* makes sense when it's pitch black already, as black as a grave. And once they've run and hidden, they still have to come *back*, they still have to try to tap the soldiers because that's how you win the game, by tapping the other team, by making them yours.

Boys are so ignorant.

I know how to win. I know all the tricks to use. It's like hide-and-seek, this game, but miles and miles better, because in the first place the tunnels are scary enough on their own because of the dark and because of the danger. And for the second thing everything echoes, everything sounds like battles and heroes. So everyone roars down the tunnels, yelling and screaming, to chase away things that are hiding out there in the dark and also because you have to scream, you have to make a noise to remind yourself where you are, that you're still you, because it's so *black*, it's so black that you can't see a *thing*, can't see your hands, or your feet, or the walls and you start to get spooked as though you're not there at all. So everyone screams and the screams make you scream just to drown it all out, just to know where you are; and then the echoes build up in the tunnels and twist around and turn in the dark and suddenly everyone's terrified in case they get lost forever and never get found again, just drop through a hole in the ground and keep falling forever, just disappear—and then at that moment, the screaming stops, everyone just stops screaming and listens, and that's when your skin starts to crawl; that's when the fear gets started because there are ghosts in there. There could be *anything*, could be *anyone* waiting there in the dark, could be robbers or animals, traps or skeletons, could be *anything*. Things there that you don't even know the words for, things that slip down your neck and your shoulder blades twitch at the thought of them. And then someone starts yelling again. It's an excellent, excellent game—but not if you're scared, like Lizzie, and not if you can't keep a secret. Because it is secret. Some of us aren't allowed in the tunnels and even the ones that are, we have rules that you can't go blabbing about. There are secret things. Not bad things, just things that nobody else can know who's not in the gang. Just secret things.

We made it up, Renegades and Soldiers. So we get to rule it. If you break the rules then you're out of the gang—there are punishments for people who break the rules. So this is how you play: two teams. The soldiers count to ten in the candle room and the renegades hide in the tunnels. Then the soldiers have to chase them, hunt them down in the dark, and when they catch one they have to identify him, even though they can't see them, they have to guess by feel who it is, by how tall they are and how fat and stuff—and they have to call out his name and if they're right then he goes on their side. But if they're wrong, he stays a renegade. And if the renegades catch a soldier and say *his* name, then he's a renegade. And whatever team ends up with everyone is the winner and that's all it is. So there's nothing *bad* in the game. Everyone played it. There was never anything bad until Toby shoved in.

Lizzie

Jenna won't leave me alone. She doesn't know what I know but she guesses, she tastes the wind; she thinks that I'm friendly with Kate, and perhaps she can use me. She was waiting for me, she followed me up the dark staircase, her hand on my back—and turn after turn I could hear her, breathless, insistent: '*Listen* to me! You need to *listen* to me!' At the third turning I swung round and slapped her hand away but she was quick and determined and she grabbed my arm and pulled me into the annexe under the stairs.

'Listen,' she said. 'The place is in lockdown. The soldiers have blocked all the gates, they've taken us hostage. They shot up the bus group this morning.' She stopped for a moment then, searching my face. 'You knew this already,' she said. 'You have to tell me what you know.'

In the annexe under the stairs the tiles are dark and the air is cool and although there is no light, the walls are carved with intricate gaps and patterns which capture a view of the internal courtyard below and the clear sky above it. They are cunning, these gaps and patterns, because the view is one way, so that women can see the life of the house without themselves being seen.

What do I know? I know what I saw. I know they blew up the bus, they shot the tourists, I know that Carlo was battered to death on the cobbles outside. But I don't know who they are, so I don't know why; so I don't know anything.

When I don't answer she starts again. 'I can get a chopper here in just under two hours. They'll come from the far end, away from the New Town—they won't be stopped, they won't be expected. They can fly over the whole medina, grab some footage, get it over the news—it'll give us protection. I've spoken to them,' she says. 'They're ready to do it.'

The *ryad* is silent around me. Kate has not left the kitchen.

'There's nothing to shoot,' I tell her. 'The streets are empty. There's nobody there.'

I look at her, blazing away in the chill of the annexe. She was outside already this morning—she's seen the shuttered market stalls, the unswept streets and alleys. But she's drunk with—what? Excitement? Glee?

'I can create the shot,' she says. 'You have to make Kate agree. We can get the guests on the roof, we can have them all screaming for rescue. We can draw international attention, we'll make people look. It's the only way to stay safe.' She is burning up with intensity, with outrage; she grips my arm to press home her point. 'They've killed Westerners,' she says. 'They can't get away with that! We're here, we've seen it, we know what they've done. We can't let them brush it away.' And she can't believe her luck, I think; she can't believe that the stars have aligned to put her and her cameraman here on this day of all days. She sees the outcome already, sees it play out, herself on the roof in an hour or two, surrounded by panic, doing a satellite phone-in live-to-air with the footage to back it up; alright then, she knows how to win, she knows how to plot her career move, get herself into the newsroom.

It flares through her again, this incredible luck, this unparalleled opportunity, and suddenly she's shouting, her back to me, her face pressed to the tiny gaps in the wall of the annexe. Her anger is aimed at Kate in the kitchen, who won't unlock the roof door, who is ruining her plan. 'I'm calling the chopper in anyway!' she yells, and she leaves me and heads back down the stairs because I am no help to her now, she needs someone with guts, with power, with intention. 'Shock and fucking awe!' she shouts and her certainty smashes through the silence of the *ryad*.

And if she's wrong, then she's wrong.

Toby

Was it that day or the next that everything ended? Certainly the mood had changed, Bradleys Head changed in the blink of an eye. 'We love you, baby—we love you to absolute *bits*!' and then the light bright freedom had melted away and his mother was right after all, the world was a terrible, dangerous place.

The others had come up the following morning. There were eight of them—five boys and three girls—and the boys were bigger than Toby, one of them bigger even than Richard; but the girls were only small, were Lizzie's size. They belonged to two different families, but they were cousins too—of each other but not of Richard and Hannah and Lizzie—and they came up every year like the Woodses did. They were noisy and rough, they played wild, rambunctious games, and Toby knew when he saw them that this was what Richard had tried to prepare him for.

They'd arrived all together, all in a mass, a volcano erupting into the park; they'd surged up the spaceship, filling it up till it couldn't contain any more. The little ones were squeezed to the edges, the girls and Toby were almost invisible; the chaos of greeting and mateship swirled around Richard and Hannah. Energy blasted out through the slatted walls of the rocket and made it shudder and groan, and Toby imagined it might leave its moorings, might hurl them all into the stratosphere. Hannah and Lloyd were squeezed up together, almost squashing against the metal, and there was something else he saw, an edge of danger, a hidden message; there was a testing of the power between one of the boys and Richard. He saw that the others were watching as well, were keen to see who would lead them. The other boy was called Ray and he was big and pushy and tough, but Richard was sanctified, surely—Richard was magic. When Ray gave him a half-accidental shove, Richard didn't fall off the slippery dip but ran down it, landing as though he had meant to, ran all the way down and jumped off the lip—and then all the big kids took up the dare and ran down the slide, which could have meant broken legs, and Ray was the last one down. He pushed at Richard, laughing, and they all tore off in a mob, with Richard and Ray at the head and the matter still unresolved.

The spaceship was silent and empty again. There was only Lizzie left, and Toby and the new little girls.

You could see the whole world from the top of the spaceship—the shed at the edge of the park and the council gardener, propped on a log with his thermos beside him. If you turned to the east like Richard's compass, you could see clear to McCauley's shop and the yard where his chickens were kept. If you turned again, you could see the hidden place where the track began, the secret track that led down through the scrub to the lighthouse; and on the third turn you could see the road that went up past the cannons and past the anchor and on to the place where the tunnels began. It was empty already, that road—the tribe had vanished around the corner, with Richard out at the front and the others bunched in behind him, shoving and yelling.

The new girls climbed down the ladder. For a moment it was just him and Lizzie in the spaceship. He spun the metal steering wheel and stared into the middle distance at comets and asteroids hurtling through the emptiness towards them and Lizzie said, 'They've gone up to the tunnels. They'll get a belting if Dad finds out.' Then she said, 'They'll come back. Mum gave Hannah some money for lunch. We're meant to have meat pies but mostly we just buy lollies.'

Lizzie didn't like the tunnels, either, he remembered suddenly; she was as scared of the darkness as he was—but then she shrugged, and ran down the slippery dip just like Richard had done. 'You can play with us if you like,' she called up. But he didn't answer.

The park was stupid without the others. Below him Lizzie was moving away from the rocket, trailed by her row of small girls. They settled themselves on the merry-go-round and started to spin.

Toby watched for a moment and then climbed down and ran up the road that the others had taken—the road that led up to the tunnels.

Lizzie

Time has stopped now. Everything outside is silent. Inside, people wait and watch each other.

The Somali girls sit, invisible on their bench.

I should know their names, the Somali girls—I should know their names at least. Two days ago I went with Kate to their camp, a huddle of broken abandoned buildings on the edge of the Old Town. The young Italians had taken us—they had been working here, trying to connect the Somalis to one of the volunteer aid groups.

The girls shared a tumbledown space with six or eight other children, or almost children. *Almost* is their chief descriptor. They are not refugees exactly—they're displaced persons, 'black locusts' the newspaper calls them; sub-Saharans who fled to Kenya during the civil war, and have wandered from country to country in search of work and safety. So they are economic refugees; which is to say not quite as desperate as the other kind, but desperate enough, for all that. They are not homeless at the moment, because they have each other and three walls and a roof, and they are not hungry, for now, because Kate has given the older girls work and they have as well the support of an NGO. They're not quite orphans, although their parents have disappeared, and might well be dead or imprisoned; what they are is stateless, unprotected, futureless. Even their nationality is a source of confusion; officially, Carlo had told me, there are no Somalis in Morocco—and yet here they are . . . They began wandering as toddlers or babies in arms, or even before then, perhaps, drifting through camps and townships and airports, following rivers of refugees, crossing borders illegally, dangerously, trying to avoid the famines and fighting and all the wars and rumours of war. They have no future, no way to build a future; no residence papers, no health care, no education. They have a sense of where they have come from, but no past that they can rely on or even remember, and their present is tenuous at best. They are Somali, yes, but theirs is a country they don't remember, a country which doesn't remember them—and they are not really safe here, either, in the camp on the edge of the town. Especially the girls, Kate says; she is nervous when they go back to the buildings at night. They're not welcome here, they are foreigners, they are *other*.

I should know their names at least. I should have remembered their *names*. But they are shy, they don't talk to the guests, and they didn't invite me into the hut that day.

Toby

'We loved you,' she'd told him last night, and they had come into focus one after another, those childish faces, fugitive memories pressed into the dead emulsion. And the chardonnay had been swirling around in his head, so he'd been lost for a while, unanchored, awash in the sound of her voice and her sharp green eyes and her laughter and raucous good humour. But he was smarter now, in the hot, hard light of morning. He was smart enough, he remembered enough, to pack the photos away, put them back in their folder. She'll cancel tonight, he thought, she'll wait till the very last minute and cancel, say something's come up; and then he realised she probably wouldn't even bother with that, probably wouldn't even call. Well, they had nothing in common anyway and she was halfway to being a drunk, if yesterday's lunch was an indication. She'd been rat-arsed before he arrived, he thought; she was off her face by the time they left the restaurant and the invitation, coming just at the end, at the Opera House, as he was turning to go—and delivered with such insistent intimacy—that was just drunk talk.

'Come back for the forecourt concert tomorrow,' she'd said suddenly, gleeful and wicked and thrilled to bits at the thought. 'I'll smuggle you in. There'll be champagne and food and I'm going to be all on my own because we're meant to bring a friend but nobody likes me. Oh go *on*,' she'd crooned. 'Be my friend again, just like the old days; be my best friend and we'll watch the fireworks and drink champagne.'

And he'd almost fallen for it, as though the old days were worth it, were worth re-enacting, were laughter and sunshine and music. He'd walked home last night all euphoric and flushed with acceptance. Except now he'd been calling her all day, like a fool, and going straight through to voicemail.

Well, that was their game, that was just what they did. Sucked you into their orbit and then pulled the rug out from under you. It was how they protected the circle, it was how they kept the intruders out of their tunnels. They were untrustworthy, edged about with thorns, and she was the worst of them, then and now, she was the one who always let him down . . .

He'd waited at the entrance, hesitant, insecure, with noises and laughter and squealing bouncing along the cold, stern tunnels. It was impossible to distinguish voices in the echoes, but he'd known it was them, known Richard and Hannah were there and the others as well, who were just jumbled boy-names—Matty and Ray and Sean and Kit and Lloyd. 'Hello?' he'd called, and he'd stepped away from the sunlight and into the darkness. The coolness played over his arms.

He was shy and nervous and scared of the dark, afraid that they'd call him in and afraid that they wouldn't, afraid that Richard might be sick of him now that the big boys were here, afraid that he might be sent home or get stuck at the park from now on with the little girls and Lizzie. His call created a silence which stretched for a lifetime until he suddenly thought to identify himself—and then there was such a rush of relief down the tunnels, a thunder of feet, a tsunami of welcome as they swarmed around him and pulled him back through the darkness, brave in their wake.

And they ran with him in the middle, surrounded, deep into the heart of the maze. There were so many turns and corners that he was lost immediately—but he wasn't afraid with this press of childhood around him, he was exultant instead and wicked like they were, protected and powerful here in the heart of the mob. They knew the lie of the warren as well as they knew the scratted backs of their rough little hands, and they thundered along the darkness whooping and wailing, the ones in the front with their fingers skimming the rough sandstone walls counting doorways and enclaves and corners. They coursed through the blackness, facing it down till a whisper of light detached itself and then it burst in front of him, out of nowhere, a stone-walled chamber with candles stuck into the floor and stuck on the ledges in groups of five and ten and twenty, a hundred candles or maybe a thousand or maybe ten thousand so that the room was as brightly and strongly lit up as daylight. He halted at the entrance and the group propelled him in and became seven children again, proud and bossy and full of themselves and the space they had made. 'It's our clubhouse,' Richard said. 'We make it every year.' So that's what the candles in Richard's cupboard were for. And nobody needed to tell him that this was a secret, this square that was cut from stone, this altar, this cavern, this home . . .

And even after all this time and knowing everything that came after, he found there was still the old rush of happiness at the memory, the old warm feeling of being included, belonging. They had been happy to have him there, happy he'd sought them out and seen what they'd made. And it was beautiful, what they'd made—beautiful, simple and pure; the darkness pitch black but pierced by candles, their flames quite still in the almost-stillness, their wax dripping onto the sandstone ledges, the scuffed and sandy floor—and the children's bright faces, candle-lit, etched in highlights and shadows and darkness and shadings and secrets. It was full of wonder, that moment, full of mirth and joy and pride; and what came after was something else, the flip side, impersonal after all and irrepressible—a contagion, perhaps; a virus that sprang from the other, the dark side of childhood.

INTERVIEW SGT MARRON 7/1/1967

Elizabeth Woods The baby was gone when we got back to the swings. I think it was gone. I am sure it was gone. The pram was gone.

Elizabeth Woods We stayed at the swings after that. We were waiting for Hannah.

Elizabeth Woods I do not know where Hannah was. She was with Richard and Toby.

Elizabeth Woods She might have been up at the shed or up on the oval. The oval is up at the top of the park near the shed. The swings are down at the bottom, close to the spaceship.

Elizabeth Woods All of us stayed in the park, we stayed there all day.

III

Lizzie

Listen—the air is still throbbing, pulsating, chopped into echoes and sobs that beat through the Old Town. It flew in quickly, the chopper, flew low and circled, just for the pictures, as Jenna had told us it would. *One flyover—just one flight over the market and then it will go.* And it did, and it did. *There you are,* she said. *Just for the pictures. Just as I promised.* And it's gone, but it's left a rip in the air behind it. Kate has vanished. The eggshell of safety is broken; and Jenna is making new plans and calling the shots.

The Somali girls sit on the bench by the wall holding hands. No-one looks at them; no-one has spoken to them. No-one has asked them where Kate has gone although they are the ones who could answer.

And I could answer. I know where she is. She asked me to go there with her, to creep through the Old Town—to climb the hill to the refugee huts and bring the little ones in to the *ryad*. *Their safety is never assured,* she'd said just days ago, drinking mint tea in the silversmiths' lane with the young Italians. *They are not from here. Nobody wants them.*

So before the choppers appeared she'd searched for me, found me, begged me to help her. *Thirty minutes,* she said, imploring. *Not* even that if we run. *Twenty minutes. They're children, for Christ's sake—they're kids! We have to do this.*

Thirty minutes—the world can explode in thirty minutes ... Trust can be placed and betrayed, a sanctuary broken, a war can be lost.

Please, she said. *There's nobody left, there's no-one else to protect them.*

You didn't protect the bus group, I told her. *You didn't protect the Italians. Carlo's body is still there, down there in the silversmiths' lane.*

The girls from the kitchen are still on their bench near the gap in the wall. I know their stillness; I touched it in my childhood, in the fraction of time that separates one moment from the next, the silence before the wail of grief and rage and hopelessness. They are sisters, twins I think, and I would have envied them once, but I'm stronger for being alone ...

Richard and Hannah were often mistaken for twins. There's two years between them, but Richard was big for his age and Hannah was not and they both had dark hair and the same green eyes and were rarely apart.

When I was born they were already at school. For a lifetime I watched them climbing up the steps to the gate every morning, their oversized school cases banging against their legs, and one day I'd finally been dressed in the bottle-green tunic and black leather shoes and I thought I'd caught up to them at last. I walked hand in hand with Hannah all the way to the convent; but Infants had their own playground and had to stay there, so Richard and Hannah still kept their distance, secure in their little green world. The Infants let out at two o'clock and Mum would pick me up each afternoon, and Richard and Hannah walked back on their own when the big kids were let out at three.

'You never played with me!' I wail one night decades later, when Hannah and I are reliving our childhood disasters over vodka and lime.

'Not true,' says Hannah. 'We played with you first chance we got. We played hide-and-seek.'

'Awwww . . .' I say, touched, and Hannah says, 'You understand I mean we played *with* you. We hid you. Outside. In the dark.' She looks back at a six-day-old infant, swaddled in a bunny rug, fast asleep in the night-time yard where the passionfruit vine runs amok in a tangle of trip wires and cubbies and tunnels. She gives a loud and sudden guffaw at the memory and says, 'The babysitter was *frantic*.'

There is just a beat of silence while I try to grasp the picture, the newborn, the poor babysitter, a soft-hearted woman of sixty-plus years, the implication of wishful fratricide—but Hannah can see the thoughts in my face and says, 'We gave her clues,' and I guffaw too, vodka spilling out of my nose at the awfulness, the appalling wickedness, and she is pleased to be appreciated and clinks our glasses together.

And that's the way of it. Whenever I look back it's always with a burst of sudden laughter at how wicked they were and how funny and how inseparable; and with the knowledge too that no-one I've ever met has quite matched up to the picture I hold in my heart of Richard-and-Hannah. They were the icon, the perfect thing. They were all I wanted to be when I grew up.

Red

I heard it as soon as they gave out the roster—Bradleys Head clear among all the streets and place names. They were divvying up the observation points along the harbour—just a routine placement, just for the heads-of-state meeting. So the blokes were all kidding around, making a ruckus like army lads always do—but I caught the name right through the noise as if someone had mentioned a long-ago friend. And Jesus, it brought back memories. Jesus, it did.

We weren't there very long; a year or so I think, just a quick little posting for my dad, and it was decades ago now, more than forty years ago. But I can see the place as if it was yesterday, and the beach and the bush—which is all gone now, I suppose—and the park where the baby was taken. The whole place was full of police and reporters and gossip all through that summer; but that's not why I remember Bradleys Head. I remember the place because that's where I fell in love.

I would have been around sixteen or seventeen. I look back now and think you cheeky little bugger, but it wasn't like that, not at all. She'd caught me by surprise as things do at that age and anyway, she was just—lovely.

It was my third day working part time for the grocer, doing

deliveries. Deliveries were tricky, because we were still new and I didn't know anyone much, didn't really know my way around yet. Our parents always encouraged us to get jobs pretty much as soon as we'd unpacked our sneakers; they wanted us to be independent, as parents did then, but more than that, they wanted us to fit in quickly. Fitting in can be hard for army kids. And I was red-headed, lanky, my hands were too big and the skin on them always mottled and peeling away. I hated my hands. I'd see them on the handlebars of my bike and wonder why God made me red-headed and freckled when everyone else was blond—except the Italians, of course. The red hair was bad enough, but my hands! Back then they seemed enormous.

Anyway that was me and this was a mid-week delivery—just a smallish one, some pies and soap powder probably, cigarettes; everyone smoked like chimneys back then. I'd packed the stuff into the box on the bike rack and the boss, I forget his name now, came out and said, *Mate, don't leave till she's bloody well paid you. Don't let her give you this next week bullshit, and no cheques either. If she can't pay cash, load the bloody stuff back on the bike. I'm not Vincent de Paul.* So I got there and left my bike at the gate—you could do that back then, just leave your bike on the street—and I knocked on the door all lanky and carrot-topped, big peeling hands that were sweating all over her shopping. And of course I was frightened to death that she wouldn't have cash.

Looking back, I think it's tough to expect a young fellow to manage that. New in town, and in-between in age, not sure of himself, and somehow expected to say, *I'm not going to let this go until you've paid me*—and not even knowing the lady's name. She was smiling when she opened the door, very young-looking and small and breezy in a bright coloured dress and she said, *Oh, it's so hot!* as though summer had caught her by surprise, and, *You'd better come in and cool off while I look for my purse.* But she couldn't find her purse so she said she'd drop in and pay tomorrow and just when the earth was opening up in front of my feet, her telephone rang. She would have liked me to go then, just put the bag down and go, but I stood my ground and she patted my arm and said, *Okay, wait here,* because it was only a day or two after that poor little baby had disappeared and people were out there searching still and everyone's phone was running hot. *Wait here,* she said, and she picked up the phone and I remember it still, big and heavy and black in her neat little hands with their pink-painted nails.

I don't think you ever really know how these things work. I don't understand it. She was a pretty little woman, and cheeky and sweet, but most of them were pretty in those days. Maybe it was just loneliness. I didn't know any girls my own age, hadn't been at school long enough—hadn't stayed anywhere long enough to really fit in, what with the army moving Dad from pillar to post. And the job, the delivery job—I know it was meant to help us find our feet, make friends and that—but mostly it just meant that when everyone else was doing stuff I was out on my bike alone.

But it wasn't just that. I was a worried kind of kid, always had been; worried about my big hands and red hair, and about the freckles all over my skin—freckles were really bad news when I was a kid—and worried about how fast I was growing, too, if I'd ever stop, and about all the sorts of things that boys worry about at that age. You know what it's like.

So I just sat and watched her talking on the phone, that was all I did. Just sat and watched her and suddenly I felt so sad and so lonely and so out of place. And then I thought to hell with doing somebody else's dirty work, and I put the bag of groceries on the table and turned and walked out the door without being paid.

And when I got back to the shop and told the boss he said, *Right—it comes out of your pay then.* But he never did dock me. It took me a long time to realise he was all bark and no dog.

My dad wasn't too happy with me that night. I didn't tell him the whole thing, just that I was getting my pay docked and he said it was my business, but he was pretty angry. He was a good bloke, but he was an army man, and in the army you obey orders, you don't just do things that make you feel better. He couldn't see any reason why I would let my boss down, which was how he saw it. *You let him down,* he kept saying. *He put his trust in you, and you let him down.*

And the thing is I could never have explained. He wasn't really the sort of person who talked about feelings much. And I couldn't have explained it anyway, except to say that the phone was so big in her hands, and we all knew her husband was gone and she was the one who was trying to deal with settling the kids in alone. She was small and pretty and brave and that was all there was to it. I'd fallen in love with her and I loved her for years and no-one ever had the faintest idea. Which was just as well.

It's going to be interesting to see the old place again. It really is. And if I get the chance, if it's quiet enough, if we get some time off, I'll get away for a bit on my own, have a bit of a look round, see if it all comes back.

Toby

That's what the candles were for, then, and all the supplies in the secret cupboard. And there were other things, too—a cigarette packet, some magazines, comics, a haversack bigger than his and bulging, a stick that was shaped like a spear, a bow and some arrows. There was writing on the wall in green chalk, but before Toby could make it out in the flickering light of the candles one of the big boys had grabbed him and shoved him against the wall, yelling, 'Renegade! Renegade!'

It was a game, a children's game like hide-and-seek. They called it Soldiers and Renegades and it was played blind in the dark without torches, so there was the breath of terror about it, a dancing of fingers along the spine—but it was innocent really, at least to begin with. Two teams: one hiding, one seeking—soldiers and renegades.

Richard and Toby were renegades—Toby because he was new, and Richard to help him. 'They'll guard the rooms near the entrance,' Richard had whispered. 'But they'll send scouts out too, so you have to be careful, you have to know what side they're playing on.' If a soldier was caught and identified by a renegade, he changed sides, and the more renegades there were, the safer you were, the more chance you had of catching another soldier and then another until there were no more soldiers left and the renegades won. 'But what if a soldier catches you?' Toby had asked, and Richard had told him, 'Then you're caught and you become a soldier like him.' So there were two sides to the game, Toby understood, and they were fluid; the game was one of teams and deception and shifting alliances. And the darkness was absolute—once he left this room with its candles he would be blind, and he knew he'd need trust and terrible courage.

At first Richard kept Toby close, grabbed a handful of shirt and ran with him through the blackness, hissing commands like 'Freeze!' and 'Get *down*!' which Toby obeyed without thought, without question. They stumbled and ran through the dark and Toby felt safe for the most part since Richard was sure of his way, knew the twists and the turns—and once they crawled on their bellies, crawled through a tumble of rock, crawled on till they reached a chamber where sunshine spilled in through a grille in the thick stone roof and the patterns of daylight fell down to the ground, blinding and magical. Toby laughed with relief at the thought that the world was still turning somewhere above them, and Richard pushed a hand over his mouth because they were renegades, they were supposed to be hiding, the others were still out there searching. He pulled the younger boy in away from the entrance, took his hand away and said, barely breathing the words, 'No-one ever comes here. Nobody knows this room exists except for me.' He showed Toby the big iron rings that might have been used to chain prisoners up, might have been where they starved them to death, and the names and dates on the walls that might have been prisoners carving their names so someone would know where they'd suffered and died, and Richard showed him the scuffed earth floor where he'd dug on previous visits, hoping to find . . . to find *some*thing—bones, perhaps, or graves where prisoners' bodies were buried in secret. 'But I expect they threw them over the cliff to the sharks,' he said and Toby was sure that never had a boy been braver or happier or luckier than he was to be here, in the sudden brightness that no-one else knew about, to be out of the dark, to be sharing this secret with Richard. Then Richard grabbed his shirt and they were running back through the blackness, back to the business of hiding and seeking.

Hannah

Oh jiminy, it's dark in the tunnels and I'm going to laugh and they'll hear me, those boys will hear me and they're so *wicked*, especially Lloyd, and last year I told him, I said I'll tell Richard, if you keep on hunting just me I'll tell Richard, I will, I swear I will, but I didn't and he knows I didn't and that's why he'll do it again.

I have to stay still. I have to not laugh. I have to be quiet as death because all the screaming and yelling has stopped, the tunnels are quiet as death and they're sneaking around there somewhere, sneaking around me and everything's black as night and the tunnels stretch out like fingers, like tentacles into the darkness. I know they're out there. I know they're hunting. And if it's Lloyd who comes in first, if it's Lloyd who catches me there'll be trouble, I know there'll be terrible trouble! I have to not laugh, I have to stay quiet, as quiet as—

Oh my gosh! I heard them! One of them just in the space outside—one of them's out there, a sound like a hand on the wall, like fingers along the wall and he's calling my name in a whisper so no-one will hear, so I'll know that it's me that he's hunting and oh, if I laugh, if I move, he'll hear me, he'll catch me for sure if I laugh, and then there'll be trouble alright, then he'll be dreadful, he'll be in serious trouble—

He's stopped. He's there at the entrance. I'll dob. I mean it. I told him last year, I told him I'd dob. He knows that I mean it.

He's stopped. He's out there. He's listening, he's waiting. There are sparks jumping out of my skin, jumping all through the darkness, out of my skin like crackles of lightning, invisible lightning and I can hear it fizzing like fire and he'll hear it too, but I'm not going to laugh.

I'm not going to move. No matter how close he comes, I'm not going to move, no matter what, no matter what he does in the dark, no matter what, I'm not going to laugh, I'm not going to move, I'm going to be still like a statue.

He's here. He's just at the wall now, he's just at the entrance, I'm going to laugh—no I won't, I'm not going to move a muscle, I'm going to be still no matter what. He's coming closer. He wants me to run, I know what he wants, he wants me to try to get past him, he wants me to start the game; he wants me to run so he'll catch me the way the game goes, the way it was last year, he wants me to run, he wants to chase me, he wants to *discover* me.

Lizzie

Thirty minutes, she said, and she waited and I said nothing; and then, as though the thought had just come to her, she said with no anger at all, with no accusation, *You are a coward.* As though it surprised her, the fact of my cowardice; as though it could take her away from her fears for Hama, away from the blood and brain matter spilled on the stones in the alley outside. *You are a coward*, she said, and then, *I didn't realise.*

So I am a coward; alright—we all have been cowards.

She went to the door alone. She turned the key, and took it and held it out to me like forgiveness, like absolution. *They'll come into the streets*, she warned. She was speaking softly, so no-one would hear. *As soon as they hear the chopper, the men will be rioting on the streets.* She pulled back the big iron latch and turned to face me again. *Lock the door behind me*, she said. *Don't be frightened. I think you'll be safe, but just to be sure I want you to lock the door behind me.*

And then she left. And the helicopter came in a short while later and tore a rent through the air that is still vibrating, throbbing like migraine, caught in the alleys and scuttle-ways and pounding against the walls of the Old Town. But there was no response; the streets stayed empty, the men stayed inside—so she was wrong about that, at least. Still, there's a fracture here in the *ryad* that can't be put right. The past is uncurling. Kate has left and with no-one here to contain it, the fear has risen up, to fatten itself.

We argue in vehement whispers; we are frightened and dangerous. We hiss in a mixture of languages—and the only one with nothing to say is the one who would lead us outside. She knows what she's doing, does Jenna. She sits in the shadows, tasting the fear as though it could feed her.

Can we trust them? Brigitte asked hours ago in the kitchen. Her eyes were big and brimming with fear. Trust doesn't matter. We are powerless whether we trust them or not.

The door of the *ryad* is locked.

I have the key.

The shutters are closed. From the street it must look like the building is impregnable. The rooms are as black and enclosed as burrows, but under the sky in the roofless courtyard we see the hours passing.

I keep wondering where the Italian girl is, and whether she's safe.

I keep wondering whether she knows about the body stretched out in the alley.

Toby

It took skill, this game. It was more than just hiding and seeking; you had to catch people and try to avoid being caught, and even with light to see by that would have been hard enough with all of the twists and turns and the sudden dead ends. But there was the darkness to consider as well and the things that lived in the darkness, and there was the constant listening for feet, for flickers of sound. And there were the bars that closed off the fifth room; Richard had told him you had to stay well away from the fifth room. 'You'll never get through alive,' Richard had whispered. 'A soldier can guard the tunnel there on his own. He can pick the renegades off one by one.' So you needed to find each other along different tracks, you needed to think and plan, you needed a memory of how the paths branched into each other, and turned away: and for that you needed a partner, an ally, a mate. There was great strength in numbers.

So they were allies, Toby and Richard. And if he hung a little way back and didn't do his share of scouting ahead, well, he ran like a boy at least, he kept his arms straight, he didn't whinge and he never even once tried to grab Richard's hand.

Hannah

He's going to do it again; I know exactly what he's going to do. He did it last year and I was just twelve and I told him I'd dob, but I didn't. He did it last year in the tunnels with all of the other kids running around us, all of the other kids all around us deep in the darkness.

I was a renegade, Lloyd was a soldier, and I was in one of the rooms and he knew he had *somebody* trapped all alone and he knew it was me, I'm sure he knew it was me. I kept still like a statue because that's how you win—if you move they can feel the space change, feel the air shifting around you, and that's when they chase you, so I had stayed perfectly still as a statue—but he came in closer anyway, slipped through the doorway, crept in closer and closer towards me and it was so *dark*, so completely *dark* and I couldn't see him, I could just hear him and he couldn't see me at all. But then he stopped, he suddenly stopped and breathed out as soft as a sigh and then he breathed in again long and slow and it sounded as though he was smelling the air, as though he could taste me mixed into the cold dark air around him and all of my body was jumping, like it was ready to fall off a cliff, like my blood had gone cold and hot all at once and was boiling. And he stood in front of me, blind and invisible there in the dark, and he whispered, 'Boy or girl?' and his hands moved the air in front of my face and he whispered again and touched my arms and the skin on my arms stood up like goose bumps. And then his fingers went over my waist and right up my chest in the dark and he whispered, 'Boy or girl?' but I didn't answer and then I could feel him pushed up hard against me, his hands all running on top of my dress as though they could melt it off and wherever he touched my skin he left bits of fire and sparks and he pushed me so tight I couldn't breathe and his heart was punching the ribs in my chest and then there was yelling and someone ran into the room in the dark and I shoved Lloyd away and he yelled out, 'Caught Hannah!' as if we'd been playing the usual game, as if nothing had happened at all. And then everything snapped back to normal; there were feet outside in the tunnels and I was a soldier and Lloyd was a soldier and we went back to chasing and catching. But my heart kept thumping for quite a long time and the rest of that day he was terribly careful around me, stayed far away from me as though I might burn him or something. We didn't get caught, and nobody dobbed; but later that night—because this was the last night of last year's holiday—later that night we had fish and chips on the beach with a bonfire and once I looked up through the flames and I saw Ray Kane was staring at me with hate in his eyes.

The air has moved at the entrance. Someone is out there, someone has caught me. But instead of the sparks that were fizzing and spitting a moment ago there's a mean and cold taste in the tunnels, there's something nasty and rotten and cruel and the air feels dead and cold and empty of fire and I know it's not Lloyd there this time, I know it's not Lloyd.

Toby

Hannah's cry had cut through the dark like the flare from a lighthouse. Deep in the tunnels, Toby was terrified, reached out and grabbed Richard's shirt and was pulled in the wake of the older boy to the cell where the yell was still echoing, outraged and tinged with fear.

He hung back at the entrance, petrified, feeling the air on his skin, overwhelmed by the war on his senses. The room was full of the pulse of heartbeat, full of the warmth of exhaled breath. There was movement instead of stillness, there was heat in the walls—and suddenly, unexpectedly, there was a light flooding into the room and it took time, it took a moment or two for his eyes to adjust. And then he could see them, the gang of them, Hannah and Lloyd and Ray and all the others, and Hannah was angry and rumpled, standing away from the wall, and Ray Kane had tumbled onto the ground and the others were caught in the light that shone on their passions, their wickedness, and the guilt in their souls.

In the light of his torch Richard was looking at Hannah, was looking around at the boys. 'What's wrong?' he asked, and Toby could see him uncertain, trying to make sense of the story. 'What's wrong?' he asked again, and the silence grew between them, around the other kids, building up walls, excluding outsiders. Ray, tasting triumph, got to his feet again, suddenly buoyant, defiant. 'Caught Hannah!' he yelled and ran into the darkness, and all the boys followed en masse—and Hannah stood in the unexpected light, indecisive, biting her lip.

'Ray tore her dress,' Toby said into the emptiness. Richard moved the torch and the beam played across her shoulder where the blue cotton seam was ripped. Hannah's hand went up to the sleeve without even looking, and the undecided look was replaced by a grin of triumph and daring. She ran towards Toby, grabbed his shoulders, yelled, 'Caught Toby!' and disappeared into the darkness.

And then, again, it was just the two of them. But there was something left in the emptiness, something aching around him, and Toby couldn't translate it then, but later he saw it was love and loneliness. And there was anger there, just beginning. He looked at Richard and would have liked to say something kind, to say, 'We can still be friends, you and me,' because it was just like the day at the lighthouse, the day she had run off and left them, her skirt tucked into her knickers, except this time she had left Richard too, and Richard was not prepared, had never been left before. 'We can still be friends,' he would have liked to say but instead, when he opened his mouth, the words came out accusingly and instead of comfort he said, 'That's *my* torch.'

And Richard ran off and the light went with him, and that's when the end began.

BBC NEWS, FRIDAY, 22 JULY 2005

A witness to the shooting at Stockwell Tube Station told BBC television, 'I saw an Asian guy. He ran onto the train. He had a baseball cap on and quite a sort of thickish coat—it was a coat you'd wear in winter, sort of like a padded jacket.

'He might have had something concealed under there, I don't know. But it looked out of place with the sort of weather we've been having, the sort of hot humid weather.'

Lizzie

It took time, it took time, but it's started now, just as Kate said it would. People—men by the sound of it—thundering down through the alleyways, bashing at walls and doors; stones and voices beating on wooden shutters. It is violent, sporadic, it comes and goes, and when it is silent we sit and watch each other.

Kate is still out there. Deep in its burrow the past is uncurling.

There are more of us than I thought—the guests, the Somali girls, Karam who carries the bags, Mohammad the driver who usually sleeps in his car by the gates. Kate wouldn't allow them to leave the *ryad* this morning, and since the door is locked they've had to obey.

I think they are glad to be here now, and not on the street.

There was a din from the mosque but none of the music or singing that comes with the prayers. It was a public announcement, I think, but when I asked the girl who serves at the table she shook her head. She has stopped speaking English now; she is lost in the waking nightmare of her childhood.

It is silent now as I write this. Silent, inside and out. If we speak, we speak in whispers and only to the people we trust—husband to wife, companion to companion. Sometimes a woman will smile outwards into the group, smile bright and brittle, a kind of voiceless comfort that means, 'We are not conspiring, whatever it looks like,' but the men hunch, silent, directing their energy inwards.

There were children in Rome—there were children carved into the stone. There were angels and gods, there were scapegoats and sacrifices.

I am alone. Reza is also alone and Berndt and Laurence. We don't form a group, and we don't join the other groups either. We wait like everyone else. We watch. And we listen. Kate is gone. I should have gone with her, but I've come back up here to the hidden place, to the women's annexe.

Below me, down in the *ryad*'s courtyard, they move into little groups that eddy and swell, and break and form again. I watch through the latticework; and if I can't hear, I can read the physical language, the leaning in and turning away, the clenching of fingers, the tightening faces. I have seen this before. I have seen the fear that causes a mob to grow into a single pulse, to beat as one.

Jenna is watching too. She ignores me now. She can do this thing without me. She watches the fear as it swells and grows and instead of calming it, as Kate would do, she will let it feed on itself like a maddened wasp, let it lurch into panic. She is brave, I will give her that. And she is ambitious.

I don't know yet if she realises I have the key.

Hannah

Thirteen. Oh, we were so bad and bright at thirteen, so full of secrets and sin, so roiling, so fizzing with life that we couldn't contain it. We could find our way blind through the tunnels, light up the dark with the fire of our indiscriminate passions, burn through the walls with the ricocheted sparks of our devilry . . . We were awash with heat and hormones that year, Lloyd and me; and the other boys caught the excitement and beat a path through the dust in our wake—and poor old Richard, unnerved by the changes, excluded, unsettled by all of our shovings and shiftings, poor Richard, lost, as the centre of power slipped into uncharted currents.

Lizzie said that it started there, the bruise in the peach, the canker, the worm. But she's wrong; we teased, of course, but there was no harm in it, no malice at all. It was just our way of building the strength of the gang, of safeguarding the tribe. Every summer would bring us a new kid, a target, a lamb, and we'd take them up to the tunnels and chase them around in the dark and scare them to bits—and after a while we'd come to the rescue again and lead them into the sunlight. After that, of course, they were ours for life—or till the end of the summer at least. They were part of the gang, they'd meet any challenge, keep any secret.

Toby was different, though. He brought out the worst in us. Or perhaps we were meaner that summer, all hormones and heartlessness...

Toby

He thought he might die in the darkness choked by the fear in his throat—and then he felt it, up through the pressed-earth floor—a vibration, a pulse of movement—and he crouched in his corner, waited with dread till it lifted itself away from the darkness and became the beat of feet, the skimming of hands along walls; but there were no voices this time, nothing for him to catch hold of, nothing for him to respond to. Nobody called his name, no one sang out a hello. They ran into the room and he could feel them around him, dancing forwards and backward, touching the earth so lightly, whirling around in the darkness; he knew the smell of them, he could taste their movement, and if the silence was unexpected, he was drinking them in through the pores of his skin, like a caterpillar, a pupa; he was reading them and he knew they were flesh and blood, he knew they were known.

And for an instant, when they reached out for him, he was glad of the clutching hands, of the pinching fingers, glad of their flesh-and-blood warmth, but then the silence was starting to draw out the air around him, and when they hauled him to his feet, he stumbled and tried to grab the hands to steady himself, and was bewildered when he fell again and again and it took him time to learn they were tricking him, tripping him up in the darkness; that mischief was being created. That he was the target.

Hannah

We chased him out of his cell and through the tunnels in utter darkness, without a sound, pushing him, tripping him, just to tease, just to torment, and we wouldn't have kept it going for long, but he slipped through our fingers. We realised we'd lost him—and that was dangerous for a new kid because there were places where the walls weren't strong, there were cave-ins where the roof had fallen through. And it was dangerous for us as well, of course, because Dad had made the tunnels off-limits and Dad was strict about rules and responsibilities. There'd be terrible trouble if we were caught. Serious trouble. 'Poor little bugger,' Dad had said. 'He's had a rough trot, so you lot look after him now—he's really been through it.' He wasn't supposed to be in the tunnels again, and neither were we; we were meant to be watching out for him, keeping him safe. So we started fighting, Richard and me, ignoring the others—fighting about whose fault it was that the teasing had gone on so long, and who started it, who should have stopped it. We were frightened in that way you are as a child when you realise that much better things were expected of you; it's a fear that leads quickly to anger, a mixture of shame and defensiveness. But in our defence, we were only kids—and he had that *thing*, that fragility, that appalling eagerness that made him fair game. But we'd teased him beyond the point where it stopped being teasing, beyond the point of tears, to a place close to terror. It happens, that's all. A group mentality takes control and it happens.

Anyway, he got out. The darkness protected him and he found a way out, a new way that didn't lead back to the room with the bars. We were searching for ages, but when we came, blinking, into the sunshine at last, he was there already, out in the sunlight, crouched in a heap near the cannon, still bawling his little eyes out.

Ray Kane was the first to spot him; he yelled and pointed and all the boys charged in a fury towards him, screaming and yelling, and Toby stood up, I remember, crying, his face all covered with snot, his shorts wet, his legs and shoes soaked in piss, and he looked so dreadfully raw that it made me sick. He didn't even *try* to run, he hadn't even gone home and dobbed—and now he just stood there, watching the mob surge towards him. I still remember the way it rose up in me, that sticky morass of feeling, half rage, half remorse, and all I wanted was just to see him *disappear* and I couldn't have cared less how, or what he disappeared *under*, but Richard took off after Ray and caught him and pulled him down onto the ground and they fought, the two of them there in the dirt, squirming and punching and kicking. Ray cut his lip in the tackle and Richard saw blood and stood up, stood over him, panting, and Ray spat at him but Richard said, 'He's just a little kid. Let him go.' Then he looked around at the rest of them and said, 'He doesn't matter to you. Just let him go.' No-one said anything else and Toby set off down the road all snotty and crying and nobody stopped him.

'We'll go back to the park,' Richard said. 'Just say that we stayed at the park. If he dobs, it's his word against ours—but he won't dob. And we didn't hurt him.' He turned and began walking back to the park, and after a moment or two everyone else started following him. But nobody caught up with him, no-one walked with him. And of course when we got to the park, the baby was missing.

We never did go back to Bradleys Head. We never saw the Kanes again, or the Hampdens. We never saw Toby either, after that summer. So maybe that was our punishment, that was divine retribution. But if it was retribution it was a clumsy, unimaginative form of punishment, because it might have been better for Toby if he had stayed with us. He might have toughened up a little bit, been less likely to show every bruise as a badge of honour. Because we were good kids really and, despite everything, they were good times. But then it all went up in smoke.

It's hot today, with that baking stillness I remember from back in my childhood. I can see it through the window in my studio, a blanket of five o'clock heat moving over the city; the Harbour Bridge is empty, the harbour is empty. The Ferris wheel at Luna Park is still, like the bright, bright water under the white hot sun.

I want my phone back. I wish they'd tell me what's going *on* for fuck's sake. I'm not good at waiting, I'm not good at hanging around, I'm totally lousy at following *orders*.

There's a couple of helicopters out there now, buzzing like lazy wasps from over the naval base and across to Bradleys Head . . .

Lizzie thinks it was our fault, what happened there—us and the Kanes and the Hampdens. She never came out and *said* so, but she detached herself from us all. She's not a fighter, Lizzie: she's more of a world-class *detacher*. I have no idea what Richard thinks—he's just a mass of pronouncements—but me, I think it was just the place itself and the time. People behaved the way people will always behave when they're caught in that eddy of fear and impotence.

The lighthouse is still there, across the harbour, outside my studio window; still abandoned, broken, unlit. The tunnels are still there too, I imagine, burrowing under the coastline. But the proud, fierce joy we had lived and died the year Toby came. We lost the *goodness*, that hand-in-hand faith in each other, that wicked simplicity. And I have to remind myself what the hell, childhood *ends*, that's why grown-ups get vodka ... But we never climbed down to the lighthouse again, and we never went back to the tunnels.

The Messenger

The Bradleys Head shops sit at the top of the hill on a sandstone plateau above the sea. The commercial centre has grown with shops and cafés set neatly along an entirely inadequate narrow main road.

There are perhaps sixty businesses altogether and it would later be estimated that he entered perhaps seventy per cent of them. He made small purchases—a notebook in one shop, a couple of pens in another, a mirror—and he made them without speaking. The suburb has an excellent library, comfortable, air-conditioned, and he stayed there for some time, reading the local papers, using the internet. There is also a small movie theatre. He bought two tickets to the afternoon screening, but it is doubtful if he used them. The single attendant who sold him the tickets thought he left straight after the purchase; she wasn't aware of seeing him return. *He didn't speak English*, she would say later. *I knew something was weird because the tickets were for an English film, not a foreign one, but he didn't speak English as far as I could tell. He just pointed and nodded.*

By this time a tactical response group had already been formed and briefed and dispatched; appropriate permissions were sought and received.

The Lighthouse

History is lived in glimpses, interrupted. You can hear fragments only, bursts of laughter, whispers of fear.
We didn't know what was wrong, but something was wrong.
It's a long story, this—a very long story. It may not end happily, it may not resolve.
Just take the things you need to keep you safe and leave the rest.
He had a coat, a hat, a bomb belt.
He had Mongolian eyes.

BOOK THREE

On the jetty, near a lighthouse, is a boy.

He leans against the guardrail, shielding his eyes from the sun. His face is raw and swollen and there are flies, gnats, midges, little things sucking his eyes and clustering at his nose.

He thinks of the goat moth caterpillar with its body turned to wood bit by bit, or perhaps of the Gordian worm that can make grasshoppers drown themselves in a pond of water, or perhaps he thinks of his mother, who knows that the devil can get inside living things and make them weak and evil. And he wonders if it was him the devil got into, or the other kids in the tunnel—or whether the tunnel itself might have called them in like a magnet, a black north pole; and once they were there in the darkness they became powerless.

I

Hannah

There was something happening when we got back to the park that day; Richard noticed it first. The place was full of people—much more than it usually was—and Richard said, 'Look!' and pointed to two policemen down near the gate.

'He dobbed! The little rat dobbed on us!' Ray hissed.

My stomach jumped into my mouth and made me angry. 'Don't be stupid,' I said. 'There wouldn't be time, and anyway we were just *teasing*, nobody *hurt* him.'

'Keep the story straight,' Richard said and his voice was urgent. 'We've been here all morning, okay? Don't mention the tunnels. Just say that we've been here all morning.'

Lizzie saw us then and ran up with the little girls trailing along behind her. 'Where have you *been*?' she said. 'There's serious trouble! A kidnapper kidnapped a baby right out of the sandpit.'

And it was true. We headed down to the sandpit to have a look in case there was blood, but before we got there a policeman shouted at us to get back to the swings and wait till he came. So we sat on the centipede swing and Lizzie told us about everyone trying to find the baby, how people were going to be searching the bush to see if it just got lost, and walking down the road in case it had been run over—and how one mean lady had yelled at Lizzie for not knowing where it had gone. 'But it wasn't our baby,' Lizzie said. 'And nobody told us we had to look out for it.'

We watched the baby's mother, who was crying fit to bust, and we watched old Mrs McCauley patting her shoulder. A little bit later Mr McCauley drove up in his car and he helped the baby's mother to get in and he and Mrs Mac drove her away.

And the park kept filling up, people kept coming from everywhere. 'You weren't supposed to leave us,' Lizzie said suddenly, and she looked like she might start crying so I ignored her. 'You were supposed to keep an eye on us,' she said and then, before she could work up to tears, she looked around and said suddenly, out of the blue, 'Where's Toby?'

And that was the problem with Lizzie—she noticed everything.

It took a long time for the police to get to us. We waited for ages. Then at last one of them came up and looked at us all, and he said, 'Are you the oldest one here?' and I said yes. And he said, 'Have you been here all morning?' and Richard said yes, we had.

'There's a kiddie wandered off,' the policeman said. 'Did you see a little kiddie, a baby, a toddler?' I said no and everyone else said no, but then Lizzie said, 'I saw it when she brought it in. I saw the pram.' The other policeman came up and they asked her questions one after another. They said, 'How come you didn't see it?' to all of us and I thought we were done for but Richard looked up all bright and helpful and pointed up to the top of the park near the shed. 'We were there,' he said. 'In the shed.' And that's all they asked.

They left a few minutes later. One of them got in his car and drove off and one of them called all the grown-ups onto the road to start to look for the baby.

'That was a lie,' Lizzie said to Richard and Ray Kane laughed in a nasty way.

'I'll explain to you later,' Richard said, but she still wasn't happy.

We hung around for a while, us and the Kanes and the Hampdens. We went up to the shed to make sure there were fingerprints there in case they did fingerprint tests. 'Leave lots of footprints,' Richard told us. 'Make sure you leave lots of footprints for evidence.' And we did; but they never came back to the shed, and the evidence blew away in the next few days, blew away in the dust. And we didn't know something bigger was already set in play—something we couldn't have understood, something we didn't begin.

Lizzie

They went looking for Kate, the guests, as soon as the riot began to subside; I could see them down through the annexe wall, I watched as they searched through the *ryad*. They wanted answers, they wanted assurance, and when they discovered that Kate had left then the ice of terror encased them—the fear that they had been tricked, had been abandoned, sacrificed. That was the moment for Jenna to stand up, to call them together—not to her, because she is canny, she knows the ropes—but to call them to an idea, a plan of action.

We can get through, she'd told me earlier. *We can get through with the cameras running. We're used to this sort of crisis, we've done it before.*

And the cameras will protect her, of course; and of course—but she doesn't say this—there'll be footage to sell, even better than the rooftop shot she had planned. She'll have terrified Westerners running through the medina, pictures of chaos to go with the shots she has already taken—the blood on the cobbles, the guns in the square. This could take her away from the wildlife channel and make her instead what she always wanted to be, a proper journalist, a force to be reckoned with. She will gather us up, she will lead us to safety—not for our sakes perhaps, but to safety anyway; and for a day or two, she will be the American Hero.

We'll be safe, she told me. *The chopper crew will cover us through the medina—they've already agreed. And they will be filming, and nobody's going to hurt us while people are watching. They're not going to harm us knowing the world will see.*

And who's to say it won't work? Who's to say it mightn't be the best chance for us? The trouble might be over anyway—the streets might be cleared already and we wouldn't know, hiding here with the door locked, hiding away like children. Perhaps the soldiers are already gone from the square. Perhaps it's already over.

But Carlo lies dead on the cobbles, down in the silversmiths' lane, and in its burrow deep in the darkness, the past is uncurling.

Jenna is moving from group to group, selecting disciples, anointing people, making connections, a hand to the arm, a fingertip on the wrist. She moves on, and in a little while they leave their places, they follow her. Words are whispered, the plan is shared in secret. She brings her group into line, not democratically, not through discussion, but through hidden negotiations, through fear and whispering.

The men will come onto the streets, Kate had said. *If she sends in a helicopter, there will be rioting.* And she was right: they came onto the streets. And there has been rioting.

Lock the door behind me, she said, when she gave me the key. *Thirty minutes*, she said. *I'll be back in thirty minutes. Watch out for me.*

Hannah

This is insane. I've been waiting for bloody ages, waiting for Lydia or someone to come, to *explain* for God's sake! To bring my computer back—I can't *work* without my computer. There's a *show* on tonight for chrissake! I have *work* to get through! I have changes to make! There are people from the committees arriving any minute—people I need to see, I need to check in with.

Rob must be frantic. Rob will be *livid*! How long are they going to keep me here?

They told me to wait. They said someone would come to see me but nobody's been.

Red

It hasn't changed all that much. After all this time . . . Smaller of course and the shops are newer and brighter, but it hasn't changed that much in forty-odd years. Not really. Not much.

McCauley's is gone. That's, well, sad in a way. That's the spot you look for first of course, the spot where you worked, the spot you defined yourself in.

He was a good man, Mr McCauley. Bit of a shouter; knew what he needed, knew when you weren't really pulling your weight—but he was a good bloke, too, he could get the best out of a lad and that's rare today. Boys need men around them. That's how they thrive. He had a bit of a temper, but I had a lot of respect for him.

Funny old place. It's funny to see how much it's stayed the same. Geography, I suppose—there's only so much you can do to it, once you've chopped down all the trees and bitumened the road. The ocean's not going anywhere. The coast won't be moving anytime soon. They've pulled the park out of course—kids don't play in parks any more but I think it was where the library is now, and the afterschool centre. Not that I played at the park. We weren't here for long, and we weren't park kids, really. We were riders and campers and trekkers, us boys.

Funny old place though, funny how much you remember, the things you remember. The deliveries, I suppose—they're engraved on my mind, of course. Once you know a path through the place, once you know how it all fits together and who belongs where, what they eat, what they like, what their lives are like ... well you know the inside of the place, the home kind of life; not weird stuff, not stalker stuff, just, you know, what cigarettes they smoke, who likes the tins of Tom Piper Irish Stew, who reads the *Herald* and who takes the *Mirror* and that kind of thing; how much milk they get, which tells you how many kids they have, how much bread, how much bacon—well, you sort of know them. And who writes a cheque, and who counts the coins out in shillings and sixpences, and who gives you a tip and who just yells out to leave it there, I'm busy. As though you're a bloody machine.

And who slaps her forehead and says, 'Oh, I'm silly! I didn't get up to the bank!'

Was it sixpences? No, it wasn't—we'd changed by then. It was decimal currency, '67—no more shillings and two-bob bits, no more pennies and ha'pennies. It was 1967, the year the papers came down on Bradleys Head like a ton of bricks. The things you remember! And it's all coming back to me now—because this is the place where they had those gun emplacements, and Dad took me up there one day, just me and him, because he'd heard in the mess about the gun emplacements and a network of tunnels where they used to store ammunition; so we went up, the two of us, in the late afternoon. And it was hot, but not as hot as the days had been; the heatwave had broken, I think—but it was still summer, still hot; and the tunnels were cool and so dark, they were black as pitch inside, although the sun was blazing away like buggery up there above us. He was a . . . He was a special bloke, my dad. He was a good bloke. He was a good father. A soldier through and through, except for this one little soft spot he had which was us, which nobody saw; I doubt if anyone ever saw his softness except for us and Mum—and not all the time, it wasn't on show all the time, but we knew it was there. This little soft spot, just for his family, this little tenderness.

He was a lovely bloke. And this time, I remember—and jeez, I'd forgotten it all!—this day, he took me up there, just me, to see the old emplacement, the cannons and stuff. It was sacred ground to him, of course; it was military stuff, secret stuff, man's stuff, and he wanted to show me, pass it on down to me in a way. 'No-one would have been here,' he told me, 'not for decades, not since the last war, not since the Japs came into the harbour . . .' And my skin was cold with the little hairs standing up on my neck. And Dad led the way through the tunnels and it was all so silent, so cold and dead, and then suddenly, out of nowhere, this one room, Dad played his torch around this one room—we were looking for soldiers' names scratched into stone, because he'd been told there was soldiers' graffiti there. He played the torch around this one room, and there were candles. Candles! Stuck on the stones and stuck in the floor, in the sand—all over the place, like a church, or a castle. Not lit, of course—but oh! If they had been! And Dad was furious. 'Kids,' he said. 'Bloody kids!' And oh, he was angry. Lack of respect, you see, and he hated civilians making a mess out of military stuff, hated to see them barge in and treat it like toys. He was angry; he was angry all the way back, all the way out. And it wasn't long after that he was sent off to Vietnam and I wonder now, it just occurs to me now, for the first time, if that was what he had wanted to tell me, if that was where he wanted to say it, the thing that he used to say whenever he left. 'Look after them now. You look after them all. You're the man of the house until I get back.'

I didn't ask if we could light the candles. I would have liked to, but I'm glad I didn't. I'm glad I showed that much respect, that much understanding. Without understanding at all, of course. But I'm glad of that.

And it's funny, the things you remember.

Lizzie

The men will come onto the streets. And deep in its burrow, the past is uncurling. *The men will come onto the streets.* And, *Watch out for me.*

I'm back in the heat of midsummer again, eight years old at the end of a bright hot day underneath a remorseless sky and Richard and Hannah are hot and remorseless as well, and livid with rage at Toby. And Toby won't say anything, doesn't speak. He just stands there and takes it.

Richard is angry because of this: because Toby's mother is mental and Toby has had a tough time, the poor little coot, and Richard was meant to watch out for him, Dad made him promise. And Hannah was meant to watch out for him too, and if Dad finds out they left us alone in the park and went to the tunnels he'll take Richard's rifle away and they'll both get a belting. So that's what the problem is. Because Dad made them promise to stay in the park. They promised to look after Toby. And they didn't, they didn't look after him. They broke the promise and told a lie, and they know I won't tell, I won't get them in trouble—but Toby won't say if he's going to dob, so that's why they're angry.

All of it's Toby's fault anyway. *I* think it's Toby's fault and so does Richard and so does Hannah. It isn't my fault because nobody told me for sure they were going up there, so I didn't know *where* they were, not for sure, and that's what I said at the park: I told the policeman I didn't know *where* they were. I didn't say if they were in the park or not. I said *somewhere around* because they were meant to be keeping an eye on Toby and me. That wasn't a lie—they were somewhere around. So it wasn't my fault.

And I told Toby not to go with them. I said he could play with us if he liked but he ran after them on his own. I didn't say what they do to the new kids there, how they scare them and make them cry—but they did scare him and he did cry and Hannah said that he peed his pants. And later, in Richard's room, she told him, 'You shouldn't have run *away*, stupid. If you hadn't made such a *fuss* they all would have *stopped*!' But that's not true—they never stop until you are crying.

Richard said, 'Mate, we were only teasing,' but Toby still wouldn't answer, he wouldn't say anything. And Richard said, 'Hey—we showed you the lighthouse, didn't we? We wouldn't have carved your name in the lighthouse door if you weren't our friend.' Then he got angry suddenly, and pushed Toby in the chest and Toby fell over and Richard said, 'Let him dob.' He said to Hannah, 'Let him dob. He's ruined everything anyway. Let him dob. Doesn't matter. It just means he'll be out of the gang.'

But he won't dob. I know he won't dob. It's too hard to dob when it's all of them against you and you're on your own. That's how they win.

Hannah

Nothing's moving outside my window. The air looks heavy. The harbour looks hot and flat and exhausted; that late-afternoon dull sunlight is sitting on top of the shut-down city. The flags and bunting they stuck up along the expressway hang down in the heat like they just can't be bothered, like they're already beaten.

Remember the southerly buster? Whatever happened to that? It used to be lovely, the ten-minute blast of cold air. There's no sign of it today—no sign at all. There's a heaviness I remember though— the kind of relentless summer that seared through our innocence, choked and smothered those final days of our childhood ...

The thin brittle grass lay parched in the yard of the police station; I remember the wire fence, the gate, the breath-sucking heat of the morning. The jacaranda was still blazing purple well after Christmas: the cicadas were screaming. Dad took us in, one by one—first me, then Richard, then Toby. He held our hands, reassured us, sat beside us. I remember the policeman, the way he listened, the way he questioned us as though there was plenty of time, no need to hurry now, no need to rush. *We were in the park. We played on the* merry-go-round. *We played in the shed.* We were important that day—more important than Lizzie and all the little girls; more important than the grown-ups, too. There was a photographer there from the paper and when the police had finished with us he lined us up along the verandah and took our photo. The baby had disappeared the day before and hadn't been found. This morning was the first full day of the search.

Our stories were congruent, synchronised. *The shed was locked. The window was open. We climbed in and played in the shed.* It was early and every hour mattered. *We played underneath it, too, in the space underneath the shed, and in the scrub around it. We played hide-and-seek.* We were helpful—the policeman told us that: we'd been helpful. *There was only us at the shed. The Kanes and the Hampdens and us. We played there all day.*

When it was over, Dad told them that he'd drop us home and then join the men on the search; and the knowledge flashed between them that this is how things change—that it was acceptable now to drive three healthy kids five blocks. We caught the knowledge as though it was a virus and took it into ourselves.

Toby

It had ended there in the tunnels, the dream of belonging, the blood-brother magic.

Next morning Hannah and Richard had pulled him into the little cupboard in the wall of the screened-in verandah. They'd closed the door and listed the punishments that would come to Toby if he dobbed, if he told anyone that they'd lied about being in the park. *We were up in the shed if they ask. We were up there all morning.*

And later, at breakfast, just to be sure, Hannah had said—so lightly, in front of her parents—*Don't you want to explore the tunnels, Toby? Can't he go back with us, Dad? He won't be scared, will you, Toby? You know we'll watch out for you.* The threat behind the words was unmistakable. He'd been told not to talk. He'd been told not to shoot off his mouth.

After breakfast Uncle Peter had taken them back to the police station. The baby that had gone missing still hadn't been found. Toby could remember the people gathering, anxious, eager to start, and he remembered the dusty grass around the verandah. It was a hot day beginning, a white sky burning with secrets and sadness and, *You, the little bloke—come in closer,* the man with the camera had said, and Toby felt the other kids retracting, bunching away from him. There was the scratch of cloth on his thighs, the sting on his legs ...

Ever been in the paper before, kids? Ever been famous? The newspaper man was chatty, but the children were canny—they knew not to trust him. He'd tried to joke, tried to keep his voice light and friendly, but Toby remembered the strength of the children, and it was brutal and unforgiving.

You were at the park, hey? Up at the shed? And you didn't see anything? Nothing! Not a detective in the bunch! He was trying to shame them into responding and when that didn't work, he turned to the weakest link, turned to Toby and said, *I'll bet you saw something. The gardener for starters, hey? Reckons he was around the sheds, you must have seen him. You couldn't have missed a bloke with a bloody great shovel?*

The big boys were watching, bunched in a group. Lizzie was there, breathing everything in, seeing without being seen. Hannah stared openly, merciless, pitiless, and the man from the paper kept at him. The questions pushed into the hot morning air one after another and Toby was all alone, unprotected, afraid of the things he might say. He felt the thump of his heart, the fear that someone would hear it—and the sick relief when Richard came to his rescue.

There was no-one up at the shed, Richard said. *Just us. We stayed there all day.*

And after that he'd retreated back into himself, and counted the days till his dad would take him back home. 'You alright, mate?' his dad would say over the phone. 'You alright there, mate?' And the tears would lodge in his throat and stop him from speaking. His dad would talk on till their three minutes were up and he never mentioned the story all over the news, never mentioned the little lost baby, the unending search or the hardening anger. And when he called, the aunt and uncle never had to go looking for Toby, never had to come back to the phone to say, 'Sorry, John, he's off with the others,' and his dad had seen something in this because he didn't mention them either, didn't say, 'Just too busy to talk to your old man, hey?'

'Keep your chin up, old mate,' he'd say, instead. 'You'll be back here before you know it. You'll be right, mate.' And the tears would slide down Toby's face like rain and he'd hold the receiver long after his dad had hung up, hold it and listen long after the only sound was the miles of empty telephone wire. 'You'll be right, little mate.'

Hannah

He was proud of us that day, Dad was: he said so. Each time we came out, each time we'd finished our stories. And then the man from the newspaper lined us up and fiddled behind his camera and I waited for Dad to butt in because there was nothing that Dad loved more than he loved his cameras; but he was in a hurry, he wanted to get us home, wanted to get himself back to the search, get this kiddie *found* as he'd say in a few days' time, red-faced and sweaty and full of rage and despair. So he let the man herd us into the hard white sun, let him point and focus and click the shutter and all he said as he got in the car was, 'That's going to be a shocker.'

Then he drove us home. He was proud of us—said we were great and we'd done a good job. But all through that morning, without a word, we'd kept the pressure on Toby—keeping him quiet, silently turning the knife. At breakfast, and in the car, on the verandah waiting to go in to give our statements, all in a group while the man from the newspaper took our picture; and Toby felt the threat and, frightened, he backed us up in our little lie. *We were up at the shed*, we said, and he didn't demur. *We played there all day.*

Mum had stayed at the house. She came out to the gate when she heard the car pull up and Dad told her quietly, 'They're sure it's him. His story doesn't hold up.' And in a voice almost too soft to hear, he said, 'Keep them inside, just to be safe. It's their word against his, after all. I'd keep them inside.'

It was Lizzie sitting beside him who heard, who made sure we knew about it, made sure we got all the ramifications. Not then, of course, not at the time—when it might have done some good, when it might have been useful—but years and years later, after we'd all grown up. 'I remember waiting,' she said. 'I remember just waiting for them to find out. But Dad believed us. He believed in us right to the end.'

That's stupid, though. That's just Lizzie—wanting to be included. She always wanted to push her way in, to examine, unearth the hidden things: always wanted to find the worm under the rock. It *wasn't* just our word—we weren't the only ones questioned. There were grown-ups there, Mrs Monckton, the McCauleys, parents of local kids, visitors. They heard what they wanted to hear. The Hampden and Kane kids were questioned too, lined up in the sun with us, waiting their turn. We're all in the shot there, aren't we? Bunched up and squinting? It was never just our word. And Dad was right. It was a lousy photo.

We weren't allowed out at night any more. The games on the beach were a thing of the past and so were the bonfires, and so was hide-and-seek-with-the-torches. During the days we were told to stay together and play in one of the yards—ours or the Kanes or the Hampdens; and by and large we did. We had our own fears after all—the search took in the tunnels as well as the bush and we lived in terror of them finding things, finding Ray Kane's father's magazine or the packet of Benson & Hedges, finding Toby's screams and tears or tracking our footprints all through the dust in the places where we'd promised we wouldn't go, on the day that we'd sworn that we'd stayed at the park. We would listen for the front gate to click, and hover while Mum went out to greet Dad as he came back, walked him through to the kitchen, sat him down, poured him a beer. The holiday was ruined and we longed to be gone, but Dad was one of the searchers—and there was a feeling among the holiday people that we were part of the township now, that this was our tragedy, too.

We discussed it a bit, that first night, Richard and I—but as days went by, the talk became tangled, grew careful and more oblique. We were silenced by what we knew, what we hadn't told ...

That's it. I've had it. I'm not waiting here any more, I'm not a criminal. They want to go up me for bringing Toby in, well they've made their point. But I'll be fucked if I'm going to hang around till they come in to lecture me. Rob can manage the set without me tonight. Lydia's got my number. They can phone me at home if they need me and pay for the call. Who do they think they are, really, these bloody Americans? 'Wait till we get to you.' Screw that, princess. Screw the whole bloody show and Toby as well. They can keep my fucking computer. I need a drink.

Lizzie

The searches always began before we were up, and never ended till long after nightfall. Meals were eaten in the meantime, five cycles of bedtimes and wakings observed, but mostly the days were still and we waited for news. Years later I asked my sister if the waiting had stayed with her too, if she thought it had changed her, but she barely remembered it. We lived through parallel times, Hannah and I. *I remember reporters*, she said. I remembered the waiting.

Those days were framed in stillness; five days and five nights, when life was on hold. The holiday was forgotten. Children were kept close to home. Fathers gathered together to search the beach and the bushland; mothers stayed on the phone from breakfast time, hunting for news. There was no information the first day, but on the second day the whisper got out that the police had some idea who had taken the child and where she might be. Mrs Hampden brought the story to our house; she and Mum talked it over in the kitchen. Then the search in the park had been abandoned; the area around the tunnels was cordoned off instead. Police and soldiers were gathering up there and the volunteer searchers, our fathers, tired out and on edge, were suddenly free.

This new development stopped the flood of uncertainty and built a bulwark of sorts against the fear and defencelessness that had threatened the town. There were new people on the streets and in the shops—gawkers from the other suburbs, and people from neighbouring areas eager to help—and I suppose the reporters were in the mix too, fired up with the thought that the Beaumont tragedy might be being repeated. 'It will be a foreigner,' Mrs Monckton had said when three days had gone by and then four with no answers at all. 'It'll be a foreigner or one of those homos.' But there weren't any homos at Bradleys Head.

There was a foreigner, though.

BBC NEWS, FRIDAY, 22 JULY 2005

Commuter Anthony Larkin, who was also on the train at Stockwell Station, told reporters he saw police chasing a man.

'I saw these police officers in uniform and out of uniform shouting "get down, get down", and I saw this guy who appeared to have a bomb belt and wires coming out and people were panicking and I heard two shots being fired.'

Red

Well, that's a view right there. Jesus Christ, that's a view! I wasn't ready for that, hidden away like a secret here, at the edge of the coastline around from the Heads—suddenly, round the corner, laid out in front of you like a picture. It's a landscape, a piece of art, completely untouched after all these years. Not a house in sight, not a cabin—just bush and the lighthouse along the way and that view. What a view! Straight across to the bridge and the Sydney Opera House, straight across to the city. And the harbour! Movement everywhere, sailboats like bright little butterflies dancing around on the water . . .

You've got to admire the army, you really do. When it comes to corralling the good bits of land, they could teach a thing or two to the bloody churches. That's a view worth millions, hundreds of millions probably—just this few acres of scrub. Clear it up, whack a few mansions across the top there, glass-fronted but not too gaudy, no blond brick or anything—Christ, you'd make a fortune. No wonder the real estate industry hates us—all this potential development locked away. Must drive them crazy! Completely untouched—just bushland and old barbed wire. NO TRESPASSING signs all over the place, decrepit, rusted to buggery—it wouldn't be government land without rusty NO TRESPASSING signs.

I wonder if Mum and Dad saw it back in the old days, ever snuck down this way, climbed down through the bush from the road up the top? They might have done—Dad was an old romantic at heart. Maybe they found their way down here one evening, watched the moon over the water; one night, just the two of them, up there perhaps, where the climb from the road is a little bit easier—just over the outcrops there where the lighthouse is. Maybe they did.

I put my hand up for this post as soon as they mentioned it—just on the off-chance, just to visit the old place again. And it's lovely—this is just lovely. Just me and the bush and the harbour. The Opera House right there, over the water, and nobody else, no noise, no people. Just me and the lighthouse there. This is just lovely.

Mrs Monckton

I don't think you should blame the boys, though everyone did, of course. Well it was wicked, of course, it was terrible, but you can understand how they felt. We all felt the same, you know; nobody liked the idea of hordes of foreigners swarming in and taking over, changing everything. They had their own countries and we had ours and also you have to remember this was the time they were pulling the White Australia policy down bit by bit, in secret, without any kind of discussion, and people minded. People *minded*. All of a sudden the floodgates were open to all sorts, open to people we'd been at war with a few years ago, and there were the men, all these foreign men, single, and they had no idea about how to control themselves, no idea about how to behave around women. Whistling and leering—it was very unpleasant. And then when the baby disappeared from the park, that's when it hit home, really, to us here in Bradleys Head. And, yes, things did blow up a bit, did get out of control and harsh things were said, I'll admit that—but the newspapers kept it alive, of course. The newspapers, that's who I blame. They kept it all burning for years. Years and years afterwards, if you just mentioned you were from Bradleys Head, people looked at you as though you were some kind of criminal.

No-one understood, you see. No-one did. You couldn't, unless you were here, in the heat of that summer, watching the searchers go out and come back day after day, four days, five days, and never a sign of the poor little creature, and never a word from the foreigner up in the cells. Never a word. And he was a single man, lived on his own in one of those mean little weatherboard houses quite close to the bush. And of course that's the other thing—we knew they'd picked him up, the gardener; we knew the police had picked him up. He'd been there at the park, you see, the day she went missing. He'd been there in the morning pruning the bushes and things, and then suddenly no-one had seen him again. He'd just disappeared, just vanished, the same time the baby went missing or near enough. And then a day or two later we heard that he'd been hauled in for questioning—so that had to mean something, didn't it? Everyone saw it. Him in the police car in full view of everyone—it had to mean something. And they kept him up there.

Well they knew he was lying. Everyone knew he was lying. He'd said he'd gone up to the shed—but nobody saw him. There were people up there, kids up there, and they hadn't seen him. So everyone knew he was lying, the police knew—they carted him off in full view of everyone and we thought, well they'll get answers now, alright, but still there was day after day after day in that terrible heat and the men out there searching and him staying silent and nobody knew if that poor little baby was dead or alive.

And the children heard about it all every day, of course they did. You can't keep that kind of thing secret. But I don't blame the kids. You should blame the people who opened the floodgates, that's who should be blamed. They put us all in danger, the migrants as well as the rest of us. I don't say they shouldn't come in, the migrants—just that there should be a plan. For us and for them. It has to be managed. And when you look around now with these terrorists blowing things up all over the shop, well you can't say I'm wrong.

They were good kids, you know. That Ray Kane—he's quite famous now, has a radio show. He isn't afraid—he'll tell it like it is. He says things everyone wishes they had the courage to say out loud. He talks for a lot of us and he was a very nice boy, a good boy, very well-spoken. And they were just kids.

They were trying to do the right thing. They were wrong, of course, as things turned out, they were wrong—but they were just kids. They learned their lesson; and they're the ones I felt sorry for.

Lizzie

'It will be a foreigner, you mark my words,' Mrs Monckton had said—and the man who clipped the hedge at the park was a foreigner and in no time at all we knew that he was a suspect. We knew he'd been seen at the park in the days before the baby went missing, and we knew he'd been there in the morning; Mrs Monckton had seen him there. And then we heard the police had caught him and locked him up in the cells but he wouldn't talk to them, wouldn't tell them anything. The hatred of him grew with every day of fruitless searching, because he could end this nightmare, give people back their lives, just tell them where she was, where they could find her. Some of the fathers said give us five minutes alone with him and he'll talk; but there were laws and he was protected so there was nothing to do but wait and talk and imagine . . .

And they didn't find her. They searched day after day, through the park, in the bush, at the cove and, finally, right through the tunnels, until there was nowhere else they could look and the soldiers went home.

I never played with the Hampdens or Kanes again. Something was broken and no-one was friends any more. I was sad for the baby and sad for its mother, but saddest of all for my dad, who had really believed they would find her, that she would be right as rain. On the night that they called off the search I patted his face when he came in to kiss us. 'You'll be right, little possum,' he said, and I'd put my arms around his neck and pulled his face down so I could whisper into his ear. 'I want to go home,' I said. He rubbed my head and I started to cry. 'It's Toby's fault,' I cried to my dad. 'He brought all the bad things with him.'

That was the longest night, I remember, the night that the search was called off. It was hot and I couldn't sleep because I was lost in the sadness of everything. Hannah couldn't sleep either and late in the night the boys came and tapped at her window, but this time she didn't sneak out like she usually did. She just lay there, perfectly still, as though nothing would ever wake her. Because that was another thing that had changed—the gang was all breaking apart.

The boys tapped and giggled and sang out her name for a while and then they went sneaking off round the side to the back of the house, where Richard and Toby slept. In the quiet I heard Hannah whisper into the darkness, 'Fuck off, then,' which was something we'd never said. 'Fuck off,' she whispered and then I could hear she was crying.

The Messenger

Towards the end of his walk, he bought food as well—some biscuits, a bottle of water. The final sighting was in the last of the shops on the street, a real estate agency. It was a brief visit; he collected a free brochure, shifted the overcoat to his other arm, declined the offer of a glass of water from the chilled Clearview dispenser, and left. He was, according to the realtor, *stressed out. Too hot—a bit cranky. Not the sort of man you want to annoy.* He might have been foreign, the realtor said. *He didn't speak.*

Later, on television, the realtor would be more certain: *He was definitely foreign—he didn't speak and he was inappropriately dressed. He had that up-against-a-wall look, too, like he wasn't relaxed, you know, like something was after him. I asked if he wanted a drink of water or something, but he just, you know, grunted.*

There was something wrong, I knew there was something wrong. And there was the coat.

Toby

The search was called off at last. The town was exhausted.

That night was terribly hot; the air outside was heavy and still. On the verandah, curled under the sheet, aching for home, Toby counted the hours in the days that were left: and before he was done, the back of his neck had pricked suddenly cold and he opened his eyes.

Nothing had moved in the darkness, not the stars, not even the shadows—but there was whispering suddenly, light little flicks on the old wooden walls like a lizard might make or a cat or a bird or a boy. Before the sound could come again Richard was up in the darkness, pulling his shorts on, grabbing his sandshoes, slipping as soft as a whisper into the hot, angry night.

Toby lay in the dark, alone for the first time then in the rickety bedroom. The windows were unglazed, the door was unlocked, and the night crept in around him.

Lizzie

Nothing is moving outside. The Old Town is waiting, listening, ready to churn into chaos. The mosque is silent.

I've been here before—I know this stillness, I touched it once in my childhood, in that tiny space between innocence and the knowledge of what was to come.

The mosque is silent. The air is dull and heavy with waiting and watching. The donkeys up on the hill have been hushed. In the Old Town nothing is moving.

I've been here before.

It was night; I remember the night, and the whisper and scuttle of boys at the window. Hannah was taut in her bed; I remember the hidden sound of her tears. I remember this: the wicked boys tap-tap-tapping, and later the shadows that ran and tumbled outside, the grey of the fence and the black that devoured them, gobbled them up, enfolded them into the terrible night. And Richard was with them by then—I do remember that. Richard was with them.

I crept out of the house and followed them, unsuspected.

And I remember this: I remember the way that the midnight bush closed around me and I was not afraid; I was there in the dark and the sky was brilliant above me, glistening with stars that shone in the blackness, looking like tears, and I was not afraid.

It returns to me sometimes, this memory, always surprising and unannounced, and behind it always the terrible surge of despair.

And a taste at the back of my throat, the cold taste of cowardice.

II

Hannah

Oh Jesus Christ, I'm shaking—I'm literally *shaking*! My knees are like water, my hands are—I can't believe it! Who *are* they, these people? Who the fuck do they think they *are*? Getting into my car to go home and they *grabbed* me, six of them *grabbed* me, *six* of them screaming and shouting, great big American *rednecks*, all running towards me, six of them screaming and shouting—they grabbed me, literally *threw* me back onto the side of my car and they had *guns* in their hands, two of them—holding their guns in their *hands*, not even holstered or anything, just in their hands, pointing them at me. They did it on purpose, I swear, they smashed me right into my *car* as though I was some kind of criminal, *screaming* at me, and they could have gone *off* for fuck's sake, those guns, they could have gone *off*, they could have *shot* me! I don't recall voting for this; I don't recall ticking the boxes—I do not recall voting to loosen the gun laws just so America could visit. What, was I busy?

And I've banged my back on *something*, my arm and my shoulder, and that's going to bruise, that's going to come up a lovely colour tomorrow—those bastards! I look like I'm crying. *I am not crying*, you bastards! *Enraged* is what I am. I'm fucking *enraged*!

I'm *shaking*. I don't believe it. My knees are like water, my hands are—with *guns* in their hands! Who *are* these people? And nobody stopped them. There's people all over the place, the bump-in crew, the service staff, even a few of the guests—people everywhere and nobody stopped them. Dragged me up through the corridor and pushed me into my office—and nobody got in their way. All that screaming and nobody heard a thing—nobody *stopped* them.

My office is trashed. They've turned it all upside down. What they hadn't taken before, they've taken now. If it wasn't nailed down, they've got it. *This is not the way it's supposed to be, you bastards! This is not the way this country's supposed to be run!*

Lydia saw it. I'm sure she was there in the hallway. I'm sure I saw her and some of the singers as well. And I screamed out for Rob—I was screaming and kicking—they hustled me up to my office so fast that my feet didn't touch the ground, and I lost my balance, and they just kept dragging me on by the tops of my arms. And nobody *helped* me. Like no-one could *see* me. Corridors full of people and no-one could bloody see me. And nobody's come. Not Lydia, not the police, nobody's come.

They've broken my door—I can't close it. My office opens right onto the corridor now but whenever someone goes past they go past softly, speed up to get past my office as quick as they can. As though it's improper to look; as though somebody died in here.

They've taken my handbag. My wallet. They've got my car keys. I can't drive home without car keys. All my stuff, they've got all my stuff . . . They kept shouting questions. Where had I been? Who was I with? *New* people, they kept on saying. Had I met foreigners? Have I? I don't think I have. Maybe I have—Toby just got back from overseas. *Overseas* is foreign to this lot. How long does it take to become a foreigner?

I want to go home but I don't want to walk through the corridors. I want to go down to admin and file a *complaint*.

It's quiet now. No more announcements.

Everyone saw it happen, but nobody helped me.

Lizzie

Listen. The wave is returning, the under-sound building again, coalescing, swelling through alleys and laneways ahead of the mob and they will catch up, they will hurl their hatred and rage at the walls of the *ryad*, hoping to bring them down around us. Listen! It is still faint, but definite now—and if I am the only one who can hear it, I know in a moment or two the French girl will hear it too, and she will look at me, eyes wide, the pupils dilated, and she will not tell Luc this time, she won't put her hand on his arm the way she did before, she won't risk it because every time he flinches she finds it harder to trust in him. She meets my eye and looks away, looks across to Karam, who never speaks, never makes contact, but shows his terror in his thin hands and the soft way he brings them up to his mouth, and then hides them under the bony shield of his elbows.

We have gathered again in the courtyard. Jenna is central to everything now; she stands in the middle, the group comes together around her. She has told us the roof is locked; her plan for the rooftop shot is gone. She has told us her new plan—the exodus through the medina.

They're coming back, she whispers at last. *Stay calm. They don't know we're here.*

And then they come back.

Hannah

They're trying to *intimidate* me, the thugs, and I won't be intimidated, I am not Lizzie, I'm not a coward. And they brought Lydia with them this time—she was holding my mobile phone, she was holding my phone and at least she was shocked, I could see that; she was shocked when she saw what they'd done to my office, she went pale when she saw my face and just for a moment she held out her hand to me, but they came in behind her, four of them, all in security jackets, and one of them took my phone from her, held it out to show me the screen, shoved the thing right into my face and shouted, '*Read it! Read it!*'

I stood there. I held my ground for a moment—but then he stepped closer, they all came in closer, and what does it matter whether I read it or not? They could read it themselves. So I read it. No pushing this time, they didn't touch me, no shoving; they just waited for me to read it and yes, I read it aloud, and that's why I hate them, because I never knew this about myself, never knew I could be so frightened, never knew that I wouldn't stand up to them.

A week ago Lydia said, 'We don't have a sense of humour about security any more.' And I'd laughed because this was *Lydia* talking and what kind of superpowers did she think she was made of?

So, alright. They know about last night's security breach. They know I brought Toby in to show him the canvas. They know he was here. And I can see what they think, I can see their paranoia at work, their post 9/11 mindset—but they are so *wrong*, they are *so* wrong, because this is *Toby*, for God's sake! What kind of a threat is *Toby*? He's not a terrorist, he's not a danger, he's not going to cause any problems! With all the stuff we put him through, all he did was come back and try to be family again: and that makes it worse because now I remember his terror, that day in the tunnels with us, I remember his fear and I remember abandoning him.

They're thugs, they are bullies. They started screaming again, held the phone right up in my face, they were screaming at me—who sent you these messages, who has been texting you? Holding the phone in front of my face, screaming, 'Read it! Who sent it? *Read* it!' over and over, louder and louder, and he'd sent a new message, and I should have just kept quiet, should have told them to go fuck themselves, I should have refused because Toby's whole heart was there in that message, there on the phone in their hands.

Stay there, he'd texted, over and over again. *Watch out for me.*

The Messenger

In addition to the shopkeepers, the cinema attendant and the realtor, the newspapers eventually tracked down a woman from the library, a Mrs Egan, who had spent some time beside him at the computers. She was an older lady, a local, less keen to talk on camera, less keen to be interviewed.

She had spoken to him, certainly: *Wasn't he hot? Had he come in for the air-conditioning? Was he from around here?* She had thought there was something familiar about him, but no she couldn't place it. He left after about an hour, she thought, and no she couldn't say whether he had an accent or not; now that she came to think of it he might not have said anything at all. *Well it was a public library and people our age still try to keep the noise down in public libraries.* She had stayed in the research room till closing time, unaware of any tension on the street. She had stayed for the coolness, she said, and also because the family history people who usually hog the computers were blessedly absent for once.

He had left around seven, but she stayed till the sun had gone down and the heat left the streets.

Toby

He must have slept for a while because it was suddenly darker still and he opened his eyes to see that the moon had moved from the window, the world outside was blacker and even more menacing—and something was *in* the room, he realised, moving around in the room and his heart leapt into his throat but before he could scream he saw it was Richard, just Richard, there by the screen door, creeping across the floor like a ghost; as unbodied and thin as a ghost, as dull and unshining. Toby could smell the fear round the other boy's shoulders like smoke, almost taste the despair as the last little bits of his magic slipped into the night. He crept into bed without taking his shorts off, and pulled the blanket up despite the heat; and across the room, Toby could feel him crying.

Hannah

I told them his name. They'd have found out anyway, they can manage a phone trace surely, even on silent numbers—so what does it matter? They'll know as soon as they talk to him. They'll *know* he isn't a threat, so I told them. 'My *cousin*,' I said, and I told them his name, and so what? They can't suspect him of anything—this is *Toby* and Toby is totally *pointless*, I told them, he's uninformed, he's worse than *I* am, for God's sake. He's been in Cambodia, not bloody *Pakistan*!

So I told them his name—so alright, I told them his name. I am not brave, after all; but I'm not craven either. I didn't *help* them, I didn't *inform* on him—he did that all by himself. He dug himself in when he started texting my phone and alright, yes, I sneaked him in last night, yes we broke the rules, but I took the rap for that and I said I was sorry, I said it was my fault, I said I was drunk—I wanted to show him the canvas. I've done it before, I said, and it wasn't a problem. But that was then, of course, and this is now; and if you do it *now* they smash your door in and shove *guns* in your face while everyone else in the building is mesmerised suddenly, hypnotised by the flags in the sunlight, the fucking *cowards*. If they can't keep us safe they can make sure at least that we're terrified into submission.

Stay there, he wrote. So now they know that he's coming. And they're keeping me here just in case they think they can use me. They said they'd be back. *Watch out for me*, he said. They told me to wait.

They've left a man outside my door and I am not brave.

Toby

Afterwards, after the funeral, after his dad had taken him home again, he'd let that memory of Richard wash over the earlier ones like the waves at the foot of the lighthouse, till all the shine of the boy-king was dulled and corroded away. He didn't want to keep the cousins there in his heart like a photograph any more—he wanted them faded, covered with ashes, burned to nothing. On the train home he would have liked to hold his dad's hand, to say, 'I want to stay with you forever,' but he was shy, so he leaned against him instead, pretending to sleep. And the next time his mother was sick they sent him away to a school in the mountains, where he grew into one of those boys that no-one remembers, a name in a photograph, there on the end perhaps, shortish and squinting a bit in the light—*that* kid, there; and then someone might say, 'Him! I was at school with him!' But that's all they'd remember.

That was all he wanted anyway; to disappear into the darkness, away from the bright summer light, away from the noise and the rough and tumble and chaos of people.

To burrow. To wait. Just to be left alone.

There was one insistent memory, just one that returned—and he let it return. He liked to mull it around in his mouth like a toffee, tasting its shape, to inhale and exhale it, catch it and keep it close on a shelf in his bedroom, or cool in the dark of his pocket or hot in his heart. He couldn't remember what led to it, or why it held such power, but it was this: it was the lighthouse, and it was the day when his father was coming to get him and take him home, it was the last day. In the morning he'd climbed down the bush track all on his own, alone, through the scrub and the trees and the thorns, under the blazing sun and the hot, empty sky. He'd crisscrossed the jetty, retrieved the knife and climbed up the terrible ladder. He'd stood for a moment there on the platform that skirted the light itself, and then he had taken the sacred knife, the magical knife, and scratched at the writing, the letters that stood for his name, ripped and ripped across them until they were all gone, ripped until nothing remained of him. *They'll fix it*, Richard had said, back in the early days, before the gang came up, when Richard was good and anointed and pure and full of assurance. *They'll fix it one day and find our names and then they'll know we were here.*

Well then, his name was gone and it was over. He didn't belong any more. He threw the blade into the water as far as he could because it was nothing, it was just rust and metal, it wasn't magic at all, and he climbed down the ladder and over the jetty. And when he was on solid earth again he looked at the world once more through the green glass marble, and then, without any words, he dropped it into the place where the flag used to go, in the mound of cement that a soldier might have been buried beneath. And it didn't matter that no-one would ever find it . . .

So if he'd been less than happy at first to get the phone call from Hannah, despite the treacherous rush of delight that surged up at the sound of her voice, it might have been because of the dangerous thought that they had come looking for him after all, after all these years, had come to release him at last from his prison deep in the tunnels, come to draw him back into the circle again; and cold at the back of this wave came the undertow, pulling away already, the danger of trusting them, the threat of the past, the darkness and smoke and all the things they remembered.

But a drink had turned into dinner and gone on for hours and it had been lovely, wonderful, charming and then at the end she said, *Come back for the forecourt concert tomorrow . . . Be my friend again, just like the old days.* And she'd kissed him, half on his cheek, half on his mouth, so that showed—what did it show? It showed something. It showed that she didn't hate him, anyway. People grew up and changed—he'd changed; he'd travelled and been a success, been pretty successful really—and it would be just him and her, and they were the good times, weren't they? When it was just the three of them, back in the earliest days—just them at the lighthouse, Richard and Hannah and him. He remembered her dancing across the rocks with the skirt of her frock tucked into the legs of her knickers. *We love you, baby—we love you to absolute* bits! she'd said, and she might have meant it, mightn't she?

And while it was true that she hadn't been answering her phone all day, she'd texted him now, out of nowhere, the words blazing hot and bright across the screen of his phone. *Eight o'clock at the lighthouse*, she'd written. *Just us two, just like the old days. We'll watch the sky burn.* Signed with an *H* and an *x* so it was like *hex*, which was so like Hannah, of course. He wasn't disappointed to miss the dinner—he wasn't all that keen on corporate events. And the lighthouse would be the perfect spot for fireworks—she'd thought of that, too. He could imagine it, the view, the isolation: the black of the harbour, and the unwritten sky.

He was comforted now by the knowledge that she had melted a little, had made the connection stronger. He texted her back right away with: *What can I bring?* And the answer returned in an instant, just like he hoped it would. *Just bring yourself,* she'd texted. *Bring yourself.*

Just him and her, then. And maybe they'd talk—but anyway, just him and her. So a new start, perhaps, a way to begin again.

Lizzie

The roar of the mob has grown with each incarnation, but it's changed its shape now, it's not a wave any more—it's a tsunami hunting down everything in its path. And this time we're not forgotten the way we had been earlier, tucked in away from the markets. This time the wave breaks out from the little town square and runs through our alley and for just a few minutes we are the target of all that rage and hatred. Things are changing; the virus is strengthening, feeding itself and the past is uncurling.

I've been here before . . .

I remember that night, and Hannah still in her bed and her quiet tears running into the pillow while I followed Richard over the fence and into the darkness, unnoticed. I am back there again, eight years old, and instead of the sky I can see the tumble of boys ahead of me, breathe in the night-time warmth of the hot dusty earth and the sting of the gum trees. And there is that smell that catches itself in the back of my throat, unnamed and dangerous, potent and alien, a smell like a taste that evaporates into the empty air. I remember the gardener's house and that taste; I remember the dark, that enveloping, cradling dark and the sudden awareness that something is happening there in the blackness ahead of me; there where the boys are, something is happening, something bad because they're divided five against one, they're fighting now, five against one, and the one is trying to stand up but he's punched and kicked, he is spat at and then he breaks free and when he breaks free, he turns and runs and is eaten again by the night.

We have all been cowards . . .

They are back, the mob, they are angrier, louder, their roars and hatred are trapped in the maze, in the burrows; the walls surround them and catch the echoes and now there is the drumming of wood or weapons against the wood of the ground-floor shutters, against the door, and the kitchen girls press close up to each other, their eyes wide and terrified. Jenna is shouting at the girls above the noise, 'What are they saying? What are they saying?' But if the girls can catch the words they're keeping them in. So she turns to us and shouts, 'Sit down! Sit down!' and I realise that we're all standing, cowering, backed into corners and walls and she shouts again over the uproar, 'They're going. Sit down!'

Hannah

This isn't my fault. This is not my bloody fault. I will *not* be suckered into feeling guilty—this isn't my doing. I didn't tell Toby to call me, *I* didn't give him my mobile number. This is Toby's fault—and Richard's fault, too, for wanting bloody *atonement*. I was happy enough with Toby out of our lives, thanks; I would never have tracked him down—and that is deliberate, that, it's precisely because I *know* what he's like, he's a train wreck and *I* can't be trusted with vulnerable things, with breakable things. So it's not my fault and this is not mine to fix.

Stay there, he wrote. *Stay there. Watch out for me.*

But I'm not going to sit here and cower, I'm not going to sit here and *cry*. That's not who I am—I am going to *kick some arse*, you bastards, I'm going to *hit back*. I'll be making some fucking phone calls, filing complaints and not to the Ombudsman either, and not to the fucking *government*—I'll be raising this with the public, the press, the news channels. The civil liberties crowd would *love* to hear about this, and so would the Trots and the radio shock jocks—and they *will* be hearing about it because I'll tell you what, this has gone far enough, this is *fascism* now, this is totally out of *control*! People are going to *mind* when they know that you're monstering people, setting the rednecks upon us, pulling out guns and monstering people, stomping their jackboots all over our freedoms—people will *mind*! This is Australia—you don't fuck with us and *our* fucking democracy!

This whole performance, just to punish us for not taking them seriously—because that's all it is. There's no way they could think we're a threat, me and Toby—but they want to make us *pay*, they'll make an example of us. This is your public dollar at work, Australia! Trapping *Toby*! Talk about lambs to the slaughter.

I'm not hanging around—I'm leaving, I'm going to get out, call up the TV stations or someone, kick up a racket, explain what's gone down, make someone accountable. It's better for Toby, too—if they're going to monster him like they monstered me I can make sure at least that it's done on a public stage, in front of the fucking cameras. Because this isn't child's play. They had guns. And they don't get to shove us around.

Mrs Monckton

We all knew that it was hopeless, of course—we all knew she wouldn't be found. After the first day or two we'd all known that she had to be dead. In all that heat, with no-one to feed her—she had to be dead. I can't tell you how upsetting it was to know nothing was being done. Oh, the search went on—they called in the army eventually—but the police were too soft, they weren't getting any results . . . We all felt it, we all did, people felt helpless quite quickly and then felt ashamed of being so helpless, and then of course we got angry. This wasn't the country we knew, now that our children weren't safe. This wasn't what we were used to; and the government couldn't care less, the police were useless all of a sudden. Something had changed, we'd let some terrible danger into the country and we wanted an answer, that's what it was, we just wanted to put things right. We wanted to make it clear that we wouldn't tolerate this, that we'd keep our children safe. And we wanted it over. And that's how it happened.

He'd been in the cells for days. The police were keeping him in—but they weren't helpful, they wouldn't tell us whatever they knew. We knew it meant something, of course, that they'd kept him in, that they weren't going to let him run off—but still, they weren't helpful. We went up there, but they just told us to let them get on with their job, just said to go home. Oh, they knew he was lying—everyone knew he was lying. He'd said he'd gone up to the shed, said he'd finished the pruning, gone to the shed, denied leaving the park at all—but nobody saw him there, that's the thing. And somebody would have, because there were people up at the shed, there were kids there and they hadn't seen him so everyone knew he was lying—but still there was day after day after day in that terrible heat and the men out there searching and him staying silent and nobody knew if that poor little baby would ever be found.

The Messenger

He keeps to the sealed road, passes under a road block into a military reserve. He carries the heavy coat as he makes his way to the old gun emplacement. He passes the cannons and finds the top of a half-hidden track that leads down to the harbour. Blackberry thorns tear his skin as he makes his way in the lengthening shadows down to the rocks near the water's edge. Where there's an ancient jetty that leads to an empty lighthouse.

Across the harbour the sails of the Opera House catch the last rays of the sun. He has opened the lighthouse door and slipped inside.

Less than a hundred metres away, hidden from the lighthouse by the turn of the coastline, the red-headed soldier considers the harbour.

GUARDIAN, SATURDAY, 23 JULY 2005

After leaping the ticket barriers, racing down an escalator and dashing on to a train, the man appeared to have either fallen or been bundled to the ground by pursuing police, one of whom leaned over and shot him several times in the head.

Lizzie

'They'll be back,' she says. The riot outside is fading into the distance. 'They'll be back, they'll keep coming back,' she says, 'and it's not safe to stay here and wait. We have to get out, get up to the *mellah*. Listen to me!' she orders. 'We have a safe house up there—right on the walls; our fixers are waiting. We can be rescued from there, we can organise cars to collect us.'

She has stilled them at least—but the panic has not subsided. The mob has passed for the moment; the guests are listening, whispering, arguing, grasping at straws.

'We'll go out together,' she says. 'I'll call the chopper back in to fly over us. We'll be protected as long as the chopper is filming— no, listen to me! We'll be visible! Once we get outside the *ryad*, we can be visible, we can have footage on all the news networks. We can walk through the tanneries up to the northern gate and no-one can touch us. No-one will touch us—no-one will dare while all of the world is watching . . .'

And I could say this: I could say, *Tell them about the bus group and the Italians. Tell them about the soldiers outside the gates, along the walls.* But if she tells them they will be scared, they won't leave and we have to leave, and it's safer in the middle. We have to leave because we're here in the silversmiths' lane, because we're not on neutral ground, because people were cowering, wet-eyed like children, tossed on the waves of the hatred outside and because no-one can see us in here. And there is something else. We are strangers. No-one protects us, not Kate or Hama, not the locals or beggars, or the children, or the girls from the kitchen. We don't belong here, we have no embassy here.

A chopper then. A camera crew and a helicopter making a shield for us, throwing a focus of light around us, protecting us.

'Kate said we should wait,' I tell her, but she ignores me.

'The mob will be back,' she says to the guests. 'We'll stay here and wait through one more attack and when they're gone, when they've gone past the *ryad*, that's when we'll leave.'

'Go to your rooms now—get your passports, papers—just what you can take in your pockets. Get ready. Get ready.'

They disperse then, all except the Somali girls, who have no passports.

'You have the key,' she says to me without warning. 'I'll need the key.'

Red

Je-sus, that gave me a start! I nearly fell over the bastard—Jesus! Wandering down out of nowhere, all on his own in the very last moments of dusk; damn nearly pissed myself and so did he. I nabbed him of course, read him the riot act—frisked him, tipped out his backpack, the whole performance; but he wasn't carrying much, just crackers and cheese and a bottle of chardonnay, and then when my heartbeat was back to normal I felt a bit sorry for him, poor bastard, I'd obviously scared him shitless, I'd been a bit rough.

'Having a bit of a party?' I asked, but he was still frightened, didn't pick I was teasing him now, he was all overcome, poor bugger, all scared and sorry. He'd only come down on the off-chance, he said, to look at the fireworks going on later over the Opera House. Sad guy—the lonely type. I said, 'You're not a local, then?'—because all the locals would know that the place is off-limits tonight, for security reasons. The council has told them, they've had letterbox drops, and I knew there would have been a couple of my blokes up on the road at the top would have stopped him, so he must have climbed over a barrier or two to get through, but I thought—let him go. He looked harmless enough. 'You're not a local, then?' I said, and he said, 'No. No. I played here a bit in the holidays, years ago. Decades ago.'

Well, we had that in common, I thought; and he wasn't doing any harm—in fact he looked ready to leave, he looked all overcome, so I said, 'Okay, mate. We'll say I never saw you. Enjoy the fireworks.' It took him a moment to catch on and then he said, 'Cheers, mate, thanks,' and wandered off round the bend where it leads to the lighthouse.

Toby

That was the last thing Toby expected, the very last thing, and it set his heart pounding to suddenly come upon a soldier like that, in uniform, there in the dusk at the edge of the water—a big man, strong, with a powerful chest and spiked reddish hair, a thug by the look of him, big boots, a thick black belt with clips and buckles all over it, pockets all over his shirt, on the sleeves, on the back—and the air of a man who could *take him out* who could *rough him up* who could *do him some damage*. All his life he'd avoided people like that, situations like that. Bloody Hannah!

The soldier had seen him at once, called him over, ready to run at him if it was called for. Called him sir. 'Sir, you're on restricted ground, sir.' Made him stand with his arms out, patted him hard and quick, up and down, across his arms and legs and suddenly, briefly, around his crotch and he felt himself shrinking away, felt his balls go tight and frightened, but then he stepped back, the soldier, and said, 'You're not a local, then?' as though they were mates. As though he already knew all about him. Well, no, he wasn't a local. Obviously. If a local wanted to watch the fireworks he'd be out on the harbour by now, swilling champagne and talking up money and skiing and sex. No, he wasn't a local and it wasn't his idea to come back here and he didn't intend to discuss it all with a uniformed thug; so he got in first, turning away before he was told to. 'I used to play here,' he muttered. 'Years ago,' and the grievance of being chased out, the unfairness, tightened his jaw and made his skin prick with disgust. But the soldier said, 'Nah, you're okay, mate. Go on, then. I never saw you.' He turned his back like a kid playing hide-and-seek and then there was no escape, Toby had to go on, go over the rocks and around the curve of the headland, whether he liked it or not. And suddenly, there it was, standing out from the shadows, straight and strong and white against the darkening sky, unchanged and unyielding . . .

Hannah

One guard. One lone guard out in the hallway—one little guard. And that right there is where they made their mistake, because let me tell you it's going to take more than one little guard; because let's assume this. Let's assume that a Homeland Security thug is a glorified nightclub bouncer; and let's assume furthermore he's a *public service*-style bouncer—well I'll tell you this: shoot-to-kill training is all very well, but it won't trump the public service employee's aversion to writing reports. If he pulls the trigger, we're going to be talking *shitloads* of written reports, and I'm pretty sure like all good bouncers he joined the service to terrorise people, not because he likes paperwork.

Alright then. Time to complete what I started over an hour ago. Time to go home. It's time to get in my car and go home.

I know every inch of this building, I know there's a spare set of car keys down in the raincoat I left in the workroom. I know that the workroom leads to the old scenery lift and the scenery lift opens up in the room where the props used to live which is now a cleaners' supply room. I know that the cleaners' supply room opens into the men's room down on the second floor—the men's toilets, I mean. All I need to do is leave this office and get to the second-floor men's loo without being shot.

All that I need to do is leave this office.

Red

It's going to be a beautiful night. The harbour is gorgeous, of course, when it darkens to black and silver, a few drifts of colours lying along the shore ... The Americans will be besotted. They flew over the Opera House a while ago, for a final look-see in the evening. Just the one chopper—just one flight, a sweep-and-swerve.

We should have been notified there—they're supposed to give us a heads-up, the US security boys; they're supposed to run everything past us, their motorcades, all their security plans, their media circus. It's always trickier, though—they like to run their own show. I'm not convinced that they should get away with it, but that's not my call ...

The little boats have all been moved out of the way. That will be our blokes clearing the no-go area—that's pretty routine. It's getting darker now—so they'll want the place empty.

They mean well, the Americans. Nicer bunch you couldn't hope to meet when we're doing the social thing—really nice guys. But they ramp things up, they're not big on compromise and that can be awkward. They get people's backs up the way they go about things, that insistence they have on getting things done their way. Determination. *Exceptionalism*—that whole *can-do* thing, it just runs amok, and it puts people's backs up, puts ours up—my lot. People get sick of being sidelined or shouted down—or simply ignored.

The talkback crowd loves it, though. Either way—right or left, pro or anti. Ray Kane's mob loves the importance, the flags, the chance to be patriotic; and then the left-wing shows just love the chance to be outraged. Maybe it's good to give them a bit of a rant on the radio; like a safety valve or something. Maybe they settle down after that, have a coffee and a smoke and sit back and feel better for getting it off their chest, I don't know. I don't really have the stomach for it any more. All the palaver this week—all the choppers, the motorcades, new anti-terrorist powers, barricade fencing; half of Australia thinks we're eroding democracy, the other half thinks we're not doing nearly enough—and we're in the middle just trying to get the job done.

I'm not prepared to get into a fight about it. Nobody's listening. You're with us or you're against us is how that talk goes. I'm not a political man, but I've travelled around a bit, and the more I see people, the more places I live in, the simpler everything seems. *People,* my dad used to say, *are not all that different except in the shouting.* Except in the shouting—that was my dad's phrase. And it's true. In all of the countries I've been to, most people just want to get on, look after their kids, put a little bit by. But you can only do that when there's peace, and it's the shouters on both sides who bring the whole lot unstuck. That demonstration this morning—I saw it on TV and Jesus, just watching it I wanted to hit someone, one of those fools with the placards. I wanted to grab him and say, 'Listen, mate, we'll protect the country from bad guys with bombs, but who's going to save it from morons with placards and too much free time?' We all have a role to play, that's what they don't understand. We all have a job to do. Okay, you don't like the fencing wire down the side of the road—well, neither do I. But be constructive. Don't just wave a placard. Go back to class, study, become a lawyer. Change things. Or join the services, make things safer, become a nurse if you like, or a plumber, a teacher—something that makes life better for people. But don't stand there yelling, you know? Don't just be a fool with a placard. Peace isn't that easy! But you can't say that, of course, when you're wearing a uniform. You can't argue back, you just look belligerent. And they'll splash it all over the evening news.

I'm not a philosopher, anyway. Dad was. But his was an easier time, he was before My Lai, he was back in the days when there were good guys and bad guys and we were the good guys and we didn't build barbed-wire camps in the desert or let boatloads of refugees drown off our coasts. That SIEV X thing would have killed my dad. And *Tampa*. That would have shamed him.

Soldiering's not what it was. The idea of service is gone—the ideal, I mean. And then Abu Ghraib, Guantanamo Bay. Renditions and torture. Waterboarding. The people who lead us are letting us down. It's harder to follow them, hard to believe in them. And fools like Ray Kane, spreading poison and whipping up rage and, Jesus, it's *dangerous*, this kind of fear-mongering; it *burns*, it can spread like wildfire. I've seen it happen, I've seen it before—even here, in Australia.

III

Hannah

This is the longest walk down the corridor, this is the longest walk and he's right behind me, angry, and twitchy because of his anger and sure he's been 'disrespected' and badly treated. But he's well trained, I'll give him that; he's good at the strong and silent thing and it was a battle at first to face him down, to walk past him, not to stop when he told me to stop, not to answer until I'd made him leave his place by the wall. And that was the breaking point, when I made him follow me, leave his place by the wall—when I went on past him, swerved out of his reach and went past him, that shifted the balance, it turned the tables, it put him into my wake. And then for only a moment the power was there between us, there in the space between us, invisible, there for the taking. And if there's one lesson I learned in the tunnels it's how to grab power. You grab it in silence. In self-control.

He followed me, and I counted the steps I took, three, four, five, and I listened to hear him, to hear how his anger was growing, and then without turning or raising my voice I told him I needed to piss. I'd be happy to piss on the floor if that's what he wanted, I said, but he should realise there would be occupational health and safety issues and paperwork, there'd be explanations to make and I doubted that any of it would make him look good on the ten o'clock news ... and so he followed me, because after all America likes to call itself civilised, and when I got to the men's loo I said this will do and I said he could wait outside. And I walked right in and that was that. I went through the cleaners' supply room and yes, the lock snapped home and the lift was right where we left it the last time we took this secret journey, Rob and I.

I have a minute or two before he comes looking and seconds after that till he finds the cupboard and opens the hatch that leads to the lift ...

I'm down. I've jammed the lift. It's a couple of seconds from here to the workroom, and no-one will be there. Rob will be up on the stage with the techies, and everyone else is part of the milling horde on the Opera House forecourt. I'm the only one left up here except for security. I'll get in, grab my keys and be off like a shot. And Jesus, when I get out I'll bloody fill the airwaves about our sad, pathetic government and their fascist American goons.

Toby

The lighthouse was smaller than it used to be, and the opposite shoreline was closer—but that couldn't be right. It stood out of the water, not more than eight metres high, attached by an old wooden pier to the cliffs of the coastline; and the cliffs were small, only three times the height of the lighthouse. There was no wilderness here—just liana and saplings that clasped at each other through the twenty-five-metre drop to the water.

The water itself was clear, and flecked with moonlight. It was not so deep, after all; the bottom was clearly visible still, alive with the dash of minnows. It was dark-looking, welcoming, cool . . .

The night had been slow to approach. It had been creeping over the water uncertainly, in fits and starts; but now it had hold, it was quick to strangle the last little whimpers of day, quick to empty the world of sunlight and fill it with stars and blackness instead. There were ribbons of light on the water, spilling out from the city's high buildings; and there was music too, Toby thought, and the echo of laughter and songs from the shore. Across the harbour, he knew, on the opposite coastline, the manicured gardens and parks edged the coast with the best real estate in the country. Behind lay the city, bank upon bank of shimmering glass dwarfing the dark smudge of trees.

So nothing had changed, then, and nothing had stayed the same . . .

It took him straight back, the lighthouse, took him straight back. There was that child inside him, still, after all these years, and suddenly he could hear their laughter and voices, the hot summer wind, the plash of the water and Richard and Hannah discussing—oh, who knew? Adventures. Ghosts. Superman, probably. Phantom Agents, Swiss Army knives and fishing and campfires.

There was no easy way across to it any more. The jetty was almost completely gone; there were little more than pylons left, and the joists that were there all but submerged in the rising tide. The rocks were slippery with weed, and the scrub ran all the way down the hill and up to the water. In the moonlight he breathed in the dusty smell of bush and heat and earth, tasting the flavour of childhood again, and he laughed aloud suddenly, surprising himself. It was such a ridiculous place to meet! There was nowhere to sit, it was dark and the jetty was so unsafe. The only flat rocks were down at the water's edge, and that would be dangerous too if the tide came in any further—and it could of course, it would; they'd be here for a while. It was a daft idea, it was imbecilic, but he was delighted, warmed by the reckless silliness of it. Because this was exactly how she *would* plan it, this is just what she'd do. Hannah would leave it till the very last moment and suddenly, out of nowhere, she'd be there, in her cotton frock, with one finger raised to hold their attention, saying, 'I've got a massive idea!' Or, in this case, sending text messages—and then, refusing to answer her phone in case somebody showed her the fatal flaw in her wonderful plan.

It didn't matter. Nothing mattered. He was just glad to be back here again, happy to be here, now he was here. He was happy all over again . . .

He claimed the area slowly, until he found the little rock ledge at the southern side of the lighthouse, a couple of metres above the edge of the foreshore. Looking up he could just catch the dim outlines of the track back up to the top, still there, after all this time. She could have mentioned that, he thought; she might have saved him the long trek over the rocks from the headland. But he was glad to see it, glad to see the way, and it wouldn't be all that tricky to walk out later. There was a torch on his mobile phone if it came down to that; but she'd bring a light, surely—she'd said she'd bring everything with her.

Just bring yourself, she said—and he had; he'd brought himself. Or he'd found himself here, in the darkening bush, his past, his happiness, waiting here all this time. He looked up at the lighthouse again, and felt four decades of bright summer days, of southerly busters, cicadas and secrets and children. Old friend! he wanted to say. Old witness, old guardian! He was drawn to it, wanted to touch it, wished he was huge enough to stand right beside it, throw his arms all the way round it. It would be warm with the last of the sun. It would be strong and silent just like his dad was, strong and silent, uncomplicated. And this was the place that he had come down to on that last day, the day of the funeral—the day his dad came back to collect him. He'd walked down the track on his own in the thumping heat to this very place—and it took him back to see it again in the gathering darkness, took him back to the earliest days, to the innocent days. Hannah, skipping over the rocks with her skirt tucked into her knickers. Richard and him, lying down on their bellies, watching paper bags full of their breath float on top of the waves for a moment and sink like soft wet balloons. Hot, damp sandwiches, the smell of sweat and tomato, the heat coming up from the jetty itself, which was hardly there any more, which he had outlasted. The mound of cement that might have a body beneath it.

Hannah

No no no no no no no! This is not how I left it, someone has broken it, someone has come in and changed it, destroyed it—I *did not do this*! I saw it just yesterday, I saw it last night, I showed it to Toby and it was perfect, just as I meant it to be, it was fine, it was perfect last night! Someone has *done* this, come in and done this, come in and attacked it and who would do that? It's ruined and who could do that, who would *do* that, why would they do it? Why would they do that to *me*?

Alright.

Alright, then. Alright. Quiet. Just get the keys. Don't touch anything. Just get home, get out of here safely, because this is crazy. Get home, get home. It's paint and canvas, just paint and canvas, it didn't mean anything, really, just let it go—just get out of here before they come back again.

Keys. Spare set of car keys in your raincoat pocket behind the door since the last time it rained—and that was months ago, wasn't it? Months ago—focus on that. Just focus. Don't make a noise, don't bring them in, for chrissake, don't let them shove you around again, don't be afraid—coat and keys and just one last look at the paint that has covered their faces, the children's faces, the little girl looking back from the door of the church with her face bleeding tears now, red splashed all over her face, on her dress—and words scrawled across the photographs too, in bright red paint—*Am I Acting Suspiciously?* And newsprint from papers I don't have access to, the *Guardian*, *le Monde*; there are new photos, press photos, plastered all over the shots of my wild, wicked children, and the same photo there and there and there from different angles over and over again: a man lying sprawled on the ground in a train, blue jeans, white trainers, a thin denim jacket that rides up to leave his back naked and terribly vulnerable. He lies on his side, with one arm fallen back behind him, the fingers open, relaxed, and his legs are bent and relaxed as well, and his head has been blown to pieces. Blood pools on the edge of the floor in the photo, runs in a thin red rivulet down through the aisle of the carriage.

Am I Acting Suspiciously?

There are other photographs. An African baby crouched in exhaustion and hunger with vultures behind her. A monk in Cambodia burns like a lotus in flames. There are boats on fire in the ocean and children floating like broken seagulls, a man stands hooded and caged, his arms outstretched and his hands trailing wire.

And there's the church, and the little girl, Lizzie, looking back at us over her shoulder. She is bleeding red tears and the paint is still wet on the paper, and just as I turn away from her, turn to leave the room, I see suddenly scrawled on the door behind me just one more word, and it stops the blood in my veins, this word, turns it thick and cold, scrawled over the door, this one word, this one word, *atonement*: and oh my God, he was here, then, I know it—Richard was here.

Lizzie

They are back, they are back and it's angrier, louder than ever, filled with hatred and rage and now there are English words in the chaos, isolated but clear and full of abuse, *pigs* and *dogs* and *fuck* and *kill* and *die*—and this is not even the worst; the worst is the chant that rises above the shouting, a beat of hatred, disembodied, turning the voices into a mass of rage that is undifferentiated, untargeted, uncontrollable. There's a pulse behind the roar and the pulse takes over, the drumbeat of feet and fists and chanting, and when I look around, I see people down on their knees, crouched down, curled over, their hands and arms shielding their heads, people who won't want to know they were cowering, won't want to know they were pale and sobbing in terror, helpless, unreachable. The beat of the chant is locked on the beat of my heart and the blood in my neck in my face is caught in the pulsing, caught in the hatred, and Jenna screams in a whisper, 'Get up! Get ready!' and people are pushing and shoving and running to get to the door. 'Give it to me,' she says and she holds out her hand, but I keep the key shoved in my pocket, turning to ice in my hand, and I ask her, 'What about Kate?'

She shakes her head and yells, 'We can't wait,' and she grabs my shoulder then and pushes me through the corridor to where the guests are already herded.

'Give me the key,' she says, and they hear the demand and that's why she's brought me to them. To have them hear it.

There is not one of us who is sane now—there is not one of us who can stand the terror, not one of us who can't feel the world crumbling around them, there is not one of us who can see or breathe or take control of their fear, counting down through the silence.

'Give her the key,' says Brigitte under the roar and the tumult. 'Give her the key.' She is shaking with fear, her eyes enormous, her face stark and white.

Jenna holds out her hand and I give her the key without meeting her eyes, handing it over without a murmur.

Outside the rage of the mob has moved a fraction away, surging against the next house and the next on its way through the town. It is trying to flush out the foreigners, the *others*.

I saw Richard in Rome, just after the bombings in London. And after I saw him I walked through the city at dawn. There are children in Rome, carved into the stone of the churches. There are angels and gods, there are scapegoats and sacrifices.

'Where now is the helicopter?' Brigitte asks and Jenna puts her finger to her lips.

'It will be here,' she whispers. 'Wait.' She is breathless like all of us. 'Wait till they're gone.'

We wait and then she reaches up to the latch, turns the key in the lock and opens the door.

We slip into the alley. There is no sign of the mob, just scrapes and bruises on the walls and heat in the air and Jenna whispers into her phone to call in the chopper.

The refugee girls have remained inside on their bench. Kate told them to stay. Kate promised them she would return.

Red

There is movement out on the water, there is an action underway up on the edges; something is moving, out from the naval base, something that wasn't planned. This is part of my world—this is what I am trained to see; the little boats there in the darkness, armed and cautious, watching and waiting, reading the signals and waiting for orders.

The threat has been verified, then. The response is already underway.

Voices are dancing over the darkness still—fragmented, tangled, buoyed with laughter and music.

Lizzie

Before we see the blood, it is in our mouths. The morning air is cold and thin but the thick black sweetness lies on our tongues and the smell burrows deeply inside us. He is sprawled on the cobbles, his brave bright scarf about him, and I think this is kinder at least than the view from the rooftop. The houses wall the alley, some of them stone or daub, some of them rendered in plaster; they are terribly old, crumbling and peeling with age, and the colours are soft, in ancient creams and yellows and such tender pinks that the laneway, which should be black and forbidding, is glowing instead like moonlight. The huge wooden doors, hasped in iron, are looming like guardians over his body, and just for a moment he might be sprawled in the easy sleep of youth. His arm is thrown out to one side as though to fend off the coming sunrise but his head is pulped in tangles of bone and hair and brain, and the cobbles that pillow his head are slick and black.

In Rome, the streets are cobbled like this but the air is full of the magic of bells and the echo of running water. *Are not two sparrows sold for a farthing? And one of them shall not fall on the ground without your Father's knowledge.*

Jenna takes charge. She stands between us and the body, her back to him, hiding him, shepherding us from the sight of so much brutality. 'Keep going, he's dead,' she whispers over and over, a prayer, a mantra, and so we walk past him, all of us, stepping over the blood that is thick in the cobbles. Our shoulders turn and hunch against the horror, but I am not the only one who sees his fingers move, who sees him pluck at the hem of the blood-soaked scarf.

'Keep going, he's dead,' she whispers and he must be dead, he must be dead and there's nothing we can do.

They are all around us, the mob—we can hear them, feel the vibration under our feet, we can smell the heat and the anger. Once in the marketplace we will be unprotected, unable to hide—and as far as the eye can see the houses are shuttered, blind to the lane and alleyways. No-one is watching, no-one will come to help us; no-one will see if they catch us, no-one will know our story.

Brigitte grips my hand. 'Where is the helicopter?' she says again, and her legs betray her, refusing to move—but Jenna is there between us, hissing. 'Come on! We have to go! Come on! Come on!' and she's pulling, dragging, pushing, a wild thing, beating us through the shadowed alley away from the *ryad*.

We move quickly across the cobblestones. It's like moving across a painting, like slipping into a photograph. Without the press of bodies, the shove and push of the crowds, without the touts and beggars, without the insistent children, the struggle of donkeys and carts—without all this the Old Town is simplified. The tiny fires are gone and the twist of wood smoke from up on the hill. In place of the drifts of scent from the bundles of mint and *fleur d'orange* there is only the smell of yesterday's garbage, the taste of blood.

Toby

Hannah would come. She was late, but she'd be here. All afternoon she'd been sending him text messages—one after another: *Eight o'clock at the lighthouse* and *Just us two, just like the old days* and *Just bring yourself*—all day long and never once spoke to him, never once picked up her phone when he hit recall, never the sound of her voice, never letting him in. And he could have left, could still leave, probably ought to leave, ought to say screw this sitting around in the dark waiting to join in, waiting to be allowed—except this; except yesterday she was lovely. And back then, too, before the other kids came, when it was just the four of them she was lovely then, too. Being here brought it all back, all the first days, when he was lonely and scared and abandoned and she was lovely, oh, she was so *lovely*—they all were. They probably never intended to hurt him that day in the tunnels—they were teasing and he wasn't used to teasing and things just got out of hand. *Atonement* the last message said. Atonement. Which was a kind of forgiveness, wasn't it? Which was a kind of apology, a way to begin all over again. And beginnings were good.

So he'd wait. There was nowhere else he needed to be, and she'd come. He was sure she'd come. It was beautiful here.

He remembered the green glass marble he'd left in the place where the flag used to go. In the darkness he found the cement mound under its tangle of vines and rubbish, cleared it out in the tiny light of his mobile phone, slipped his finger into the cleft as Hannah had done all those years ago. But it was empty. His fingertip reached to the end of the burrow and nothing remained. Well then so what? It was gone. But he felt a frisson of—sorrow? Anger? Not anger. Disappointment. That was all.

He sat back in the darkness. He waited.

Hannah

They're using the PA system—and this time it's not routine, this time it's for me and Richard. They're sending messages out through the building and I can see movement outside, specks of light against the black harbour. Little police boats I think, or it might be the navy creating a no-go zone around the peninsula.

We are clearing the building. Keep your hands in the air and await instructions.

He was here in the dark without me. It must have been Richard who took my passkey—the night that we came here, the night before he went off to Rome: the night that we fought. And he used it last night. He got into the studio, somehow, he got to the canvas.

The red paint drips down on the photograph, down from the shot of the man who is sprawled on the floor of the train. Am I Acting Suspiciously?

We are clearing the building. Keep your hands in the air and await instructions.

The man's face has been blown to pieces; the thin denim jacket twists up to reveal his innocent back.

We are clearing the building.

I can hear dogs.

Keep your hands in the air—

He's still here. He must still be in here. He's here and they know he's here and I have to find him. And there at the top of the painting, across the canvas, in thick black paint in his own hand— *Domine dirige nos.*

Lord, lead us.

Oh stay still, for God's sake, wherever you are—stay still wherever you are, oh don't let them catch you; they're *armed*, they have guns and tasers and there are no limits now, they can do what they want, they can trap you and kill you. Oh God, stay still—stay till I find you. Stay where you are—watch out for me . . .

Lizzie

Jenna is pushing us, making us run, she is hissing at us to be quiet. I've lost my bearings, I don't know where we are—somewhere, I think, at the back of the tanneries, lost in the tangle of filth and rot that leads down to the meat-sellers' market. This is the meanest part of the Old Town, crumbling, fetid, rank with decay, and the cobbles are slimy and sunken and treacherous. The alley is roofed, linking old shacks and derelict storehouses and the daylight is only vestigial, kept at bay by the ruin and shadows and crumbling roofs. Shades of grey merge into black and in the gloom we lose our little selves and become a body, an underground creature sharpened by terror, a worm, a nematode, pushing against the darkness, blind in our panic, trying to speed away from the rage that is sweeping in waves around the medina.

The men will come onto the streets.

Watch out for me.

The past is uncurling. I am eight years old. I remember the dread again and the fear and the knowledge of what was to come. I remember the taste of cowardice that caught in the back of my throat; I remember the smell that evaporated, that joined with the darkness around me.

I remember running away.

The past is uncurling.

The first child is glimpsed only, crouching down in the shadows. He is dark-skinned, ragged—he might be a rock perhaps or a pile of refuse, something that's fallen in through the holes that gape in the roof. The second child is further along, and older—and this one I do remember from my visit with Kate and Carlo and Roberta. He was laughing then, but his face is empty now, with no hint of recognition. And Jenna hisses, 'Keep going, keep moving, they're coming—we need to get through the marketplace.'

There is a stream that runs under Rome, that was sacred for centuries before the city was dreamed of—an exuberant, powerful stream which became first a women's place and then a Mithraeum, then a Christian sanctuary when that faith was still new and unlawful, and then a church and later still—but still centuries ago—it became a basilica. The power and magic withdrew by degrees—the stream was rerouted, filled in, in an effort to chase out the old gods and vouchsafe the new—but the scars they left can still be seen. The Catholic basilica is open for worship; the underground church is gated; the Mithraeum is hidden and hard to find. The stream itself can only be glimpsed behind plexiglass walls.

This was a place of redemption, Richard insisted. This was a place of renewal, a chance to atone.

The Somali child pulls his robe around him and when we go past he becomes invisible. Stay away, I think. I can't help you. And I can taste it again, the smoke and the stench of cowardice.

Toby

It was dark, completely night. From his place on the ledge he could see the obsidian harbour. The boats had vanished, but there in the distance out on the opposite shore the sails of the Opera House were bathed in pools of white. *We'll watch the sky burn!* she had said, and now with the lights like flames on the water the memory came suddenly, out of the darkness, unbidden—that other night so long ago when the sky had burned with all of them watching together, silent and powerful.

It was still, that night; there was no wind, there was no breeze. It was after midnight, and morning was hours away. There was none of the exultation of fires on the beach in the quickening dawn; none of the pride of those hidden campfires out in the secret-filled scrub. This was momentous this fire, it was huge; it was brimming with feelings he couldn't interpret, with rage and fear and destruction ...

He remembered the silence.

They'd sat in the car, the four of them, nobody speaking, eyes straight ahead. He'd thought at the time that the silence was pointed at him—the intruder, the cuckoo; but now, looking back, he could see it was all around them, outside the car as well as in. On the street the adults stood and watched without speaking;

the other kids, too, the Kanes and Hampdens, all of them there in the midnight, just standing and watching, not running around, not whooping and leaping about like flames in the blood-stirring conflagration. So maybe the silence wasn't about him at all. Maybe he'd misunderstood . . .

The morning after the fire, Richard had sought him out diffidently, almost shyly. They hadn't spoken for days—not since the tunnel, not since he'd run away from the gang. 'We could go down to the lighthouse, if you like,' Richard had said, and Toby knew beyond doubt, beyond question, that Richard was out of the gang as well.

'We could take the rifle,' Toby said, looking away.

'It's got no bullets.'

'We could take it anyway, in case we need it.'

But they didn't take the gun. They weren't warriors any more.

He could see them now, in his mind's eye, two little boys treading down the path to the lighthouse, and one of them carried the weight of the world on his shoulders.

In the shrouding darkness, it could have been yesterday; he remembered it all—the heat beating out from the white of the lighthouse, the glare of the sun on the water, the hot dusty smell of the earth. They sat on the jetty, the two of them, watching the water that lapped and sucked at the barnacled pylons. It felt like the first days again, and Toby was hot with relief at the thought. And if the older boy was different now, was muted, no longer anointed, the younger one still felt the magic in him, would follow him anywhere. But it needed to be said, so Toby took it on himself. 'I don't like those other kids. Ray and them.'

There was silence. Richard looked away over the water. He put his hand in his pocket, withdrew it, and there on his palm lay the green glass marble. After all these years Toby could still feel the wonder at how the world could be caught in a green glass globe and held in his hand.

'You can keep it, if you like,' Richard said. Then he got to his feet and thrust his hands deep in his pockets again. He set off alone across the perilous jetty and up the dirt track to the road.

The marble burned in Toby's hand. Richard walked away through the bush alone and the earth dissolved around him, began to shimmer and turn to water, dissolved in the green of glass and tears. But why was that? Toby wondered all these years later. Why would he cry? It was a talisman, wasn't it? A symbol of love, a badge of belonging. And didn't he keep it? He would have wanted to keep it, surely; it would have been precious, a treasure, a gift of protection against the world and all its loneliness . . .

Why look for it, then, in the place where the flag used to be?

IV

Red

There were those who wondered why the fire was allowed to burn so long, to do so much damage. Fire is a treacherous servant, even at night. They regretted it later and spoke out, some of them—Mr Woods and my old boss, Mr McCauley, for starters. They told the papers that they were ashamed. But they watched, at the time—and we watched as well: the local kids, and all of the summer ones, too. Children dressed in pyjamas or standing against their bikes in the darkness, slipping silently out of parked cars—fifteen or twenty of us and everyone quiet. The heavy black night pressed around us and we watched, mesmerised by the fire.

It was dark, well after eleven, I think, and the air was hot and still. The house burned and nobody lifted a hand to save it, even though this was a night in the middle of summer, the height of the bushfire season—even though everyone said that the state was a tinderbox. Fires in the bush were forbidden; fires on the beach were guarded, were built into pits in the sand. And that was the strangest thing, I remember—the gardener's house in flames and nobody trying to stop it. I still remember that feeling, the grown-up people in front of me, black and dense between me and the fire—I remember wondering how the fire had started, and when, and why they were letting it burn; and I still remember the realisation that something was changing. That this was a line in the sand.

It's my greatest shame that I didn't ride home straightaway and get my dad. It's my greatest regret.

The glass in the windows was broken. The night air was feeding the flames and they surged to the ceiling. The house was bursting with fire, was overflowing. The hose lay coiled on itself by the tap near the fence.

And then afterwards—long after we'd all gone home, when the firies had finished the mopping up, making sure in the uncertain light of the grey false dawn that the embers were out and the danger was over—then they called my dad because he might know about this sort of thing; they called him out to help him explain what they'd found. They were upset, he told me later, and they were right to be upset because there's a world of difference between a simple house fire and a petrol bomb.

Lizzie

They are coming around again—we can hear the pulse growing, feel the beating of feet in the walls around us and they are circling us, tightening the noose, but we are so close now, we are so close to the end of the tunnel. Around the next corner the marketplace lies wide open and empty and if we are quick we can cross it without being seen, and we have to be quick, we have to get over there now, before they return, while they're pounding through alleys, back in the tangle of lanes, because there's no chance if they see us out here in the marketplace, unprotected; there will be nowhere to hide.

But Jenna stops suddenly, stands at the entrance and won't let us pass. 'Not yet, not yet,' she says. 'We need to wait, we need the cameras.'

Beyond her the marketplace lies bare and bright, an empty rectangle. The houses and shops that line the cobbled square are closed, their windows shuttered. On the opposite side, there are alleys—but wider, clearer, uncovered and running straight up through town to the top of the hill and then down to the house by the walls and the cars that are waiting to take us to safety: and now behind us, around us, we hear them coming closer and faster, above the sound of the chopper, closer and louder and pounding like surf again, like a drumbeat, like blood. They are burning the *mellah*, I think, because I can smell the smoke—and still Jenna keeps us here, keeps us waiting.

Brigitte cries, 'Where is the helicopter?' It sounds like a child's cry, tortured and frightened and lonely and then—oh, at last!—the chopper swings into the sky above the walls and the throb of its rotors beats back the hatred and rage of the mob around us.

And she leads us now, down through the end of the alley and into the marketplace. The chopper swoops towards her, a man with a camera leaning out of the gap in its side, harnessed and vulnerable and we are terrified, bunching away from the whoop and chop and thud of its blades; but Jenna is pushing us forward, pushing us out where the camera can see us, where it can protect us.

There were children in Rome, carved into the walls of the catacombs; there were cheeky-faced fat little putti.

There were flames as well, cold in the stone. And the angels hovered above them.

I'll tell you something my grandfather told me about the little moss piglets. They are small, so small you can't see them without a microscope. Their scientific name is tardigrades. And the thing about tardigrades is, if there's no water or if it's too hot or too cold, they don't die. They curl into a ball and stop. They just stop until everything's better. And when it's better, they start again.

I left home when I was nine. Not formally, but not as a runaway either. I caught the school bus to my grandfather's house one day and stayed in the garden until it was dark and too late for me to walk home. The next day I did the same thing, and the day after that—and eventually it became accepted that I'd spend most of my weekdays there and go home on weekends. Then I stayed for the weekends as well. Hannah told everyone I'd been adopted out, and at school she refused to talk to me, told all her friends to ignore me. I didn't care. My grandparents were old but they felt *safe*, they felt cocooned. They never mentioned Bradleys Head or the fire and neither did I. And then after a while, after a few months, I went home again on my own.

I didn't forget the fire, though. It burned every night in my dreams. We'd stand there again, my brother, my sister and me, our mum and dad and the other parents, old Mr McCauley, the Hampdens and Kanes and mean Mrs Monckton—all of the people I knew, all of the people I'd always known. We'd stand there again, together, and we'd watch the house burn in silence.

Then and for many years after I thought that I knew where that silence had come from. I thought it was born in the tunnels, deep in the guts of the game that we played in the dark, in the tunnels, the chasing game. I'd only played it once, the year before—and it was terrible, so terrible I screamed until Richard made them stop chasing me, came to find me, held my hand all the way to the outside. 'Just don't *run*!' Hannah had hissed at me, embarrassed, infuriated. 'If you don't *run* they'll chase someone *else*—' But if you didn't run you were left in the tunnels all by yourself, in the dark with the ghosts and whispers all around you.

Of course I ran . . .

Hannah

It must be pitch black outside now and there's a vibration, a pulse in the air that I thought was fear, was my heart beating loud and quick, but it's louder and quicker, it's in the walls around me. I've come to the passageways, come to the tangle of tunnels that leads away from the workshops and out to the loading dock for the lift to the stage—and I know the place well. I've explored it all, drunk and sober, I know it as well as I know the back of my hand, as well as we knew the labyrinth down at the old gun emplacements at Bradleys Head when we were kids.

Stay there. Watch out for me.

And Richard knows this place too, knows its passageways—not well, like I do, but he knows they exist at least. He's been here, I brought him, he knows that they're here and if he's afraid now—if he's scared of their PA announcements and tasers and dogs—then this is the place he would run to.

Stay there. Watch out for me.

There'll be nothing moving, out on the water. The boats will have been herded away, their tiny lights lost in the churn and wash of the sirens down at the water's edge. Above us the choppers are beating the air, making the darkness deeper; their lights will be spilling over the Opera House sails, and sliding down into the cold black harbour.

From the opposite shore it must look like the sails are burning.

There was a night once, just like this, and it's all around me suddenly; but it was long ago, so long ago—we were just kids. There were feet in the hallway just before midnight, there were voices cutting the darkness, and lights were turned on suddenly and the front door slammed and there was a hint of smoke in the air. We followed Dad down to the car, and Mum wasn't happy, said, *Go back to bed.* But Dad said, *No, let them come, let them come. Let them see how much damage a fire can do. Let them learn.*

Lizzie

The chopper is over us, pounding the town and punching and rending the air, covering us with the terrible shelter of thunder. This is not the time to rethink, not the time to regroup—we are through, we have crossed the marketplace and we have to keep running now, up past the spice shops, away from the open space, away from the mob; we have to keep running up to the fields, to the break in the walls—but we are hovering suddenly, vulnerable here at the mouth of the laneway, the very edge of the marketplace, we are in danger still because Jenna and Tom are angry, *now* when we're almost safe, they are fighting and shouting under the thud and roar of the chopper. And then Tom rips the camera off his neck and thrusts it at Jenna and pushes past us without a word and disappears into the spice-sellers' street away from the marketplace. And we wait, uncertain, shivering, with the chopper circling above us, circling and filming, and we look to Jenna for orders.

She gestures for us to follow Tom so we do, running to catch up with him, to leave the mob behind on the other side of the marketplace, the chopper between us and them—but I turn back and in the cold bright light I can see what the fight was about.

She has stayed. She is poised with his camera, there at the edge of the lane. She is determined and small and totally undefended.

She is ready to shoot the moment and I can see the shot that she's planning. The chopper over the rooftops, the mob about to burst into the open space; and she sees that the frenzy will feed itself there, that the chopper will madden the mob with fear and fury. The rampage will start in earnest then, the hunt to destroy the things that define their rage, the strangers, the infidels, and she is there with her camera to capture it. And there where the alley tips into the edge of the marketplace—there are the children.

There are the children. They are lost in the dark of the alley, little ones, down from the refugee camp, silent, invisible; two little boys—and then three and then four . . .

They have tried to follow us. They are not safe.

The Messenger

It had all been planned. He was focused; he was meticulous. This has not been the work of a single night; transformation takes time. Clearing the broken rubble, translating mechanics; inventing the new dialectic to resurrect it without arousing suspicion, avoiding defences, finding his way through the dark. This was an angel's task, a messiah's task—this was sublime. *'The Lamp, enclosed in Glass; the glass a brilliant star, lit from a blessed Tree, an Olive neither of the East nor of the West whose Oil is well-nigh luminous though fire scarce touched it.'* It was never a war between prophet and carpenter: it had always been words and symbols, mistranslations and human errors. It had always been failures of courage, lost amid moments of terrible evil.

He has calibrated the weight. He slips it over the edge. The chain draws after it and a great vibration begins as the mighty lamp begins to turn. As the action begins, he prays for himself and prays as well for the boy he remembers: *'Fear not, for I have redeemed you; I have called you by name. You are mine.'*

He wants the glass to shine; he will gather the fragments of light, compress them, force them together until they explode, magnified over the harbour. He wants to see the lighthouse incandescent against the water—to recreate it, see it accuse with the wrath of God's own fury. He wants to force humanity down to its knees at last.

In the closeness and heat of the chamber, alive with the knowledge of power, he whispers into the darkness: '*I am the light.*'

Down at the water's edge, the soldier watches the night unfold. He is not a major player; he is at best a witness, a sentinel. If he plays a part tonight it will come from his past, from the lessons he's learned.

Lizzie

The mob is closing in, is almost in view. The beat of their feet has been lost in the thud of the chopper, but we can hear the shouting, the wave of fury, amplified, trapped in the walls and cobbles, mixed with the drumbeats of hate and she stands there, Jenna, the camera raised to her face, her feet strongly planted, and I am so close to her now I can hear her heartbeat. Only the force of ambition can hold her in place. And the chopper circles away and returns, a vulture that thuds in low and full of menace, scanning the marketplace, and we watch as the children are flushed by the noise from their hide in the rubble, transformed into birds, little broken things fluttering, crouching, trapped by the panic that lurks in their nightmares of rampage and war and dislocation. I am horrified, overwhelmed by their fear and their terrible vulnerability, and I grab Jenna's arm and scream at her, 'Send it away! Send it away!' But my voice is lost in the gale and she shakes me off, pressing the shutter. She is mesmerised, shooting off frame after frame as the monstrous thing swoops and circles, fanning the tiny panic below; she stands firm, like a rock, and she moves her camera to capture the mouth of the lane where the mob will burst through any second, enraged by the roar and threat of the fury above them, and come face to face with these stateless children who don't belong here, who are not wanted here, who have left their hiding places like little black beetles and followed us because they thought we would see them and guard them, that we would watch out for them.

There is a stream that runs under Rome, a powerful stream, a place of redemption. They have rerouted it, and the scars can still be seen behind plexiglass walls. When they found him there, the walls were broken—and Richard was streaming with blood and exultation.

They called the police. They took him to hospital. My name was on his phone. I was on my way to Morocco when they called. They told me to come. They said that he needed me.

At the hospital he told me—what? To worship and not to worship. To trust the priestless gods, the voiceless gods, to venerate the humble and tear down the mighty. To atone, above all to atone. I hardly knew him at first—he was terribly thin, lit up from the inside, and fragile, so bright and fragile I thought he might shatter. His mouth was taut and dry but his lips were rimed with spit and murmuring and his bandaged arms were white on the white of the sheets.

I stood back, against the door, but, 'Your sister is here,' the nurse told him brightly.

He looked at her and I was invisible. 'What I tell to you in the dark, you will speak in the daylight,' he said. 'What I whisper in your ear, proclaim from the roofs.'

The nurse, whose English was good, as good as mine, just patted his arm. 'Be brave,' she said to me. 'Come closer. Let him see that you're here.'

So I came forward, leaned over him and gave him a kiss. I smoothed the hair from his forehead and with a jolt of fear I saw the boy I had worshipped decades ago—saw him lost again and adrift in the midnight bush, and the sky that was brilliant with tears and maybe that's why it's me he's called out to, I thought. Maybe that's why I'm here. I took his hand in mine.

'Are not two sparrows sold for a farthing?' he asked. 'And one of them shall not fall on the ground without your Father's knowledge.'

'Richard—' I said, and he looked up at me then, and suddenly he was lucid and calm again.

'They shouldn't have called you, Lizzie,' he said. 'You've never been much of a fighter. You don't have to stay, I don't need you. Hannah is coming.'

I sat with him all through the night. I left as the sun rose.

I didn't go back to see him; Hannah was coming. There'd be no need. There'd be nothing that I could do, no place for me. I left my email address at the desk in case anyone needed to contact me, and a note for Hannah in case she wanted to talk.

And I waited three days, but she never called.

BBC NEWS, SATURDAY, 23 JULY 2005

SHOT MAN NOT CONNECTED TO BOMBING

A man shot dead by police hunting the bombers behind Thursday's London attacks was a Brazilian electrician unconnected to the incidents.

The man, who died at Stockwell Tube on Friday, has been named by police as Jean Charles de Menezes, 27.

Two other men have been arrested and are being questioned after bombers targeted three Tube trains and a bus.

Lizzie

They burst from the alleys, the men, a storm of righteous fury just metres away from us, seventy metres perhaps or eighty, and closer than we are now to the lost little children who flutter like birds, dehumanised, broken and just for the moment still invisible. And we are invisible too, I realise—all of the force of the mob, all their focus is trained on the chopper above them, swinging and circling and filming, and they would bring it down if they could, they would rip it apart with their hands, they would crush it completely, and finally Jenna has eaten her fill of this rampage; she slings the camera across her body, holds it against her hip. 'Come on!' she screams, and her face is ablaze with excitement and danger and triumph. She brushes past me and races in the wake of the other guests up through the spice-sellers' street, as the chopper acts as a decoy, distracting the mob.

Down in the marketplace the children are hidden behind the fountain now, like a bas-relief of terrified angels crouched against ancient stone. *Stay still*, I think at them. *Wait; the chopper is moving away, it will drag the mob in its wake, they will be gone and the air will be clear of the thud and shudder and oh, stay still*, I think, *stay still*, but the oldest child is beginning to move, he's losing his nerve, he is going to panic and then they'll see him, they'll catch the movement and make him the focus of all that fury. I turn to see that Jenna is at the top of the spice-sellers' street and I ought to follow her now, follow her quickly, but then it comes back again, cold at the back of my throat like the stench of cowardice, like the taste of petrol—like the knowledge of what is to come. *You are a coward*, Kate had told me earlier. *I didn't realise.*

There is something I have to remember, there is something that needs to be said—and I'm back there again in the bush, in the night, near the gardener's house and there, at the fence, there was fighting—five boys against one and the one was Richard. In the darkness my face was hot and stinging with tears. Richard broke away from them, swearing and shouting, and vanished into the night, and so in a fury I ran to Ray Kane who was laughing, who'd dared to punch and kick and spit at my brother. I slapped him as hard as I could and he hit me back and I tasted it then, the tang in the air that was oily and dangerous. And yes, I knew what was to come—I remembered the bull ants at home, remembered the taste in the air, the way my dad had lined the three of us back against the fence and out of danger. *You're never to do this*, my dad had said to us. *This is something that only grown-ups can do.* Then he'd tipped the can and struck a match and thrown it to burn the bull ants out of the vicious nest that had grown up under the laundry line— tipped the petrol can and struck a match and that was the same hot smell, the dangerous oily smell of the petrol.

Ray Kane slapped me and pushed me over; the other kids laughed. In the darkness I got to my feet and ran after my brother. And so the two of us left the empty house in the darkness—left it unprotected there with the tribe of boys and their terrible power.

From his hiding place behind the fountain he's seen me, the oldest child has seen me before I can turn away; he's locked his terrified eyes on mine and I hold up my hand to tell him to stay, to wait, but he's waited too long, and he breaks and runs through the open towards me, the little ones following him, and the chopper is turning away from the marketplace now that its work is done, now that Jenna is safely away, but the mob is casting about for targets, and it is enraged and unrestrained.

There is no choice after all, so I leave my sheltered place and run through the shadows and down to the children. So many children! Six of them, seven, some of them tiny and all of them wide-eyed and terrified, clutching and grabbing in silence. Our hearts pound together in time with the pulse in the eldest boy's neck which is drumming a visible terror just as the blades of the chopper had drummed their powerful danger into the air and we grab up the littlest ones, he and I, and run down the cobbles under the eastern wall of the marketplace. Silent as smoke and not looking backwards, not stopping to think, we leave the open and slip deeply into the tangle of tunnels. And I don't know if they've seen us, don't know if they're following us, because we've been eaten up in the darkness and the laneway is strewn with rubble, and there might be safety here or terror, there might be hope or fear.

The houses are shuttered.

There are no eyes to see and no-one is watching.

Toby

'*I have called you.*' It comes from nowhere, soft in the darkness—a man's voice, shockingly close at hand. Toby jumps and his heart leaps against the wall of his chest, begins thumping in terror. The tiny light from his phone is eaten at once by the shadows—and then he can see, oh God, on the water, walking across the water, there, impossibly, blackness against the blackness, walking like Christ on the shivering water, untethered—and, '*I have redeemed you,*' it says. '*I have called you by name,*' and Toby is caught again in his mother's night-time web of evil and prophecy, ready to crouch like the child that he used to be under the terrible heavens, crouch like the child who sobs in the tunnels unable to hold his own destruction at bay.

The black presses in around him—the boats with their lights and laughter have all disappeared, and, 'Don't be afraid,' the voice says, suddenly earthly, warm with concern. 'Don't be afraid.' And the years fall away in the beat of a heart: and it's *him* after all this time, it's just Richard again, on the remnants of jetty, Richard walking out from the lighthouse, walking on water along the submerged and insecure joists, it's Richard, the hero, the king, who catches his arm and saves him from falling, who holds out his hand and shows him the marble, there again in the tiny light, in the warm stinging love of childhood, there on the palm of his hand the green glass marble that holds all the earth, contained and safe and complete. He closes his fist around it, holds up his hand for silence. '*I have called you by name*,' he says, and he's smiling just like he used to smile, and he's strong and anointed again.

He offers the marble to Toby, snatches it away before he can take it. He laughs and says, 'Come with me,' and pulls him up onto the fragments of jetty; and Toby, weak with relief, is laughing as well, grabs hold of the edge of the other man's thin denim jacket and follows him over the joists in the night and up to the lighthouse.

Not far away, at the water's edge, the red-headed soldier stoops in the darkness.

He puts his hand to the earth. A vibration is building under the night—a sound on the edge of sound, like an imminent fury.

He stands for a moment, his back to the bushland, his face to the empty water.

Hannah

*L**ord, lead us.* That was Richard's talisman. That was his prayer for years, ever since that terrible night, since the night of the fire. *Domine dirige nos*—and yes he would try to lose himself, to fade into the maze of tunnels. To hide, to be safe.

Domine dirige nos . . .

The house had been burning a long time when we got there. The roof was starting to crumble, but the fire was still inside the walls, contained; the trees were untouched in the garden, standing black in the night against the flames. It never got out of control—there was never that panic, that surge of energy we'd see when a careless spark in the bushfire season could threaten entire neighbourhoods. But it changed things, it destroyed things utterly.

When we pulled up, people were gathered across the road in the dark, just watching, looking. 'Stay in the car,' Dad said. 'Keep the windows up. We'll be back in a jiffy.' We didn't move, and I thought it was strange how he didn't notice that, didn't wonder why we were suddenly so obedient, sitting and watching without making a fuss, rather than ignoring the warning and opening doors. Lizzie slipped into the front seat, and Richard and Toby and I were all in the back seat looking ahead, past the fire and into the dark of the night. The flames ate the shell of the house from the inside, and nobody spoke.

There was no attack on the fire, no attempt to stop the flames seething out through a breach in the fly-screened door. The front yard could have been an ocean, a desert. When sparks exploded from the roof, the crowd retracted away in a single movement and surged again back to its stance, like a caterpillar rolling deep in a burrow. Sometimes someone would stamp out an ember, would grind it under a boot; for the most part they watched.

The hose coiled neat like a snake by the tap at the gate.

We could see inside the walls now. The curtains melted and dripped like icicles in the heat of the fire; ribbons of flame shot along the rug under the window. The books on the table were burning. Newspapers, years old and carefully husbanded, burst into flowers of orange and lost their unreadable headlines and bloomed and turned to ash in a single instant. The gramophone burned in patches, droplets of flame that flared out of nothing, arced in a pattern over the carpet, over the table, down the wall; and in the corner the music of Europe, the dances, the divas, conductors, composers were fused together in tortured blisters and imprisoned in twists of black plastic ...

They've shut off the access doors. They've shut the whole Opera House down, it's in lockdown. The lift is frozen, now. There's no way back up.

They'll be creeping along the halls with their guns unsheathed and I don't know if Richard's aware that we have no compassion for crazies now. People get shot or imprisoned without any access to lawyers.

Things are different now, things are fearful and merciless.

They've turned all the lights off.

It's quiet.

The PA announcements have stopped.

They're coming. They're coming, I hear them. Close by, a few doors away. I can hear their radios, hear them opening doors, calling out.

They have reached the door that leads to this tangle of passageways nobody uses, the mean little annexes too small for anything, too small for storage. The old hands knew this area once, but nobody else ever sees it, no-one comes down here.

Stay there. Watch out for me.

Toby

It was not such a difficult climb, despite the darkness. The jetty was dangerous, yes, but Richard was with him—and so it was simple, an easy matter, a blind man could do it. And when he left the ladder and stood on the tiny apron in front of the door he didn't have time to think of the blackness around him, the fall to the water, because Richard was there behind him, pushing the door, and it opened and they were inside for the first time, inside the lighthouse.

There were candles. That was the first thing he noticed: stumps of candles, scores of candles in clusters along the wall, enough to show up the floor and the walls that curved unbroken around them, the low perimeter ceiling and the ladder that disappeared into a gap in the platform above—and enough to take his memory back to that secret chamber under the gun emplacements, that sacred place all those decades ago. And Richard was there beside him and he was complete again, his past handed back to him, his memory validated. There had been power and grace and nobility in the boy that Richard had been, and Toby had seen it and loved him and yes, had been right to love him, and right to trust him and right to follow him.

It was loud inside the lighthouse, a painful vibration, a grinding of metal on metal. A massive weight on the end of a chain slowly descended and clockwork gears caught and ground. Richard smiled across the shadowed years and walked to the internal ladder that led all the way to the light itself and he started to climb, knowing Toby would follow.

Red

At the water's edge the red-headed soldier tries to decode the story; tries to read the threat he can feel in the black rubber darkness. In the sky above the Opera House, a flat beam of light spills over the sails. Closer in, around the bend of the coast, black inflatable boats pull into the shore without help from the motors; they vanish and then they appear again, dancing back from the coastline quickly, lightly, without the weight of their cargo.

So. Inflatables, night vision, special communications. Not his mob, not ordinary soldiers—TRG then? One of the specialised anti-terrorist units? One of the secretive US security details? Soldiers are being unloaded there in the darkness all around him—this much he knows. They are on target, staying out of sight of—what? The bushland? The lighthouse? He feels the vibration thrumming under his feet and his spine turns to ice.

He's been briefed, of course; he can guess what the job is tonight: *At 11.15 am, give or take, a middle-aged man of average height, clean-shaven, dark-haired, pushed a pink square of thin cardboard over the counter at Lawrence Dry Cleaners inside Wynyard Station.*

And: *Witnesses said that he seemed intense . . . He was sweating and angry-looking . . . he became increasingly agitated . . . He was lost, but he looked, you know, angry. I didn't know if he spoke English. He looked sort of foreign.*

And a woman: *We didn't know what, but something was wrong . . . He didn't look right.*

At 11.15 am, give or take, a middle-aged man of average height, clean-shaven, dark-haired, pushed a pink square of thin cardboard over the counter at Lawrence Dry Cleaners inside Wynyard Station. He looked sort of foreign and a general alert was issued.

And now there are fighters here, armed and deadly, primed to kill: and the red-headed soldier has broken the cordon, allowed a civilian into unauthorised territory, put him in danger.

Toby

There were candles on the perimeter edge of the second level too, and the light was dim, but almost enough to see by, almost enough to work by.

'What on earth are you doing?' Toby asked, and Richard explained the procedure to him simply and gently. High in the lighthouse, pulled by weight and chain, the ancient clockwork was grinding, metal on metal. The platform rotated—the massive plate that once held the old lamp was turning.

Toby was stunned, looking at workings which seemed so ad hoc, so provisional. They were centred around a huge gas cylinder, jury-rigged to form an oversized pressure lantern standing in front of the lighthouse's old polished Fresnel lens. All it would take, Richard said, was a flame to bring the lighthouse to life again.

He had orchestrated events; he had primed a timer to open the valve, to set off the spark: and there would be chemicals set to ignite in a burst of light, that would catch the mantle, that would kettle themselves through the lens, which waited here useless and blind and forgotten. A searing beam of light would shine over the harbour. '*The glass a brilliant star,*' Richard crowed. '*And the light shines in dark and the dark comprehendeth it not.*'

And it was going to work, Toby thought; in theory, at least, it would work. It would light up the sky, it would rip through the night like a lighthouse was meant to do—and yet... 'You can't do this,' he said. 'They won't let you—the council. Whoever. They'll charge you with trespass or something. There'll be a law of some kind—a national security thing. There'll be so much trouble!'

Richard laughed quickly and turned away for a moment towards the harbour. He drew strength, Toby thought, from the blackness—or else from the bright creamy silhouette of the unmoving sails. 'You needed to see this,' he said, and he turned to Toby again and said, with infinite gentleness, 'You needed to see this. I have called you by name—you need to bear witness. We need to atone.' He rested his hand on Toby's shoulder as soft as a blessing and Toby felt the sear of returning memory, felt his skin was reddening suddenly, blistering, felt as though scars were forming and glowing hot as he watched and Richard said, 'Yes, you see? You remember the fire. You know how it happens.'

And the terrible night came back to him.

It was still. It was dark. He remembered the powerful silence. They were hushed in the car—the three of them bunched in the back seat, Lizzie alone in the front. There were other cars parked in the darkness and there on the verge, in front of the house, a crowd of people watching their red-hot anger in silence, watching it burn.

Why were they there? He could hear Uncle Peter's voice, daytime-loud in the midnight hallway: 'Let them come, let the kids come, Susan—they should know what a fire can do.' And the silent drive, and Richard's face terrified, ashen; and when they reached the gardener's house, when they saw the flames leap through the darkness, he felt the tremors that ran through the other boy's body, unending, one after another, great waves of despair.

And that, he thought at the time, was the worst, the final moment, the house destroyed—that must be Richard's undoing; but then just an instant later it started, that terrible little-girl scream, Lizzie screaming, again and again, pierced through with horror, her eyes turned to the body in flames that was visible suddenly, writhing and twisting—there in the furthest corner away from the watchers—there, dear god, *look*! *There!*—framed in the hot, red light, framed by the shattered and curtainless window.

They all piled out of the car and the breath of the night swept down towards them; and then they could smell his terror and taste it too: in the burnt-flesh stink of the wind and the smoke, they could taste his terrible dying.

V

Lizzie

There's no noise. No sound. The chopper has circled away. I don't know if the mob is still with it. I don't know if they're running around the walls or are doubling back through the alleys.

I have lost my way. I am back in the darkest places.

There was a fire at Bradleys Head. A man burned to death because that was better than facing the mob outside. *But we weren't a mob, I cried later, we were just people, just Mr McCauley from up at the shops, and us and the Hampdens and Kanes, and the locals and holiday people.*

I saw Richard in Rome. There were tortures carved into the walls. There were demons and devils, scapegoats and sacrifices. *You're not much of a fighter,* he said to me. *Hannah is coming.*

I don't know what to do now. I don't know where to take the children. I don't know where Kate is, or how to get to the *ryad* or who will help us.

The bus was blown up in the square. Carlo is lying alone in the dark on the cobbles. His arm is thrown out to one side; his head is pulped in tangles of bone and hair. *You are a coward,* she told me, and yes, we have all been cowards.

The mob is returning.

Toby

'It wasn't our fault,' Toby whispered—because that's what the years had taught him, that bad things just happen and no-one is really to blame. 'It wasn't our fault,' he said and he looked at Richard, soft in the light of the candles, and saw the torment of decades behind his determination and again heard the tap-tap-tap at the midnight window and saw Richard leaving and creeping in later as thin as smoke and caped in despair... And he remembered the moment, later again, in the car, in the dark, when he'd looked across, seen the tears sliding down Richard's face and he didn't need words to promise that he would be quiet, that he could be trusted with this, that he'd guard this secret forever.

Which was why it had hurt him so much the next day, when Richard had come with him down to the lighthouse, stood just in front of him and handed him—instead of his soul, instead of his admiration, instead of his trust—the emerald-green marble. Which had no magic at all; which was only glass.

'You can keep it if you like,' he'd said, and he'd turned away, the transaction finished, the payment made. Toby had stayed a long time down at the lighthouse, leaning against the guardrail, thinking of darkness and fire and death, and longing to be a rock or a stone or something that didn't hurt so much. And later he'd wiped his eyes and known he'd never believe it again, that he could belong, that he could be one of the gang, be befriended ...

Mrs Monckton

I remember the fire. We all do. We've never forgotten it. It was a dreadful thing. A hot night; a fire. It was dreadful. Of course it was years ago now but they still bring it up all the time—even all these years later.

It was nobody's fault, it was just—a tragedy. It was a tragedy. A baby was missing, you know—a baby was missing. That gets forgotten. And we'd searched for days, everyone, people had searched for days, the men, in that heat and the hopelessness. They were heroes, you know.

Well and then the fire came; and we were all damned. And that was that.

Everyone blamed the kids, but it wasn't their fault—they were too young to think of the consequences; they were just kids. It's the police I blame for what happened. They should have listened to us, they should have kept him locked up at least until they had answers. Just for his own good, you know, as much as for us. Just locked him up until the baby was found, the poor little lamb. In any case, I don't believe he was innocent. Everyone says he was now, but I don't believe it. There were too many questions unanswered. I know they found her later, the baby, they found her; and they knew what had happened then, said it was one of those terrible things, post-natal depression they call it now, and nothing to do with him after all. But still—I don't know ... If he was innocent why did he hide in the house, even after the fire took hold? Why did he stay inside, if he was so innocent? Not even to call out, not to try to save himself? That's a guilty conscience—that's what it says to me. That's someone who knows there's worse to come, that's someone who knows what to fear. And he was lying. He said he was up at the shed in the park—but the kids never saw him. How come the kids never saw him? If he was innocent, if he was up at the shed, how come the kids never saw him? I'm still not convinced.

We gave him a funeral, you know. The town did. Gave him a very nice funeral. There was no family, you see, him being a migrant and everything—he was alone. But we gave him a very nice funeral. It seemed strange at the time, after all he'd done, all that we thought that he'd done. But then later, much later, the mother went up to the hospital with the cuts on her wrists and they called the police in and—oh, this was weeks and weeks later—she told them her story. They went straight to her house and found the baby there where she'd said it would be. She'd buried it there a full day before she had even reported it missing, can you imagine? A whole day of wheeling that pram around just pretending, the poor little thing. Such a shame. Such a shame. She must have been crazy—it happens, of course. But she came forward, a good girl, came forward and told them the truth and then it was over.

And we were glad he'd had the funeral then. We felt better because of the funeral.

Lizzie

It is silent and dark. We are lost in the depths of the alleyways back in the stink of the slaughtering places. The children crowd tightly around me. The Old Town is silent. No-one is watching.

I don't know where the mob has gone. I can't hear any sound at all. The vibrations are gone, the silence is filling the air around us, catching itself in the walls, coming up from the cobblestones, channelling down through the mouth of the alley like water. I know they are out there. I know they haven't gone back to their houses. If they are silent it's only because they are tracking us now, they are hunting us down.

The chopper has gone. We are lost in the tunnels along the butchers' street where the walls smell of fear and blood and the sun is kept out and the air is secret and cold and dead. I am seven years old and lost in the tunnels, screaming while feet thud around me, ghosts and whispers and flickers of fingers, screaming and screaming till Richard finds me, takes my hand and leads me outside.

I am eight years old, I am watching a house in flames, and trapped in the nightmare.

Bad things just happen.

Beside me the children are still and deathly quiet, and suddenly soft on the air I can feel the movement of feet, feel the whisper behind me, the chill of terror along my back and I turn and there in the shadows is Ali—who led the bus group down to the square in the darkness this morning and watched them burn.

He is eight years old. He can't be dangerous.

Hannah

They are here—they are here. I wait in the dark till I taste the bitter grey metal, the heat of leather and sweat in the air, then I've had enough and I run—not carefully now, not quietly—up through the tunnels under the stage, up the ramp past the orchestra pit and into the auditorium and surely they hear me, surely they'll follow me, up the aisles and I scream out my name, that I am not dangerous, that I will not resist arrest, that I want to get out and be safe—and there it is, the door to the foyer, the glassed-in foyer that looks out over the concourse, and there on the concourse the crowd is corralled, the crowd who had come for the show and the food and the fireworks; and God! I am safe because they are watching, they can see me and surely they will not allow this to happen again. So I stand at the full-length window, my hands in the air, my back to the crowd, and I am unarmed, unthreatening, and yes, it's over, I think: oh God, it's over. I've turned them away from Richard, wherever he is, and he will be safe. And they have come up with the dogs, through the almost-black of the aisles, they've followed me into the foyer and yes, they are angry, and yes, I imagine they'd love to shoot me or set the dogs on me, but no, it's too late, the crowd can see us and there would be witnesses; they couldn't say it was accidental, they couldn't say it was provoked. So all they can do is swear and shove and push me hard against the window; and maybe there, behind them somewhere, down in the tumble of empty darkness, maybe he'll have the sense to curl into himself like a little moss piglet, burrow down, keep quiet, just *stop* till everyone's gone. Till this night is over and he can slip safely into the darkness.

The lights are off. The foyer is black. There is movement outside, there is suddenly black against black in the air, the drum of rotors shaking the glass as the choppers shut off the cold white glare of their floodlights and swing in unison, turn away from the Opera House, heading back to the naval base.

Stay there. Watch out for me.

Red

The boats are out of sight now. In the darkness across from the curve of the shore, the soldiers have regrouped and moved through the bushland as softly as ghosts.

Alone in the darkness, the red-headed soldier is creeping up the track to the lighthouse. Mistakes can be made in the heat of the moment—things can go terribly wrong; and if there's a terrorist threat in the darkness tonight, he knows that there's also a man with a backpack, a harmless man, passive and easily cowed, and he's let the man walk into danger. *You let him down*, he hears again, in the long-ago voice of his father. *He put his trust in you and you let him down. You look after him now.*

He slips quietly through the bushland, aware of the thrumming under his feet. He's aware of the silence, the bulk of the lighthouse, the lap and retreat of the harbour.

Inside the lighthouse, the candles flicker and gutter unseen. Above them, the light is prepared.

Across the water the city is waiting, vulnerable, mesmerised.

Toby

'I never told anyone,' Toby said into the shadows that moved around them. His eyes had grown used to the half-light now—he could see the chamber more clearly. Richard was setting the trigger, starting the timer. As he worked in the flickering candlelight Toby saw for the first time that the walls had been covered with words, the words written over and over, the lettering tiny and tightly packed, black ink on the white walls, in a pattern of angles and swirls—and over it all, in an echo of Hannah's canvas, there were the pictures; newspaper images, prisoners hooded and shackled, dogs and airplanes. And there were children, their faces streaked with ashes or charcoal—so it was a moment before he could see them, see Hannah and Lizzie, see Richard, the kids that they ran with, himself on the edge of the group, squinting into the sun. 'I never told anyone,' he whispered. 'You know that, Richard, don't you?'

'It was us. It was all of us,' Richard said, and the candlelight jumped and settled again as he spoke. 'We unleashed the bad thing. We let it out of the darkness. We let it grow.'

And there, on the wall behind him, another newsprint photo. A man on the floor of a railway carriage, his head in a river of blood, his light denim jacket rucked up, his back smooth and innocent, clear and exposed, his face blown away.

Toby was close to panic all of a sudden, close to panic at being alone in the middle of nowhere with this man who was crazy, really, wasn't he? Crazy? His scalp was already clenching and clawing with terrible dread because it was crazy, insane, to be here, to break in here, to rig up the lighthouse like this, go to this kind of trouble. 'I never told anyone,' he said, and his breath was patchy, his voice uncontrollable. He realised with a sudden drop of his gut that it was late, that the fireworks should have begun already, something was terribly wrong. He put out his hand and said, 'Bad things just happen. You know that, Richard. Bad things just happen. And we were just kids,' but he could hear the fear in his voice like an echo down the years, and Richard had heard it too because he sat back and then said to Toby gently, 'Don't be afraid.'

Richard laid out a mat of newspaper. He pushed it across to Toby. 'You must help me,' he said, and he took two plastic bags of powder and dropped them down on the paper and then a knife to open them with but Toby sat frozen and suddenly Richard was thwarted, frustrated, just like he used to be. 'It won't *hurt* you,' he said, and he sounded for all the world like his twelve-year-old self, angry and scathing and full of dislike—or like Hannah, there in the sun at the edge of the tunnels. 'It won't *hurt* you. It's light, I'm bringing the lighthouse to life, for Christ's sake, I'm burning the shadows away, I want people to see.' He was breathing fast, he was sweating now in the terrible closed and glassed-in cell, and he looked like he might have snapped, he looked truly insane, so Toby backed away, up against the wall, and said no, said we should go down, we should go down, Hannah is waiting, she's meeting me here. And Richard caught himself, caught back the words that were always so ready to come spewing out of his mouth these days, caught them back and instead said, soft and forgiving, '*Eight o'clock at the lighthouse. Just us two, just like the old days. We'll watch the sky burn.*'

So it had been Richard all along. Hannah wasn't coming, she didn't know he was there.

It had been Richard texting his phone, calling him here; and they were alone.

Lizzie

We stare at each other for minutes or maybe for seconds and all in a heartbeat the child on my right hand crosses the chasm between us, lets go of me, moves to Ali. And then another child crosses as well, big-eyed and breathless, and then another, and as Ali turns away from me they follow him, clustering closely, tightly, around him.

I want to speak to him. I want to ask where Kate is, and if she is safe—but he's eight years old and he watched the bus burn this morning down in the square. And then we can feel the air moving again, the thunder and pulse of the mob; and behind it, above it, the shuddering thud of the chopper returning.

And he's ahead of me now in the shadows, this little boy. Tiny and quick as a fish, he finds the path through a tangle of go-downs and scuttle-ways, down through a rubble of steps and debris under tunnels that lead from the markets and up to the tanneries. He knows the secret pathways like the back of his tough little hands and he ducks and weaves and around us the now-distant roar of the mob is shifting and changing direction. He carries the smallest child, clinging silent and tight, on his back, and the one in my arms is silent as well and the older ones too are running, and running without a sound, without even a whimper, and I remember that they have known fear before, these children, they have known terror. Ali turns back to make sure I'm with him and then he ducks to the side and I follow and just in time because he's found the gap in the wall of a house that must have been empty for decades, for centuries maybe, that threatens to fall all around us, collapsing under the echoes and rage of the mob that is getting closer. We slip through the courtyard and out through the gap in the wall at the back and I know where we are—in a flash, I know we've come out at the back of the *ryad*, out near the kitchens, out near the laundry, and we are safe. Ali thumps on the shuttered window and Kate is there—and we pass the children through and Ali is through and I am through at last and shaking with fear and relief.

I grab onto Kate like a lifebuoy. She says, 'You're alright. You're alright,' and turns away to comfort the children, to soothe them. Hama is behind her as she pulls the children to her. 'You're safe,' she tells them over and over but they won't believe it again, no, not for a moment.

And above us, the air is cut into pieces, pulped by the chopper that's flying in low and determined—and outside the *ryad* and all around us the tunnels erupt in its thunder.

Toby

It was done, it was finished. The powders were mixed, the procedure was set in play. Toby was frozen, trapped in the other man's fire. In the heat of the chamber Richard had stripped himself naked; his body was lean and slicked with sweat and glowed in the light of the candles and he smiled with such brilliant clarity, such gentle joy and pride, that Toby was still unprepared when he said, 'They will kill me tonight. I have called you to watch me die.'

Toby tried to get to the ladder then, tried to escape—but Richard was there before him and punched him hard on the side of his face, which sent him back and onto the ground, and then Richard reached down and touched Toby's cheek where the fist had struck and said to him, 'Trust me.' And he would have said more, but Toby grabbed the knife from the floor, braced his back against the wall and held the blade out between them, burning and sharp in his hand.

There was no-one else on earth. The harbour, the coastline, the crowded boats, the music and laughter, the tiny lights were all gone. The world was contained in the arc of the lighthouse. The time for fireworks had passed without notice; the little sailing boats had slipped away in the dusk. Outside in the night, in the bush, little creatures were scuttling away to safety, looking for burrows and tunnels and crawl-ways, looking for darkness.

'Toby.' Richard said his name softly, disbelievingly. He took a step forward, and Toby raised the knife, held it higher, closer, held it as though it would tear the other man's throat, but Richard moved closer and Toby—who was a coward, yes, who had never been brave, who couldn't bear pain, couldn't bear to *see* pain—closed his eyes and hurled the knife at the pressure lamp, hoping to hit it perhaps, to knock the thing over; and he missed entirely of course and heard his last hope go skittering off the ledge and bounce impotently on the floor below them and Richard pulled him to his feet and slapped him across the face, slapped him hard, and he stumbled again and almost fell and opened his eyes. And yes, he had made things worse. The softness had gone and Richard was full of righteous fury.

When he spoke now his face was in Toby's face and flecks of spittle flew from his mouth like sea foam. He was brilliant, shining, lit up from somewhere inside and his voice was loud with wrath and accusation. '*Ye allow the deeds of your fathers*,' he stormed. '*For they indeed killed them, and ye build their sepulchres.*' Then he paused for a moment, seemed to pull himself in by an effort of will that was dreadful to watch, that showed the terrible strain of the burden he carried. '*I will gather the lame, and assemble the exiles and those I have brought to grief.*' His breath came fast and light like a woman in childbirth; his eyes were full of pain and pleading. '*Atonement*,' he said in a whisper, as though he were praying—as though he could pull some protection out of the word, as though it contained absolution. '*At one* with the victim, Toby—*at one* with God.' Then he set his watch to the timer, and climbed down the ladder to the candle-filled chamber beneath, pushing Toby ahead of him.

When they reached the ground, he shook Toby lightly, released him, forgiving him.

'The hour is come,' he said gently. 'Watch out for me.'

GUARDIAN, WEDNESDAY, 17 AUGUST 2005

Evidence given to the Independent Police Complaints Commission (IPCC) by police officers and eyewitnesses and leaked to ITV News shows that far from leaping a ticket barrier and fleeing from police, as was initially reported, he was filmed on CCTV calmly entering the station and picking up a free newspaper before boarding the train.

It has now emerged that Mr de Menezes was never properly identified because a police officer was relieving himself at the very moment he was leaving his home; was unaware he was being followed; was not wearing a heavy padded jacket or belt as reports at the time suggested; never ran from the police and did not jump the ticket barrier.

But the revelation that will prove most uncomfortable for Scotland Yard was that the 27-year-old electrician had already been restrained by a surveillance officer before being shot seven times in the head and once in the shoulder.

Red

Out in the darkness, the red-headed soldier hears movements, quiet, soft, on the edge of sound. He knows the surveillance methods, knows the specialist forces are trained in silence and secrecy.

He can feel them around him, settling into position.

Instinctively his hand goes to his hip and for the first time he is grateful for his gun—not to shoot, but because he remembers the man with the backpack, remembers his easy capitulation to signs of authority.

He just has to find his man, keep him down, keep him quiet and safe until it's over.

Lizzie

It makes pass after pass, the chopper, run after run; it circles the town like an eagle, a guardian angel. The chaos of power beats down and hammers the ancient medina and when it hovers above us the roar is trapped by the walls of the courtyard. Here in the *ryad*, the children scream, but their screams are lost, blown away in the thud of the rotor. It captures the pulsing of blood and turns our fear to rage, and after the fourth or fifth pass the power remains, no longer ebbs in the air. We have caught it and taken it deep inside. It has changed us. It beats in the body, deep in the cells, in the veins, in the arteries. We are creatures of noise, of thunder: and then the little ones turn to stone as I watch, their jaws tightening on their screams. They have felt the strength of rage and hate and terror and they will survive it.

At the fifth pass I turn to Kate. 'They're just filming,' I scream above the noise. 'They're only filming. They're keeping us safe.'

'They're making it worse!' she shouts and her face is dissolving in rage. 'Why are they ramping it up? Why aren't they calming it down?'

There is a sudden lull. They have moved away, over the edge of the Old Town. We straighten up and I say to Kate, 'They're not armed. They're just taking pictures—they're not going to shoot.'

'Nobody knows that,' she says. She spits the words through clenched teeth. 'And nobody trusts you here.' And the gunfire begins.

Toby

There is nothing but silence. Toby listens, trying to pick up whispers of sound from the earth outside. He is filled with the fears of his childhood, nights of terror and prayer and superstition.

'You are with us or you're against us,' Richard says, and he has covered his nakedness now with the heavy black overcoat, its weight incongruous still in the heat of the night. His eyes flash with excitement, with fervour; he holds out his hands, each one clutching the wool of his garment. 'I am a man in an overcoat,' he says, and he laughs against the simplicity of it, proud and strong and triumphant. 'Do you see, Toby? Do you see? They will shoot me for that.' Toby tries to answer, to soothe, but Richard hugs him quickly, plants a child's kiss half on his cheek and half on his mouth, and then he opens the heavy iron door.

'*I will send them prophets,*' he whispers into the darkness, '*and some they shall slay.*'

It's a hot night. Icy hairs play along Toby's neck. Richard counts down the seconds, his eyes on his watch, only looking away for an instant to raise his eyes to the gap in the floor above, where the ladder points up to the chamber that will soon, any moment now, any instant, be full of the blazing light of God, full of Richard's truth, full of Richard's fire.

Red

The little rock ledge at the southern side of the lighthouse, above the foreshore, is the only place to sit and wait in the night, and it's empty. The red-headed soldier stands for a moment and fear settles quick around him.

He has pulled the gun from his belt. He can see through the blackness. There is a moment, he knows, before the fuse is lit, before the dice fall . . . He can hear the earth, he can read the vibration beneath him. He can smell danger.

It's his father who comes to him, always, shows him the way to slow down, to wait. He is the soldier; he is the one who must conquer his fear and his darkness. *Think*, his father would say to him, speaking as only the dead can speak, clear and clean and divorced from the interruptions of life, the chaos and misunderstanding. *There's more to this than shooting. Take your time. Look after him.*

But the lighthouse door is opening and the play is about to begin . . .

He hears the men in the shadows around him, closer than he had imagined and greater in number, fixed and determined. There is a sudden breath of movement above the jetty. The lighthouse has opened its door—and framed in the dimness he sees the open hands, the outstretched arms, the form of an angel, draped and winged and powerful and behind it, cowering, terrified, lost in the dread and terror, the man he has searched for; and even before the words can form in his brain like bullets he's screaming out to the hostage to *get back inside! Get down!*

Hannah

They have dragged me away from the crowd to the wall of glass that looks over the harbour and I am pinned with my back against it, and they are shouting with rage and hatred, ripping my shirt away, kicking my legs apart and their hands all over me, grabbing and probing, searching for dangerous things, for wires or guns, for a bomb belt—and over and over one of them screams at me, 'Who sent this message! Who has been texting you?' and he's holding my phone and they grab my hair, turn my head and he shoves the phone in front of my eyes, still screaming, 'Who sent you this message?' and I can't read the words on the screen, but I tell him, 'It's Toby, it's only Toby.' And I taste the lie as I say the words, I can see what he's done, what he's planned, I can see the gene in the Gordian worm, and I lick at my lips that are split and bleeding, reach a hand to my shirt where they've ripped it away from my shoulder and I'd walk away, let them shoot me—but he can see the lie on my face too, and then at a word the dogs are jumping and growling and snarling, the guards shove me back off-balance, the man with my phone screams, 'Who sent this?' and I say, 'Toby. Toby sent it,' and he grabs my face and slams my head backwards into the glass. I tell them, 'He works at the embassy,' and there's a fire of pain in my leg, and another—the dogs, I think, and that's going to bruise—and the tunnels and caverns beneath us are empty, I know, so I look outwards, out through the darkness, out to the magical places—and there in that curve of the harbour, there on the edge of the waterline, there, where the body lies under the mound, where the world is held in a green glass marble, there in the fire and secrets of childhood, I know what the message means and I can see it before it happens.

The Messenger

Look, now. His coat is incongruous; it is heavy and soft around him.

He steps onto the jetty, naked under the coat, his arms outstretched—and look, his hands are empty, his palms are innocent, open. He raises his arms and all in an instant the timer has lit the flame and his work is done. The lamp of the lighthouse blazes—a white-hot beam that pierces the darkness and burns around him and there in the brilliance he stands and the overcoat casts a shadow that falls like an angel's wings about him.

He is there for a moment, forever. Look at him, black in searing light, his arms outstretched, his hands raised open unto God—his face consumed with love and the righteous perfect flame: and then with no further signal, no word, the night is ripped apart by gunfire.

Hannah

I close my eyes in the instant before the flash, the explosion that rips the sky, that tears it apart—and even the soldiers flinch, turning away from the light, their hands over their ears. And down on the concourse people are screaming, seeing the flash of light and bracing themselves for the shock, for the sound to come bearing down in a wall of fury. But it never comes; there is no sound, no destruction, only the light. And I am the only one standing, watching it shine in the cowering darkness.

In my mind I can see him there and I know that it's too late now, it must be too late, there have been choppers and guns and orders, and now it's over and *oh my God, Richard*, I scream, but inside my head where it can't be heard, over and over and over—*oh my God, Richard.*

The Messenger

There, look. He lies on the rotted planks of the jetty. His blood spills across the stanchion and into the water.

And all this was planned.

The boy who once loved him is cowering inside the lighthouse, turning to water.

Soldiers are swarming through bushland; they are alive with shock and release. You can see them lit up like flames, triumphant, alert for another attack, surrounding the body, untangling the overcoat, checking for heartbeat or pulse or blood flow.

They don't know yet, in the darkness, won't see for hours, not until daylight, won't see in the hidden curve of the land the shell of the soldier cut down by their crossfire, red-headed, lanky, his gentle hands large and covered with freckles, his dead body slick with the blood that has pooled in the earth beneath him.

The Lighthouse

They are not unconnected, these stories. A man boards a train. He looks out the window.

Remember him. The myth will absorb the man.

It's a long story, this, a glimpse of a longer story.

It may not end happily, it may not resolve.

There are hidden things—there are shadows and imprints; impressions, interpretations. There are tiny things—there are plagues and bacilli and fear, there are slogans and wars.

A man boards a train. Remember his face. You will see it explode like a soft red flower.

Create him a coat, a hat, a bomb belt . . .

Create him Mongolian eyes.

On the jetty, near the lighthouse, is a boy.

He leans against the guardrail, shielding his eyes from the sun.
But the guardrail is old and terribly dangerous and
when you look again

the boy is gone.

Acknowledgements

To the earliest readers—Anne Fletcher, Bruce and Laura Cunningham, Anne-Maree McDonald, Stuart Maunder, Anita and Andy Harmon and Michelle Morgan—my love and gratitude for your insights, suggestions and constant support.

To my agent Gaby Naher, to Jane Palfreyman and to Catherine Milne, Ali Lavau, Sandy Cull, Ann Lennox, Simone Ford and all at Allen & Unwin, my thanks—you made the book shine.